AFTER THE LIGHTS GO OUT

"Intense, brutal, compassionate and moving, this foray into a savage form of sport and the scars of racial trauma . . . will linger in the mind long after"

CRIMETIME

"A swiftly paced triumph complete with a surprising one-two punch of a conclusion. This is simply brilliant"

PUBLISHERS WEEKLY (STARRED REVIEW)

"John Vercher writes with the intensity of championship rounds. [*After the Lights Go Out*] had me hooked from start to finish"

KEVIN POWERS, AUTHOR OF *THE YELLOW BIRDS*

"Exactly the type of book one needs about the fighting life and what it costs those who get paid to give and receive punishment . . . Brilliant"

RYAN GATTIS, AUTHOR OF *THE SYSTEM*

"John Vercher writes like a fighter, a dancer, an athlete . . . Here is a novelist at the height of his power"

WILEY CASH, AUTHOR OF *A LAND MORE KIND THAN HOME*

JOHN VERCHER is a writer on race, identity and social justice currently living in the Philadelphia area with his wife and two sons. He holds a BA in English from the University of Pittsburgh and an MFA in Creative Writing from the Mountainview Master of Fine Arts. His debut novel, *Three-Fifths*, was shortlisted for the CWA John Creasey (New Blood) award and was a *Sunday Times*, *Guardian* and *Financial Times* Book of the Year.

AFTER THE LIGHTS GO OUT

JOHN VERCHER

PUSHKIN
VERTIGO

Pushkin Vertigo
An imprint of Pushkin Press
Somerset House, Strand
London WC2R 1LA

First published by Pushkin Press in 2022
This edition published in 2023

1 3 5 7 9 8 6 4 2

ISBN 13: 978-1-78227-756-9

Offset by Tetragon, London
Printed and bound by Clays Ltd, Elcograf S.p.A.

www.pushkinpress.com

For Mom and Dad

Nothing fixes a thing so intensely in the memory as the wish to forget it.   —Michel de Montaigne

MY MIND PLAYING TRICKS ON ME

L ast year, he left his groceries in the trunk for two days. He'd just gotten the call—a number-one contender fight. After alternating wins and losses, he'd strung together four in a row, evading a cut from the roster by the slimmest of margins. The old-timer, the journeyman. Not a has-been but a never-was. In spite of—no, because of the doubters and their calls to leave his gloves in the middle of the cage. No one would have thought less of him if he'd quit on his own terms. The game had passed Xavier "Scarecrow" Wallace by. Too many young bucks on the come up looking for a steppingstone to the next level. The cage had no place for old toothless lions fighting for their pride.

And then four in a row. No tomato cans, either. Championship kickboxers. Jiu-jitsu aces. Each one the next big thing. But none of them had the grind in them. All talent and hormones. Cardio made cowards of them all. Xavier dragged them into deep waters, the championship rounds where lactic acid torched muscles. Where deep breaths provided no oxygen, only the desperate need to breathe deeper. Faster. Shoulders ached. Submissions lacked squeeze. Punches lost their snap. Kicks sloppy, thrown with languid legs, hinging and pivoting at the joints from sheer momentum. Break the spirit and the body follows fast behind.

But he'd paid a cost for his time in the deep end, too.

Worse than the patchwork remnants of stitches in his fore-head; worse than the accumulation of crackling scar tissue above his jagged orbital bones; worse, even, than the seem-ingly interminable, intensifying headaches. Worse than all that was the forgetting.

Mild at first. Patches of time gone, sketches of memories swiped from a chalkboard where only the faintest outline of the words and images remained. More and more often, feeling that he'd been somewhere, done something, though never sure how, when—or if. The ravages of age, he told him-self, nothing more. Some days he almost believed that.

When the contender call came, he'd been ready. The weight didn't come off as easy as it had a decade ago, so he'd kept his diet tight. A fight meant keeping it even tighter. Temptation beckoned when the refrigerator was bare, so it was off to the grocery store for the usual suspects. Packs of skinless chicken breasts. Sacks of brown rice. Sweet potatoes. Leafy greens. Broccoli. Gallons of distilled water. He'd tossed his plastic sacks of calorie-bereft blandness into the trunk and drove to the gym to tell Shot the news before heading home.

That night had been restless. He conjured images of the fight to come. No matter how many times he'd ascended the stairs to the cage, his fearful mental rehearsal was always the same. Involuntary and unwelcome. And never was more at stake than now. A contender's bout meant media days. Press con-ferences. Local television appearances. He played those out, as well. The questions about his age and how many more wars he had left in the tank. His thoughts on his opponent, attempts to spark the inevitable trash talk. He lay flat on his back in the darkness, eyes wide open. A hot breeze wafted through his open bedroom window. Sweat beaded on his bare chest. The broken air conditioning window unit sat like a headstone in tribute to its own demise. Even in the dead of night, the humidity of a late Philadelphia August hung in the air like fog, pressing up against the wood siding of his father's Montgomery County bungalow.

Resigned to sleeplessness, he peeled the backs of his legs from the sheets and pushed himself to a sitting position on the side of the bed. He gripped the edge of the mattress and closed his eyes as he waited for the spin to slow, then stop, the positional vertigo another unwanted trophy, awarded after years of concussive blows to the head. His doctor had told him the spinning originated in his ears, something about crystals floating loose, a condition requiring a specialist's treatment. Xavier imagined a long-haired socks and sandals-wearing type with a stringy goatee waving a shard of glass over his ears, collecting a seventy-five-dollar copay for five minutes of work. He told his doctor he'd take his chances. His physician then offered him a medication, but the side effects included dizziness. Xavier stopped seeing him altogether.

The spinning stopped and he stood. A cacophony of pops and clicks sounded in his joints, ankles to spine. He tried but failed to ignore the swell of pressure behind his eyes, the steam whistle of tinnitus in his ears, an unwelcome and worsening addition to the forgetfulness of late. From a pile of clothes at the edge of the bed, he donned a paint-splattered tank top and basketball shorts and stepped into the short hallway leading from the bedroom to the kitchen. Canvas tarps covered the floor. A roller sat in a pan. Paint congealed in the well.

The roller sizzled against the wall as he crossed it back and forth, up and down, the motion hypnotic, sage green covering the off-white. The first coat completed, he was no more ready for sleep than before, but the tinnitus had grown louder. He moved to the kitchen where he leaned his hands on the counter. His eyes squeezed shut, he willed the whistling to go away, but the intensity increased. He sat on the floor, long legs

stretched out in front of him, and rested the back of his head
on a cool cabinet door.

And then awake.

Not in bed.

Eyes open. Neck stiff. Ass sore.

Sweat had stuck the skin of his scalp to the cabinet door
and he peeled his head away. He wiggled the stiffness from his
knees and stood, gripping the edge of the faux granite coun-
tertop to steady the room. Through the window over the sink,
the high bright sun shined orange through his closed eyelids
as he waited out the spin. The carousel ride over, he scanned
the room and saw the roller in the pan. The hallway walls had
more paint on them than before.

Didn't they?

The fumes, perhaps. That made sense. They'd made him
drowsy, and he'd sat. He should have opened more windows.
That seemed like something he might have told himself at the
time. Of course, that was why he fell asleep. On the floor.
In the kitchen. Perfectly reasonable. Unlike the time on the
microwave clock. 3:24. In the afternoon.

That's impossible.

He walked from the kitchen to the living room, ducking his
head under the jamb, and retrieved his cell phone. The clock
on the screen read the same as the one on the microwave.
There were a number of texts and calls from Shot. Xavier
had missed his morning workout. And his afternoon training
session.

My bad, Shot. I'll double up on the roadwork. Hitting the trail
right now. Catch you at the gym tomorrow.

He watched the screen. The speech bubble appeared, the
dots darkening and fading in sequence before disappearing.
Xavier's face tightened. Then:

K.

"Fuck," Xavier said. No way to make the drive to Mana-yunk now. Rush hour would be a nightmare by the time he got to Lincoln Avenue. Another headache swelled at the base of his skull. Back in the kitchen, he grabbed a gallon of dis-tilled water from the pantry and downed two ibuprofens. A pair of running shoes sat by the front door. He scooped them up and stepped out into the summer haze.

AN HOUR LATER, HE'D RETURNED home, sweat-soaked and ravenous. The heat of the asphalt trail had burned through the bottoms of his shoes, propelled him forward, faster than his planned pace. The sun's relentless blaze had weight and rounded his shoulders. He peeled off his tank top, dropped it to the linoleum with a wet slap, and downed more than half of the gallon of water in loud glugs as the plastic imploded. The remaining water he poured into a pot on the stove. He ignited the gas burner and went to the refrigerator for a chicken breast to boil and noted that it was his last. The vegetable drawer was equally sparse, and his bag of rice in the pantry was down to his last serving. To the grocery store tomorrow then.

The next morning, the list he'd taped to the refrigerator reminded him of his errand. He headed to his car, opened the driver's side door, and was hit with a potent smell. A sour odor, like the meat drawer in his refrigerator when the power had gone out in the middle of a summer some time ago (when *was* that?). He poked his head in the backseat, the odor stronger there. Some sweaty rash guards and shorts sat lumped behind the passenger seat. He knew that smell, and it wasn't this one.

He popped the trunk. There sat the groceries he'd forgotten he'd bought the day before. Chicken spoiled in a cloudy pink puddle of its own juices. Wilted broccoli glistened with slime. Cooked under the summer sun.

|6| J O H N V E R C E R

He held the waste at arm's length as he hauled the bags to the trash cans next to the garage. The stench rose up out the can in a whoosh as he dropped them in, and he gagged. He left the door open to air out the car and sat on the edge of the driver's seat. He recalled wanting to go for groceries. He remembered knowing that he needed to. Yet he didn't remember having gone. He'd been busy, he rationalized. His mind preoccupied with the fight, among other things. The groceries had simply slipped his mind. Just like falling asleep in the kitchen, it could have happened to anyone.

Sure, it could have.

THE MEMORY OF THAT DAY had faded like many others since, and he'd not thought of it again—until this morning.

Late (again) for work at the gym, Xavier opened his driver's side door. The trapped heat blew a stench against his face like a blast furnace—but it smelled nothing like the reek from last year. He reflexively slammed the door shut and held one nostril closed as he blew snot out of the other, but the odor lodged in his olfactory. The smell of shit and piss was unmistakable, but there was something else, too. Something he couldn't place.

He walked toward the trunk, stopping to look in the backseat. On the floor behind the driver's seat was a pile of feces sitting in a pool of urine. Across from the mess, in the same space on the passenger's side, was a dog with grayish blue fur, curled into itself.

"What the fuck?" Xavier ran around the back end of the car, whipped the rear passenger door open, and held his breath. "No, no, no, no," he said, wishing the dog had been some kind of mirage, brought on by the haze and glare of the high morning sun. He kneeled on the cracked driveway and hovered his hand over the dog's body, skin pulled tight across the ribs. Xavier went to rest his hand on the dog when the ribs moved.

He jerked his hand back. A hallucination, surely, born of wishful thinking, but he lowered his hand again, and the curved bones rose to meet his palm.

"Hey," Xavier said, softly.

The dog's whip-like tail pulled away from where it had curled against the hind legs, lifted, and then dropped to the floor with a thump.

A little louder. "Hey."

The tail thumped twice more.

Xavier slid his hands under the dog's head and hind quarters and gently lifted him out of the car. Its skin was hot to the touch through its thin fur coat. He cradled the dog to his chest and could not differentiate the dog's rapid heartbeat from his own. Xavier lowered his nose to the top of the dog's head and breathed in.

Through the smell of the dog's own fluids, there was a scent embedded in the fur on its crown, one that unleashed a torrent of recollection, though one stood out more than any other. When he first saw the dog, he wondered who would put it in his car, what kind of person would leave it there to suffer in the summer sun. The scent told Xavier what kind of person would do such a thing. He didn't need to see the rescue adoption papers sitting on the passenger seat with his signature to discover the answer.

The dog was his.

GRAND CHAMP

The dog shivered despite the heat radiating from its skin. Xavier's sweat soaked his shirt as he carried the dog the short walk up the uneven sidewalk to his father's back porch, pulled him close while his hand searched for the handle of the screen door. He heard a rustle and saw movement in his periphery. Ray, his father's next-door neighbor—or rather Xavier's neighbor now—sat on his back porch. He made a show of turning the pages of his newspaper, pretending to mind his business when he most decidedly was not.

Xavier had first met Ray on a return trip from the grocery store. Xavier had gone to pick up his father's medications, along with an assortment of frozen dinners and liters upon liters of diet soda. Ray had been raking leaves in his tiny front yard and Xavier lifted his chin at him and waved. He hadn't yet noticed the white embroidered MAGA on Ray's red baseball cap, perched high on his balding head. The hat had his full attention when Ray asked with no small sense of entitlement if Xavier lived in the neighborhood. Xavier smiled tight-lipped, a practiced response to like-minded questions from the many Rays he'd encountered, a mask he wore when explanations were in no way owed but nonetheless demanded.

Xavier told Ray that he was in fact Sam Wallace's only son. Ray's face registered a mélange of surprise and disappointment. Whether the man's expression was because his neighbor's son was Black, or because he felt he no longer had a good enough reason to call the police, Xavier didn't know. Nor did he care. Arms encumbered by the groceries, Xavier had fumbled for the keys, used the wrong one twice, conscious of Ray's watching him until he slid the right one home and made his way inside. Xavier imagined Ray back in his house, grumbling something in racist, peering through the aluminum blinds bent just wide enough to see whatever Black shenanigans Xavier would most assuredly be up to.

"Don't let me find that thing's shit on my lawn," Ray called out. Xavier's fingers grasped at air as he cradled the trembling dog. His arms burned from the strain. He shifted the animal, pressed his thumb down on the door handle's release. Ray snapped his newspaper. "Or in anyone else's yard for that matter. This is a decent, clean neighborhood. And I better not hear so much as a whimper past eight P.M. You know we have a noise ordinance around here, don't you?"

Xavier leaned his rear against the door and closed it behind him. Ray continued his screed unfazed by the lack of audience. Xavier stepped into his bedroom, just off to the left of the back door. The dog still in his arms, he pulled the sheets from the mattress and dragged them down the hall to the kitchen. Once there, he piled them into a make-shift bed with his foot and gently laid the dog down. From the cabinets he pulled down a bowl and filled it with cold water. Xavier placed the bowl by the dog's muzzle and lay down on the floor in front of him, their faces inches apart. The dog's dried nose flared, each breath a struggle. One eyebrow lifted, then the other, as he looked to the water bowl, to Xavier, then back again. His eyes interrogated Xavier, asked him why and how, pleaded for answers. Xavier heard the unspoken questions, ones that echoed his own, but those answers on the chalkboard, like many as of late, had been partially wiped away.

YESTERDAY HAD BEEN, RELATIVELY SPEAKING, one of Sam's better days at the nursing facility. Xavier hadn't been able to make it that week as many times as he would have liked—or at least as many times as he told his father he would have liked. As the end of his suspension neared, Xavier stepped up his training, the intensity and frequency as though he was in camp, ready to take a fight any minute, though the chances were remote given the circumstances of his exit. The promoter had told him as much. Still, he had to stay in fight shape. Being unprepared when the call came was a luxury for fighters under contract. If that meant missed visits to Pop, then so be it. To see his father's decline was difficult. Not being there to see it remedied that particular malady.

There were, of course, days where Xavier simply forgot to go—and then there were the days that he forgot that he forgot. Yesterday was not one of those.

Lying on the floor across from the dog, he remembered that he'd remembered to be at the nursing home for a family care conference with the team coordinating Sam's care. The nurses and therapists told Xavier his father's emphysema had worsened, and in his demented agitation, he had been pulling his nasal cannula out, which caused him to desaturate. When Xavier asked them for a translation of all the words that weren't "agitation" into English, one of the care team explained that it was getting harder for his father to breathe on his own and that the Alzheimer's symptoms made him pull out the oxygen tube from his nose. When the staff tried to help him, he'd become combative. The lack of oxygen caused him to pass out, and only then were they able to replace the cannula.

If all that hadn't been enough good news, he'd also grown increasingly verbally abusive of his new roommate, unable to recall (and even then, understand) that once his money had run out, medical assistance meant no more private room. The team conveyed the situation to Xavier with a rehearsed compassion, their words spoken in a mixture of kindness entwined with the fatigue of delivering bad news.

Xavier folded his hands on the conference table and hung his head. "I'm working on his house to get it ready to put on the market. That might get him enough to put him back in a private room, right?" The care team exchanged glances across the table. "What? It can't be *that* expensive."

"No, it's not that," said his social worker. "I mean, yes, it *can* be that expensive, but that's not the concern. Not the main one, anyway."

"What is?"

"He hasn't just been abusive to his roommate. There have been some issues with certain members of the staff."

Xavier lost patience with the verbal gymnastics. "I'm sorry for that, but he's an old man. I know that's no excuse, but can't you just—"

"He's been calling members of my nursing staff racial slurs," said the director of nursing. She was a thin older Black woman with short-cropped salt-and-pepper hair. She sat tall, her hands folded in front of her on the conference table. The way in which her white co-workers looked down at their notepads told Xavier that she'd long moved past making them comfortable as the only Black woman in the room. He thought of his mother, and at once felt kinship and rejection.

"Yeah, no, that doesn't make any sense." Xavier peered across the table at her badge. "Mrs. Thomas. You sure you didn't, I mean your staff, or whoever, they didn't just mishear him? I mean, come on. Look at me."

"There was and is no misunderstanding, Mr. Wallace. I know this is a challenging time for you and that there may be certain realities that are difficult for you to accept."

"So, since no one here wants to come out and say it, the reality you're suggesting I need to accept is that my father, who married a Black woman and loves his Black son, was secretly a closet racist and now because of his Alzheimer's, his filter is off? Do I have that right? Do you know how fucking ridiculous that sounds?"

All but Mrs. Thomas shifted in their seats, straightened papers in front of them, cleared their throats. Mrs. Thomas's regard, serene but intense, remained trained on Xavier. Her look disarmed him. She did not speak, and though he tried meeting her gaze, the weight of her silence pulled his head down. His anger withered under her unspoken admonition. He broke the quiet with contrition.

"Does he have to leave?"

The social worker spoke again. "No, no, nothing like that. Well, not really. Not yet."

Mrs. Thomas shook her head, exasperated at the social worker's equivocating. "We do not have an advanced dementia unit here, Mr. Wallace. If your father's condition continues to progress at this rate, if he becomes a danger to himself or my staff, we will have to have a discussion about finding him a facility that can better take care of his needs."

"I'd like to see him now. Can I see my dad?"

Mrs. Thomas pressed her lips together and breathed through her nose. "Did he go back to his room after therapy?" she said to the young blonde across the table.

"I think he's out in the courtyard with some of the other residents. The dog rescue is here again today. He actually does really well when they come to visit."

"He had a boxer when he was a kid," Xavier said. "Sully.

Talked about him all the time. Chased leaves like they were cats. He said he would have named me after that dog, but my mother wasn't having it. He was all, 'I guess naming him after a comic book character is okay, but not the greatest four-legged creature on the face of the earth.'" Xavier laughed to himself and the care team at the table smiled. He talked to excess when he was anxious, like venting pressure in a pipe. He chewed at the inside of his cheek and his eyes stung. "Sorry, I'm rambling. Where is the courtyard?"

The occupational therapist rose, followed by the rest of the team. Xavier thanked Mrs. Thomas, who bowed her head at him. The therapist held open the door and walked him down the hall. She went to open the glass door to the courtyard for him, but Xavier put his hand out. "Not yet," he said. She excused herself to go see her patients. Xavier watched the scene beyond the glass.

Sam sat in his wheelchair. He wore a white T-shirt and a pair of linen pajama pants. He craned his head back, failing to dodge nuzzles and licks from a brown Labrador mix as wide as it was tall. When the dog's loving attack relented, Sam vigorously scratched behind its ears and around its cheeks. Other residents looked equally enamored with their canine companions, tossing tennis balls, stroking heads. Xavier smiled at all the pairings.

The representative from the rescue, a slight middle-aged blond woman, her hair pulled back in a tight ponytail, watched the group as well. A dog sat obediently at her side, a blue-gray Staffordshire, its head so massive it obscured the neck, the dog a bobblehead doll version of itself. Xavier couldn't take his eyes off the pit, nor the pit him. He'd been around enough dogs to see there was no malice in the stare, no predatory sizing up. Only an intense curiosity that pulled Xavier through the door almost as strongly as the desire to see his father.

He approached his father's wheelchair from behind and placed gentle hands on Sam's shoulders. The muscles were taut from the endless exertion of lifting his lungs to let in air, but the skin hung loose around them, the fibers beneath deflated of the strength they once held.

"Hey, Pop. How you doing?"

Sam looked up, his smile bright despite the nicotine stains. His cheeks rose, concealing his eyes in a mess of crow's feet. When he saw Xavier, however, his eyes widened just a bit, the corners of his mouth dropping. Xavier recognized the look.

"Well, hello," Sam said. Xavier circled the chair to squat down in front of him. "It's been a little while." He ended on an upturn, a question more than a statement.

"It's okay, Pop." Xavier scratched behind the ears of the dog who'd been mauling Sam with licks. It leaned in and rumbled with a satisfied growl.

"She sure likes that," said Sam. "You keep that up, you'll have to take her with you."

"She looks pretty happy here with you."

"If only I could have a dog. I used to have this boxer. Greatest dog in the world. Dumb as a can of paint, but God, I loved him." Sam laughed. He looked off somewhere, to sometime before the courtyard. "When the wind blew, he'd skitter off after leaves so hard, he'd split his nails. Damn near yanked my shoulder out the socket. But there was not a more loyal, lovable dog in the world. But so dumb. I had it bad for that one. I almost named my boy after him."

Xavier swallowed hard. "Sully."

Sam's head snapped back to Xavier and set free a tear that clung to the edge of his eyelid.

"Xavier?"

"There he is," Xavier said. Sam outstretched his arms and pulled Xavier in for an embrace, trapping the dog between them. She wagged her tail as though the hug was for her. Xavier pulled away and wiped at his eyes. Sam did the same.

"Are you taking me home today?"

Xavier considered whether to tell him (again) that the house was for sale. That they had this conversation almost every time he came. That it was beyond Xavier's ability to care for him, to keep him safe. Each iteration of the conversation leached a little more joy from his father's face. Part of Sam remembered what was happening though he wasn't conscious of the remembering.

"I'm taking good care of the house. Don't worry about it."

Sam patted Xavier's cheek. His palm was warm. "I'm not worried about it. I'm worried about you. I don't like you there by yourself."

Xavier laughed and flexed his bicep. "I can take care of myself, old head."

Sam fidgeted with the draw string to his pants. "Nobody's tough enough to beat being alone."

Xavier let go of his pose. Despite his façade, his solitude shone as a lighthouse through his father's fog. Eager to change course, Xavier glanced behind him at his blue-furred friend. "Tell you what. Why don't I see if I can find myself a friend to take home? Then maybe you won't worry so much."

Sam didn't look up. Still seated in his chair, he was already off somewhere else. He resumed scratching behind the ears of his canine companion.

Xavier walked to the woman and the pit. The dog raised its head to take in his height as he approached, and his body moved from side to side, asynchronous to its wagging tail.

"Who's this guy?"

"This gentle giant is Loki."

"And is he as mischievous as his namesake?"

"Very good. But definitely not. This big fella is a saint."

"So why isn't he out there with the residents?"

"No one wants to visit with a rescued fighting dog. They're usually too afraid. Comes with a stigma that's hard to shake, no matter how much of a good boy we tell them he is. Same at the rescue. Everyone passes him up. I bring him to every event I can so he can at least spend some time out around other people."

The woman gave Loki's leash slack. Xavier sat on the ground, legs out in a split. Loki, a pile of coiled muscle, lifted off his haunches and came nose-to-nose with him. Xavier slid his fingers between the sweet spot where Loki's ears met his head and scratched. Loki lowered his head. Xavier ran his hands down around the dog's thick jowls and massaged with the heels of his hands, sending Loki listing from one side to another, pushing his massive jaw muscles into the pressure. Xavier brought his forehead to Loki's, and the dog pushed against him until he felt as though they were holding each other upright.

"Wow," the woman said. "That's a first."

Xavier trailed his fingers down Loki's face. The tips ran over hairless patches down to Loki's crinkled jawline, and the dog lifted his head, his neck a mottled mix of pink and gray skin, crisscrossed with scar tissue. Xavier moved his scratching there. Loki's rear paw thumped the ground in pleasure.

"What happened here?" Xavier asked.

"Loki was a champion, the way we were told it. Until he met another pup a hell of a lot meaner. It tried to rip his throat out. Left this poor fella with no bark. Only his bite. Except after a fight like that, he didn't have it in him anymore. And you know what happens when a fighting dog can't fight."

"God damn it," Xavier said. He patted Loki's barrel chest.

"Exactly. One of our volunteers saw him staked outside in a yard in the middle of a snowstorm. No doghouse. No food. Not sure if they were trying to get his mean back or if they just didn't want him to die in their house. Either way, his skin was pulled tight as a drum over his bones. Our volunteer called the SPCA and after talking with them, we decided to take him in. It was touch and go for a while, let me tell you. But this dog just didn't quit."

"Still had that fight in you, huh, boy?" Xavier gave Loki's jowls a vigorous rub, and the corners of his mouth turned up as if in a smile.

"Seems you know a little something about that?" the woman asked. Xavier looked up and she pointed at her own ear and then to his. He pinched the hardened cartilage that filled his ears.

"Yeah, you could say that. You a fight fan?"

The woman shrugged. "Kind of. I don't follow them too closely, but when the hubby gets a pay-per-view, I'll sit on the couch with him and watch until I fall asleep. See a lot of ears like yours. Are you a pro?"

"Some days, maybe," he said. She tilted her head quizzically. As Xavier pushed himself up to stand, so did Loki. He placed a paw on Xavier's knee as if to pull him back to the ground.

"You've got a fan."

"Feeling's mutual." He shook Loki's paw. When he released it, Loki placed his paw back on his leg. "Guess I'm not done, huh?" Xavier sat back down, and the woman handed him the leash. Loki walked between his spread legs and turned in a circle before plopping down and rolling to his back. Xavier relented and rubbed his stomach. Loki's hind legs pumped. Xavier looked over his shoulder for his father. Sam petted his dog, the old man's face brighter than Xavier had seen it in some time. Xavier thought about the empty house, so many of his father's belongings packed in boxes there was nothing left to absorb the sounds of his feet on the laminate floor, or the cacophony of his own breathing on the quietest of nights.

"What do you say I take this guy off your hands?"

"The adoption process can take up to a month, unfortunately. There's paperwork. We have to do a home check, that kind of stuff."

Xavier looked down at Loki, still belly up, his jowls and eyelids flipped back in a happy yet crazed expression. Though he'd only met the dog moments ago, the thought of leaving without him filled Xavier with an odd anxiety that was at once recognizable and unfamiliar.

"It's the perfect house for a dog. It would just be us. No kids to pull on his ears or yank his tail. Just two tough guys." His laugh sounded sadder than he'd intended. "You said so yourself—no one wants to take this guy home. I do. Can't you call the boss at your rescue?"

"I *am* the boss at the rescue," she said. She folded her arms and looked at the two of them together, Loki writhing on his back in delight under Xavier's rubs. She smiled. "Give me a minute to go grab the paperwork."

"Thank you." As if he understood, Loki popped up, stood on his hind legs, and rested his paws on Xavier's shoulders. His tail sliced the air in a bluish blur. Xavier wrapped the leash around his knuckles. "Come on, Loke. There's someone I want you to meet." Xavier walked Loki back over to his father and the Labrador mix. Sam looked up to see them approaching and his smile dropped away. He held his hand up.

"We're good here. Tell your lady boss over there that I don't need to be visiting with any pit bulls. That's a thug's dog." He wagged a thin-skinned finger at Loki. "I don't know why she'd bring that thing here, anyway." The dog in Sam's lap whimpered. Then a growl rolled from her throat. "See, that beast is making her nervous." Loki's jaws opened in a wide-mouthed yawn and he shook from head to tail, unbothered. The Lab mix barked. "Get that damn thing away from me!" Sam shouted at Xavier.

A high-pitched whine, one that had become all too common as of late, keened in Xavier's ear. Pressure swelled behind his eyes and his temples ached. Xavier brought his wide hand to his face and kneaded his fingertips into the muscles above his eyebrows. "Come on, Pop. Just relax. It's fine. It's me."

"I don't know you. You and that mongrel get the hell out of here!"

The woman from the rescue appeared at Xavier's side, paperwork in hand. A nurse's aide jogged up and stopped behind Sam's chair.

"Everything okay here?" the aide asked.

Xavier took the paperwork from the rescue organizer and backed away a step. "Yeah, we're fine." He searched Sam's face, hoping for some glimmer of recognition but found only fury. "I was just leaving." Blinking back tears, he looked to the organizer. "You take credit?"

The headache worsened as he approached his car in the lot. He hoped the asphalt wasn't too hot for Loki's paws, but the dog trotted along, looking at Xavier the whole time, wanting only for more of his attention. The car exhaled hot breath when Xavier opened the passenger side door. He leaned in and turned the ignition, then cranked the fan up full blast in a futile attempt to cool the car. Stale dry air swirled about, the air conditioning long in need of repair. Loki sat at his feet.

Xavier pressed the heel of his hand into his forehead. He hadn't wanted to believe the care team at the nursing home. He couldn't accept that his father had gotten so much worse. The whine in his ears turned into a steam whistle, the pressure behind his eyes threatening to push them out with each beat of his heart, which had taken up residence in his skull. He retrieved a bottle of migraine medication from his pocket and swallowed two pills dry. The car was as cool as it was going to be. He opened the driver's side door and Loki bounded across the console. He plopped down in the passenger seat, panting and grinning.

The distance to home wasn't long, but the drive was interminable. The medication didn't touch the pain, only made him drowsy. He didn't want to take the pills before he drove, but he'd hoped they would blunt the edge of the maul buried in his brain stem. At stoplights, his drooping head jerked him out of the drug-induced nod.

Then, minutes from home, it happened.

The traffic light turned green, and Loki disappeared from his sight as half the vision in Xavier's right eye went black. He slammed on the brakes, grateful no cars were behind him, and pulled into a gas station parking lot. Loki came back into his view as Xavier turned his head to the right. Loki stopped his panting and cocked his head at Xavier, seeming to sense his distress. Xavier dug his knuckles into the tension wires of muscle at the base of his skull, desperate for relief. Loki's tongue slapped against Xavier's forearm. Then he gave his hand a wet-nosed nudge.

"I'm all right, Loke." Minutes passed and Xavier opened his eyes. He saw the entirety of the parking lot in front of him, and Loki in his periphery. The pain and pressure continued undiminished, but with his vision returned for who knew how long, he had to get home, and quickly. He rubbed Loki's jowls and pulled out of the parking lot.

By the time he parked behind his father's house, he had fought the waves of nausea as long as he could. The high early afternoon sun blazed through the windshield. The bright light sent daggers to the back of his brain. Ray sat on his back porch, eyeing Xavier up.

"Fuck," Xavier said. All he wanted was to open the door and puke, get his dog inside without any of Ray's bullshit. He knew Ray was looking for a reason, any reason, to call the police. Vomiting from his car in the middle of the afternoon would be all Ray needed to report him for a DUI or some other nonsense. He closed his eyes and rubbed the crucifix on his neck between his thumb and forefinger. When he opened his eyes Ray was still there. "Yeah, I didn't think it worked like that." Another stabbing pain caused him to dry heave. He patted Loki and opened his door. "I'll be right back, boy. Just need a quick minute to get the house ready for you."

He slammed the door behind him and fast-walked to his back porch, clearing two steps at a time. The wooden screen door clacked off the siding and he gave Ray a mental middle finger as he charged down the hallway and into the bathroom off the kitchen. He barely got the lid up before he vomited his spinach and egg-white flatbread sandwich into the toilet. Cold water splashed his face. The strain increased the pressure in his head, and he gagged harder in a brutal, endless cycle. His stomach hollowed out with each heave, back arched like an angry cat, neck muscles strained. When nothing but bile remained, he sat on the floor and rested his neck on the cool edge of the tub. He rolled his head back and forth, digging for some respite from the tension, but there was none to be had.

Then the cut in his vision returned.

Xavier went to the kitchen sink and poured himself a glass of water to take another dose of medication, but his hand numbed. He lost his grip on the glass and it shattered in the sink. The headache tried to push his skull through the skin of his face.

This is it. My brain's bleeding. I'm done.

He hand-walked his way down the hallway to his bedroom.

Just a minute. I'll lie down for a minute.

Feet still on the floor, he lay back on the comforter.

And he lost a day.

LYING ON THE FLOOR, THE memories back in a rush, he pleaded with the dog.

"Come on, Loki. You got to drink, man."

Loki's panting had quickened. Xavier ran his finger along his cheek, down the soft fur between Loki's eyes, and touched his dry hot nose. Loki stared at him, but when Xavier sat back up, the dog's gaze stayed fixed on a horizon only he could see.

"No, Loki. Come on. Look at me."

I could take him to the vet. And then tell them what? That I left him in a hot car? They'd have me charged with animal abuse. Not that he'd even make the drive there. Thank God it cooled off at night. Tough son of a bitch. I don't deserve this damn dog. Fuck it, I'm taking him.

"Let's get you some help. Then we'll get you some place you belong."

Xavier went to stand but Loki laid his paw across the back of his hand, then propped himself up onto his belly and scooted over toward the water bowl. Xavier slid the bowl closer. Loki dipped his head in and took a few small laps. He chuffed and water splashed out. His tongue darted in and out, faster and faster.

"Easy, Loke," he said. "Don't make yourself sick." Xavier stroked his back. He winced as his hand glided along the ridges of Loki's spine. Loki's tail shushed back and forth across the laminate floor. "All right, Loki. All right."

ME, MYSELF, AND I

Who are you fooling? Yourself, that's who.

About what? How about the fact you didn't want a damn dog in the first place. Only reason you brought that mutt home is because your daddy made you feel bad. You're a grown-ass man, and he's still got you out here acting like a little pussy over some dumb shit. That or you just wanted to fuck that white chick that ran the rescue. Like taking that broke-down dog was going to make her let you slide.

"I forgot he was in the car." You didn't forget shit. You knew good and well that dog was in there.

"Oh, my head hurts."

"Oh, I have to throw up."

"Oh, I have to lay down, so I can fall asleep and let that dog cook out there so I don't have to see his face when I take him to some shelter where they're going to put him down and I can blame it all on the headaches and the forgetting."

You're a straight up bitch, you know that? You going to take an animal you didn't even want because you're lonely? And then when you realize that bringing that thing home was some dumb shit, you pretend you forgot it. Always pointing that finger, never mind all the other ones pointing right back at you.

"I didn't take steroids. It was tainted supplements."

"I didn't choose Pop. *She* left *us*."

Always someone else's fault except poor, brain-dead X. Cry me a river.

You better wake your ass up.

No, I mean for real. You're here sleeping.

You sure that dog isn't dead? Just because he drank some water?

Matter of fact, are you *sure* you brought him back inside?

How do you know he isn't still out in that car slow roasting?

Better go check.

Unless you don't really want to.

I'd understand.

PUNKS JUMP UP TO GET BEAT DOWN

Xavier opened his eyes and sat up, wincing at the pull in his lower back.

Where is he?

His vision adjusted to the dark and he saw a shadow lying at the foot of his bed. The shadow lifted its head and wagged its tail. Xavier breathed out, relieved, and wiped a sheen of sweat from the top of his bald head. He lay back and looked across the room to his clock on top of the dresser. Just a few hours short of sunrise. He closed his eyes again but his mind conjured visions of Loki in the back of the car, straining to find the ghost of his bark in his mangled throat, silently crying for help, curled behind the seat across from a pile of his own waste. No longer waiting to be rescued. Waiting to die.

There would be no return to sleep for Xavier.

He performed his routine for getting out of bed. His hands helped his legs to the floor. He waited for the ache to leave his joints and for the vertigo to subside before standing. Loki commando-crawled across the mattress and laid his head on Xavier's leg, looking up at him. Xavier massaged his neck and Loki's tail beat rudiments on the bed.

Feet and paws exchanged pads and clicks down the hallway to the kitchen. Xavier hoisted a bag of dry food from the pantry and filled a deep bowl, then opened a can of wet food and dumped it on top. Once Loki had drunk his fill of water yesterday, Xavier had realized he had no actual dog food, so he cooked up ground turkey and mixed the meat with rice. He'd never seen an animal eat so fast. The pile that now filled Loki's bowl was probably too much food, but after yesterday—and after all the days that came before yesterday—Loki would eat like a king at every meal.

They took a walk too early in the morning for Ray to tell him to pick up after his dangerous dog, after which Loki spent the morning gutting with surgical precision all the squeak toys Xavier bought for him. Xavier looked away from watching DVDs of old Pride and UFC fights to see Loki holding yet another squeaker proudly between his teeth, the cotton entrails of another victim hanging from his jowls. Xavier looked at his cell and saw hours had passed. It would soon be time to head to Shot's to help train his stable of boxers, kickboxers, and mixed martial arts fighters.

He knew he couldn't shirk his penance, but he couldn't leave Loki at home. That dog would never be alone again if Xavier could help it. Short trips to the grocery store and the like would have to happen—but a full day at the gym? He hadn't thought this whole dog thing through.

He packed his gear, leashed up Loki, and headed toward the back door. Xavier stopped in front of a calendar taped to the freezer. Slashes crossed out days past. A circle surrounded the last day of the month, the day he might get "the call" telling him his suspension was up.

Xavier uncapped the marker stuck to the fridge and lined through today's date. He looked down at Loki.

"Any day now."

Close to the car, Loki put on the brakes, as he had when Xavier had taken him to the pet store for food. Despite how thoroughly he'd cleaned out the car, it represented a tomb for Loki, one that likely still smelled of death. Xavier had finally had to lift Loki and place him in the front seat. The dog had shivered the entire way there and back.

Xavier squatted in front of him and took his face in his hands. "Never again, Loke. I promise, okay? Never." He massaged the back of his ears. Loki inhaled, then breathed out, content or defeated, Xavier couldn't quite discern. Either way, Loki rose off his haunches and jumped in the passenger seat.

Lincoln Drive was light on traffic. No one riding Xavier's tail to keep him from enjoying the foliage along the Wissahickon. He laughed when Loki stared up through the windshield at the monolithic Henry Avenue Bridge and ducked when they drove under it, as though his massive head would somehow bump the bottom. Xavier told himself he'd bring the dog to Forbidden Drive, maybe take him down to the creek. He wondered if Loki knew what it felt like to have his paws in the water. He imagined him chained up and starving in some random yard, then again curled in on himself in the backseat of the car. Xavier's brain had betrayed his memory so many times as of late, yet his mind wouldn't let that particular image go. He patted Loki's head and turned onto Main Street.

SHOT'S BOXING AND FITNESS CLUB resided in a renovated warehouse at the bottom of one of Manayunk's steepest hills. Xavier shook his head every time he parked beneath the marquee, never quite used to the "and Fitness Club" added to the signage. He exited the car and made for the entrance. Loki trotted by his side.

Inside, Xavier lifted his chin at the receptionist, phone tucked between her shoulder and ear as she scanned a member's keycard and stared at Loki in wide-eyed wonder. Xavier ignored her incredulity and veered toward Kansas, the older part of the gym, where sweat-swollen floorboards creaked under his feet. The red, white, and blue canvas ropes of the boxing ring sagged at the center. The blood of amateurs, journeymen, and the occasional honest-to-God champion stained the once brilliant white mat the gray brown of a discarded cigarette filter. Heavy bags hung from exposed girders, duct-taped midriffs retaining their innards. Rusted dumbbells sat under a row of weighted jump ropes. Xavier breathed deep the aroma of worn leather speed bags, the hot breath of exertion that hung in the air—the smells of suffering and glory. Stripped down, lean, and hard. Where Xavier slept was simply a house. Here was home.

On the other side of the reception desk lay Oz in all its technicolor gaudiness. Treadmills lined windows looking out onto Main Street. Rubberized dumbbells. An all-purpose exercise room with glossy floors. Aerobic steps. Ab rollers. Heavy bags on plastic water-filled bases. The mirrored walls echoed electronic dance music, nearly drowning out the shouts of encouragement from the cardio kickbox instructor. Young urban professionals threw kicks and punches in the air, mean-mugging, imagining the physical embodiment of their own self-loathing.

Xavier knew Loki's presence would demand explanation. Across the floor, Shot held the heavy bag and called out coded combinations for Clayton, one of his protégés. Xavier stood at the door to Shot's office and waited. He scanned the multitude of framed photos that covered the walls on either side and above the door.

Shot standing over vanquished opponents, a conqueror in twelve-ounce gloves and satin shorts, eyes alight with fury.

Shot hoisting a belt heavenward with two others looped over his thick shoulders.

Shot shaking hands with the mayor.

A young champion in his prime. In the before time. Before it was all taken away.

There were photos from the after time, too. By then, his muscled chest had already melted into a softened belly. By then, the glint in his eye was artificial, the flash of cameras that only ever seemed to capture his face when his glass eye drifted. Pictures of Shot at the grand opening of the gym, a smile on every face of those in attendance, save Shot's. Shot posing with grinning gym patrons who paid a premium to have his uninterested fake face-off with them hung on the walls. Though physically present in the photographs, Shot was always somewhere else, looking past the camera, perhaps to the wall that held his silhouette, the shadow of the fearsome fighter he once was.

Xavier, as of late, had come to recognize that look in his own mirror. The thought raised gooseflesh on his arms, and he looked away from the photos. Shot hadn't yet seen him. He'd stepped away from the bag for a moment to correct Clay's stance. Clay shifted his feet and threw a pair of low hooks but Shot stopped him again and pushed him aside. Shot rounded his shoulder, brought his fists to face, then snapped off two thunderous body shots to the middle of the bag to show the young buck what was up. Clay blinked as the punches cracked. The bag pistoned up and down. The chain holding it clinked musically. Xavier felt for the kid. He saw defeat collapse Clay's face. The kid knew that as bad as his punches seemed a moment ago, they now looked even worse in comparison to Shot's. Everyone wanted to train with a champion. Until they didn't.

Shemar Oscar Tracy—Shot—had been a fire hydrant of a heavyweight, a head under six feet, with Tyson-like speed and power, but none of his head movement. He'd wade in, catching ones and twos to the head to get in range. Once there, the grenades at the ends of his arms fractured ribs and bruised livers. His power turned men to infants, fetal on the mat. A champion on the local circuit, Shot's star burned hot. He acquired belt after belt in the alphabet soup of boxing promotions and his pockets got fat and deep. Nightly dinners in Center City and bottle service at the clubs. Xavier had watched in amazement as men and women alike thronged to his corner tables, the fellas wanting pictures with the champ while the ladies kissed his cheek and whispered entreaties in his ear for a rendezvous in the bathroom.

Fast money led to fast cars and Shot liked to drive fast. He roared his engine down the streets of Philadelphia with Jack Johnson bravado, attracting Jack Johnson attention from local law enforcement. Xavier remembered the call from the hospital. A detached retina was a common injury in fighters, the doctors said. There was really no way to determine if it was a result of the repeated blows to the face from the officer's baton, the defense attorney said. And the jury agreed.

"Scarecrow!" Shot shouted from across the gym, snapping Xavier from his reverie. He lifted his chin at Shot and smiled, though he cringed inwardly at the sound of his nickname. Even as a grown man, the sting of the handle's origins never faded. Most assumed he'd been dubbed Scarecrow for his long limbs and seemingly limitless flexibility, practically immune to leg and arm submission attacks.

The truth was far less clever. Through his years of junior college wrestling, no matter how much he'd hit the weight room, no matter how hard he'd dieted, no matter how many sprints and Airdyne bike sessions, Xavier's midsection never carved the way his peers' did, and they never missed an opportunity to remind him. He was always soft bodied in comparison—lanky appendages attached to a straw-stuffed sack. As a fighter, he tried to embrace the creepy component of the nickname, the macabre mystique that accompanied his quiet demeanor, making him a competitor to be feared. But those past mockeries, as mockeries were wont to do, echoed louder than any sign of respect.

"Clay's not turning his hip on the hook," Xavier said.

"Yeah, well, you the nigga that's supposed to be here on time holding the bag for him, ain't you? What are you doing here?"

"What do you mean? I came to work."

"I mean what you doing *here*," Shot asked, pointing at Loki. "I don't recall sending out a 'bring your pets to work' memo."

"He's a good boy. He won't bother anyone, I promise."

"Why you ain't just leave him at home?"

"I can't do that."

"What do you mean, 'can't'?"

Xavier glanced at Clay, then back to Shot. "Can we go into your office for a minute?"

Shot led the way, eyeing Loki over his shoulder. Loki eyed him back.

With Shot seated in the weathered leather office chair behind his old metal desk, Xavier related the last twenty-four hours. Shot laced his fingers on top of his head, puffed out his cheeks, then blew the air out in a whoosh.

"Damn, X."

"Yeah."

They sat in silence for a moment.

"So . . . any thoughts?"

"About what?"

"About what? About what I just told you, man."

"I think you a grown-ass man and you going to do whatever it is you got to do."

Xavier shook his head. "Wow. Insightful. Thanks a lot."

"What did you expect me to say?"

"I don't know, Shot. Show a little compassion? Give me some advice? Act like you care?"

"Act like I—" Shot laughed, disgusted. "You ain't got the sense that dog does, do you?"

"Excuse me?" Xavier stood and the back of his chair clattered against the floor. Loki popped up on all fours, hair raised. Shot stayed seated.

"Man, you better sit down." They stared at each other for a moment. Xavier collected himself, put the chair upright, and sat. Loki followed suit. Shot scoffed. "'Excuse me.' Excuses is all you got lately, cousin."

Xavier sucked his teeth and looked off to the side. "Man, go ahead."

"No, *you* go ahead. Rolling up in here late like it's your name on the front of this building. Like you don't owe me for giving you this job in the first place. Soon as you got comfortable, you just start coming and going when you please. But you family, and I ain't said nothing. Now today, not only is you late again, but you stroll in here with some broke-down dog like this is one them restaurants down the street with a water bowl out front. And now you got the nerve to come in here and ask *me* what *you* should do? Negro, please."

"Man, what is your problem?"

"Right now, my problem is you. Coming in here whining because you got some headaches and forgetting shit."

"Whining?"

"Did I mumble? Whining. Acting like you don't know this," he said as he tapped his temple, "is part of the game. You don't want to fight, don't fight. That's your call."

"Oh, okay, then I'll just open a gym and sell out to all the other gentrifiers in the neighborhood. When you starting the goat yoga classes, Shot? I want to make sure I sign up before you run out of spots."

"Okay, you got jokes now. You know what else is funny? You not wanting to admit that you scared of ending up like your pops, drooling and pissing on himself in a home, so you putting it on me to tell you to stop fighting. Well, I'm not doing it."

Xavier rose from his seat again. "Yo, who the fuck do you think you are?"

Shot slapped both hands against the desk. Xavier and Loki flinched. Shot pushed off the desk and stood as well.

"Nigga, I *know* who I am. You better act like you know, too." Xavier sat once more. Shot circled the desk and leaned on the front of it. He rubbed his hands over his face. "Look, I shouldn't have said that about your pops. My bad. But X, you know as well as I do, this shit with your head is the bill coming due, man. We in the hurt business. You ain't really thought that just because you was doing MMA and not boxing that you wasn't going have to pay that bill someday, did you?"

Xavier stared at his feet. Loki stared up at him. His tail swooshed, once, twice, then stopped.

"But okay, you want advice? Bet. I'll tell you what I would do. I'd give anything to have your 'problem.' Yeah, that's right. Bug your eyes out at me all you want. I said what I said. Fact of the matter is I would trade that," he said, touching Xavier's forehead, then under his own glass eye, "for this, any day of the fucking week. If it was me? Boy, I'd fight until I was dead. Until they had to carry me out that ring. At least that way I would have had a say in how I went out."

Xavier took a breath. Shot's truth landed like his liver shots. Like always. "You're right."

"I know. Always am."

"It's just . . . we've seen where this can go, man. Goodridge, Seau—shit, Benoit. Not going to lie, Shot. I'm scared."

"You should be. It's scary. I get that. But, hey. Look at me." Xavier did as he was told. "I got you, cuz." Shot held out his hand and Xavier took it. Shot pulled him up into a hug.

"You got me," Xavier said, unsure whether he was asking or telling.

A knock on the door and they parted. Shot yelled for whoever it was to come in. A wrapped hand appeared around the door before Clay peeked his head in and pushed the door open. His sweat-drenched tank top clung to his frame, all lean muscle, sinew, and bone. "Hey, y'all. Sorry to interrupt." He said.

"What up, Clay?" Xavier said.

"What up, Scarecrow. Where were you at earlier?"

Shot cleared his throat, annoyed. "Nigga, what do you want?"

"Oh, my bad, Shot. Uh, Lawrence is here. Said he's ready to get some rounds in."

Shot rolled his eyes. "This fool. Tell him I'll be out when I'm out." He turned to see Xavier shift from one foot to the other. "You got to piss or something? What's wrong with you?"

"Come on, man. I need this today."

"Need what?"

"You know the suspension is up soon. The call could come any day and I've *got* to be ready when it does. Let me give Lawrence some rounds. I won't mess up your boy, swear to God."

Shot hissed. "Like God means something to you." He pointed to Xavier's chest. "Don't even know why you wear that damn thing."

Xavier's hand moved to the crucifix around his neck. He rubbed it, then tucked it under his shirt collar. "All right then, I don't swear. But I promise I'll be cool. Let me get in there."

"You mean to tell me after all we just got done talking

about, you want to go in there and get your head knocked around?"

Xavier couldn't explain the emotional swing—except he could. The past year he'd been through too many moments where he'd go from sadness to elation to rage in the space of an hour. But now was not the time for yet another revelation.

"Fight until you die. Isn't that what you just said? Besides, it's *Lawrence*. He isn't knocking around shit."

"You better put some respect on that boy's name. He's better than you think."

"Yeah, yeah. We talking or we sparring?"

Shot side-eyed Xavier, then looked past him to Clayton. "Hey yo, tell him X will be out in a minute to give him some work."

"My man," Xavier said. He held his fist out and waited for Shot's bump. It hung there for a few uncomfortable seconds before Shot touched his gnarled knuckles to Xavier's.

"He's got a big fight next week. Go easy. You feel me? I can't have him getting hurt."

"Man, I already said I would."

"Cousin. I know how you get."

"What do you mean, how I get?"

"Cuz, please. You a shade lighter than a paper bag but you more militant than Farrakhan. Stinking up my gym smelling like bean pies and shit."

Xavier laughed and waved him off. "The fuck out of here."

"Ain't nothing funny, X. I know how much it pisses you off that that white boy thinks he Blacker than Wesley Snipes at midnight. I don't like that bullshit either, but it's whatever. He can fight and he's moving up. The last thing I need is you fucking my shit up *again*. I had to pull some David Blaine-level street magic to get that heat off me after what you pulled."

Xavier dropped his head. "I feel you."

"No, you *owe* me. I just haven't figured out exactly how yet because you my people." Xavier glanced over at Loki lying on the floor, head on his paws. The dog lifted an eyebrow at Xavier, then at Shot, then back to Xavier, watching the tension bounce between them like a tennis volley. "All right, Reverend Brother Malcolm Kaepernick. Give him some rounds. But do *not* knock his ass out."

Xavier hurried out of the office toward the locker room. He emerged clutching his shin guards and boxing helmet in his gloved hands. Loki snapped playfully at the chin strap hanging loose at Xavier's side. He approached the small training cage in the far corner of the gym.

Already inside, Lawrence danced around the cage, shadowboxing with rapid uppercuts and retreating jabs, showing and proving for the young fighters who hovered on the outside of the fence. His practiced punches sliced through the air and snapped at the end. Xavier and Lawrence shared the same weight class, but their physiques were a class apart. Lawrence stood a head shorter, his skin pulled tight across his musculature with all the look of constant training and a disciplined diet. The constellations of acne on his back and chest told an entirely different story. Lawrence smirked when he saw Xavier with his gear.

"Man, you best tell Shot I'm trying to get some real rounds. Ain't trying to play tag with no senior citizen."

"Let me ask you something, *Larry*," Xavier said. "When the cops pull you over, do you drop the wannabe act and talk like the rest of the white suburbanites from the Main Line, or do you double down on the cultural appropriation? Oh, wait, that's right, you white boys don't get pulled over, do you? Even with those dumbass cornrows on your head."

The boys in Lawrence's corner brought closed fists to their

mouths and let out a collective drawn out *damn*. Lawrence waved them off, indignant.

"So, if I'm supposed to act white, that means I should talk like you, right? Because when it comes to me and you, everyone knows I'm the Blackest one here."

"Is that right?"

"That's right. And my name is Lawrence, not Larry. But I guess you know all about getting called by the wrong name, huh, Tom?"

The boys outside the cage oooh-ed, egging on the confrontation, spoiling to see the two throw hands. Others training on the bags stopped their drills and made their way cage side.

Xavier clenched his jaw while he wrapped his hands. He once thought he'd left the Lawrences of his life back in high school. The white boys who filled the trunks of their Honda Civic hatchbacks with enormous speaker boxes, bass lines rattling their windows so hard they had to have them resealed, who strutted the halls, their walk and dress an unflattering imitation of whatever rapper they idolized that week, putting on a modern-day minstrel show, who told Xavier how as a mixed kid who listened to "white music," who talked "all proper" because his Black mother taught college English and would not tolerate slang in her home, who had a white father, whose hair didn't kink as tight as the other Black kids' but was still so exotic and touchable, who wasn't naturally athletic at basketball, football, or track like he was supposed to be, who seemed to only date white girls, whose skin they pointed out wasn't much darker than theirs when they returned from their summer vacation at their parents' beach home, whose dick was seen as small (all things considered) during showers in gym class, that they were Blacker than he was. It had been hurtful enough to hear from some of his Black peers. To hear the same from the Lawrences in his world had been maddening.

Xavier hadn't been a fighter then. Far from it. A scrawny kid, he'd found no place in group sports. Obsessed with martial arts since his first brush with Saturday morning Kung Fu theater as a toddler, he'd begged until his parents signed him up for Tae Kwon Do at the YMCA in the ninth grade. The art granted him no protection from the bullying, no boost in self-confidence. Instead, he found further scorn and derision as kids followed him down the school hallways, taunting him with *kiais* before knocking his books out of his hands.

Xavier wasn't a fighter then.

But he was a fighter now.

Shot appeared behind Xavier. "How about you both shut up and gear up. Tired of hearing y'all's bullshit."

Lawrence slid on his helmet and secured the chin strap. "Yes, sir, Mr. Tracy."

"*Yes, sir, Mr. Tracy, sir,*" Xavier said.

"Keep playing with me, X," Shot said.

Xavier laughed. The fingerless MMA sparring gloves were dense with extra foam, heavier than the regulation four-ouncers. Xavier pushed the padding back and down repeatedly, as far away from his knuckles as it would go. He'd take care not to hit Lawrence too hard in the face, but it was open season for a liver shot or two. Xavier donned his helmet, slid on his shin guards, and pulled the straps tight.

Shot opened the cage door for him. "Remember what I said."

Xavier put in his mouthpiece and bared a blue-and-black rubbered grin. He patted Shot's cheek and mumbled, "Yes, dear."

Shot slapped his hand away. "Man, go ahead."

Xavier told Loki to sit and made his way up the three metal steps to the cage. The door closed behind him. Shot slid the lynchpin home and locked them in.

"Five-minute rounds," Shot called out.

"That's a long time to run away from me in this little cage, old head," Lawrence said. He extended his arm as an offer to touch gloves. Xavier did not reciprocate. "Oh, it's like that?"

"It's like that."

"Bet."

Xavier took the center. Lawrence bounded on the balls of his feet, side to side, then in and out, left hand down by his waist, his right a cocked pistol hammer. Xavier watched Lawrence's chest, keeping his body within full view. Lawrence committed to the in and out, feinting with his back hand, watching for Xavier to react. Xavier matched his lateral movements, cutting off the cage, slowly moving in. Lawrence backed into chain link and hot-footed it out and away, creating more space, and sidestepped around Xavier again. One of the kids yelled from outside the cage.

"He don't want none, X!"

"Man, shut up," Lawrence shouted. At that, he changed his footwork, and moved diagonally. Xavier had adapted to his initial pattern and in that split second, he looked at Lawrence's feet. All the opening Lawrence needed, his front hand flashed from his waist to the bridge of Xavier's nose, a stiff up-jab as hard as a cross. Xavier's head snapped back, the world gone white in an instant. His eyes leaked and the inside of his nostrils went wet, snot or blood he couldn't tell, but he wouldn't (couldn't) bring his hand to his nose to let Lawrence see the jab had affected him.

Lawrence saw it had. He shuffled his feet back and forth, stutter stepped in and around Xavier. The structureless choreography distracted Xavier and he looked down to Lawrence's feet again. Lawrence made him pay with another lightning jab followed by a straight right that put Xavier back two steps.

"Eyes up, X," Shot shouted. "You too heavy on your heels."

Xavier heard Shot, but only just. He was right. His feet felt stuck to the mat, his calves and thighs leaden compared to the springs in Lawrence's legs. Lawrence was faster. Sharper. Xavier plodded after him, no longer controlling the center of the cage, but giving chase. Lawrence faked the jab and Xavier's hands went up, leaving space for a looping hook Lawrence hid behind the feint. The punch caught Xavier behind the ear and turned his headgear. His knees buckled and forced a retreat. A faint whine started in his ears.

"Watch the power, Lawrence," Shot said. "We're sparring here."

"Man, I ain't even hit him hard, Shot. Told you he don't belong in here with me." Lawrence waved Xavier in. "Let's go, X. I ain't even sweating yet."

You going to let this fool punk you like this? Just because Shot said go easy? You bitch made for certain.

Xavier adjusted his helmet and stepped back to the center, a new lightness in his legs. He bounced back and forth, floating toward and away from Lawrence, making him adjust and readjust his distance. With each bounce the whine got louder.

He's dropping his back hand when he jabs. Make him pay for it.

Xavier stepped forward and intentionally looked down. He saw Lawrence's hand rise from his hips as though in slow motion, slipped his jab, and delivered a thunderous right cross down the middle. The boys outside the cage shouted, and Lawrence fell back against the fence. He brought his fingers to his nose, checking for blood. The corner of Xavier's mouth upturned.

"X! I said easy!" Shot shouted.

Easy, my ass. Fuck this white boy up.

"Nah, I'm good, Shot," Lawrence shouted. "Come on, motherfucker."

Yeah, that's it.

They met in the center, exchanging jabs, followed by low kicks to the other's lead leg, both looking for a power shot, but neither finding a home for one. Lawrence jawed at Xavier, told him he was two-steps slower, nothing but a ball of string to a tiger.

Ain't no tiger. Just a pussy.

Xavier hardly heard him over the steam whistle in his ears. Every blocked shot, every impact to the outside of his glove, every bounce on his toes, every punch thrown sent shocks through his temples and cranked the dial on the screaming in his skull.

Lawrence faked a low-kick and went high. His padded shin smashed into Xavier's face and sent him to the mat on his ass.

Get your sorry ass up.

Instinct kicked in and he stood. Shot yelled from outside the cage but Xavier could no longer make out the words. A different voice found purchase in his brain. Adrenaline dumped into his bloodstream. Rage streamed down his nerve fibers.

An image flashed across his mind's eye. Lawrence's face leaking blood from openings both natural and not. And Xavier wanted to make that image real.

Xavier sold a shot for the double leg takedown and Lawrence bought it. He dropped into a sprawl and his jaw met Xavier's uppercut on the way down. The impact drove his teeth into the underside of his mouthpiece and sent his helmet toppling to his corner. A chorus of *oh shit*s sounded around the cage.

Before Lawrence could fall backward, Xavier slammed his forearms down onto Lawrence's collarbones, wrapped his hands behind his head, and held his neck in a tight clinch.

Do it.

Xavier yanked Lawrence's exposed head down to meet his

rising leg. He felt the firm ridge of the bridge of Lawrence's nose against his knee, then felt it give up shape and form with a wet crunch. He lifted Lawrence's head and held it there for less than the span of a breath, though it felt like minutes. Xavier looked into his glassy, dilated eyes, and for a moment felt a fleeting ache of regret, one that disappeared as he brought Lawrence's cheekbone crashing down into another knee strike. Lawrence collapsed to the mat. Xavier followed him down and sat on his chest in full mount.

More. Don't stop.

Xavier's arms were pistons in an engine. The back of Lawrence's head bounced off the mat, then met it again with violent speed. With each blow, the hard parts in Lawrence's face went soft, and the whistle in Xavier's ears abated, enough to hear the cage door open, to hear Shot's screams behind him. A thick arm slid under his chin and tightened around his carotids, the familiar smell of cocoa butter on the skin telling him it was Shot.

But he couldn't (wouldn't) stop punching.

SO WAT CHA SAYIN'

Xavier opened his eyes.

Had he slept?

Was he in the house?

The ceiling was not his ceiling. The ground was not his bed. He was home.

He lifted his head. Clay held Xavier's feet above him in a recovery position, shaking blood from Xavier's legs to his brain. Clay wasn't watching him, though. He looked off to the side of the cage where Shot and two other fighters from the gym stood around a body supine on the floor, legs hovering stiff above the mat.

"Clay," Xavier said. "What happened?"

"Aye yo, Shot," Clay called across the cage. "He awake."

Shot turned to look over his shoulder. Fury carved lines into his forehead and he strode toward his cousin. Xavier scrambled to a seated position. He fought another wave of vertigo and stole a look through Shot's legs to see Lawrence on the floor of the cage, his face a swollen and bloody mess.

"What . . . Clay, what happened to Lawrence?"

Before Clay could answer, Shot was on Xavier. He pushed Clay aside, gripped Xavier at the armpits, and lifted him to his feet. He brought his nose to Xavier's and spoke with quiet menace. "You happened to him, cuz." He put a finger to X's chest and burrowed as if to pierce his heart with it. "*You* did that shit."

Xavier became aware of a bone-deep ache in his hands and the throb of bruises yet to surface just above his knees. He'd been in a fight. That much was certain.

"Shot, I don't—"

"Uh uh. No. I don't want to hear that shit."

"Shot—"

"Get out my face. Right now. Go back to the locker room and don't you go no-God-damn-where. I got to wait out here until the fucking ambulance shows up."

"Shot."

Shot walked away from him. He kneeled by Lawrence's side while Xavier watched. Lawrence's legs gave up their rigor and his feet turned slowly side to side. Clay stood two steps away from Xavier, mouth open, arms slack, as if he feared moving from where Shot had placed him so unceremoniously. He looked back and forth from Shot to Xavier, seeking permission to move and speak.

Xavier turned away, ashamed of the carnage he'd forgotten he'd wrought, and stepped toward the cage door. Lawrence's battered visage flashed in his mind. A dizziness different from his vertigo spun the world and took him out at the knees. Before the mat rose up to meet him, he felt an arm around his waist and thin but strong shoulders under his arm. Clay walked in step with him to the edge of the cage.

"Clay, that's not me, man."

"Nah, I get it. All that mess he was saying to you. I would have wrecked him, too. Most of us in here was waiting to see when his mouth wrote a check his ass couldn't cash. Dumbass wannabe had that shit coming." Clay helped Xavier down the stairs where Loki sat, tail sweeping the floor at the sight of him. "Thought he was going to jump over top of the cage when Shot choked you out. Why he don't bark, though? Looked like he was trying to, but nothing came out except for like this weird whine."

"Long story. Another time."

"Yeah, all right."

Xavier grabbed Loki's leash and followed Clay toward the locker room. Xavier knew Clay intended comfort with his words, but they missed the mark. At first Xavier had seen training Shot's up-and-comers as beneath him, especially when he'd been so close to breaking through to the big time. But he eventually enjoyed the job. Most of the kids had come from circumstances he couldn't have imagined growing up in, and he stepped into the role of mentor as well as trainer. Xavier showed them fighting could channel their anger and keep them from the dangerous life that awaited them if they let their justifiable rage cloud their better judgment. And yet, he'd just done everything he told them not to do. Worse yet, Clay admired him for it. He felt nauseated.

When they reached the locker room, he bolted for the nearest stall and retched hot bile until his back ached from the strain. Clay asked from the other side of the door if he was okay. Xavier assured him he was, thanked him, and told him he could go. Once Clay left, he exited the stall and sat on a bench in front of a row of lockers.

He picked at the edge of athletic tape that bound the wrist strap of his gloves. Lawrence's blood stained the white a ruddy brown. He unraveled the tape, spooling it around his opposite hand, the tape twisting on itself into a rope-like braid until it sat in a coiled heap at his feet. Gloves off, he unwound his wraps and added them to pile. Loki sniffed at it, then snorted through his nose before turning in a circle and resting at Xavier's feet.

Xavier opened and closed his fingers. He winced at the

ache traveling down the bones of his hands. The layers of padding had done nearly nothing to lessen the impact of the punches he did not remember throwing. He massaged his knuckles, pushing back the fluid that had already begun to collect there. He felt the grind of calcium deposits accumulated from the countless bone bruises and fractures he'd collected over the years, healed improperly because casts and surgery required insurance or money, neither of which he possessed. That his fighting created injuries he couldn't pay to fix was an irony never lost on him, never so poignant than in moments such as these. Except he'd never had a moment quite like this one.

The locker room wall faced the parking lot, and Xavier heard the wail of a siren come closer, then stop. The sounds of raised voices and the rattle of gurney wheels slid under the door. The commotion died down. Xavier gripped the bench with his sore hands, bowed his head, and waited for his cousin. He would not wait long.

Shot appeared in the doorway. Loki sprung to his feet, but Xavier pressed down on his rear. Loki relented and sat. Shot pushed the slow closing door until the latch clicked home, then turned the deadbolt. He sat on the bench next to Xavier and rubbed his ashen knuckles. His palms glided over the deep grooves of scar where the skin had split many times over. Shot lowered his head. His thick shoulders arched over his neck. Shot bore a weight that bowed his spine. Weight Xavier had put there.

"You have no idea what you just did."

"What did the EMTs say?"

"What?"

"About Lawrence. What did they say?"

Shot laughed, disgusted. "What did they say about Lawrence? You are unbelievable, cuz."

"Yeah, I mean did they say . . . like, how bad? Is he going to be okay?"

Shot spoke with unnerving calm. "I don't give a shit about Lawrence, Xavier. The one you fucked up here, the one I care about, is *me*." He smacked his palm against his chest.

"You don't care? I don't understand."

"Fine, you want to know about Lawrence? Lawrence probably ain't never fighting again. I've seen enough of this to know when someone got broken so bad they ain't coming back. But that's whatever."

"It's whatever?" Xavier asked, incredulous.

"*It's whatever*. He's done and I got no use for him. Now. But I *had* a use for him, X. And what you did just now is you killed me, dude. You fucking killed me."

"Killed you? How did I kill you?"

Shot screamed, "Would you stop repeating every God-damned thing I say?" Xavier flinched. Shot breathed deep, then exhaled. "I told you he had a big fight. I told you. I should have known better. I should have never put you in there with him."

Xavier spoke in a near whisper. "Shot, what are you talking about, man? What is really going on here?"

"What do you think, X? I got to spell this out for you?"

He didn't. There'd been whispers and rumors for years. Fighters like Lawrence in Shot's stable, fighters who most always won the bouts they weren't supposed to and lost the ones that should have been money in the bank. Xavier wouldn't hear it. He knew the fixers had come sniffing in Shot's prime, but Xavier knew his cousin's love for the purity of the game was a defense their offers couldn't penetrate. Xavier never entertained that his cousin, so strong, so proud, would ever succumb, even in his forced retirement. Xavier had faith. He was loyal. Not that either of those things mattered.

Not really. Because faith wavered. Loyalty could be swayed.
Neither were as strong as the power of Xavier's denial, particularly when it came to the truth about someone he loved.

"No," Xavier said.

"Yeah."

"Why?"

"Why? Because a boxing gym barely covered the rent
before this jawn got gentrified. I was sleeping here, dude.
Even when I finally gave in and put all that Zumba shit out
there, I was still barely making it. Do you even know how
much it costs to keep fucking avocados and soy milk stocked
for their smoothies and shit?" Xavier snorted, in spite of himself. "Don't laugh. Ain't shit funny."

"I didn't mean it like that. My bad."

"You damn right it's your bad." Shot paced in front of
him, then screamed. "Fuck!"

Xavier jumped in his seat again. "I'm sorry, Shot."

"That's great. I'll be sure to tell them you're sorry. Should
take care of everything."

"It wasn't your fault. Can't you . . . I don't know. Can't
you reason with them?"

"Who do you think bankrolls these fixes, X? Some Center
City financial cats with money to throw around? These are
hard motherfuckers, X, and you—*you*—just took money out
of their pocket."

Xavier ran his hands over his head. "Okay, it's on me
then."

"What you mean it's on you? The only reason you got a
dime to your name right now is because I'm putting it in your
hand. You don't got near enough money to make this right,
and what you got is mine any damn way. I'm only giving it to
you because you family. Your ass should be working for me
for free with what you pulled last year."

Xavier looked away from Shot's hard stare and rubbed his hands together until dead skin fell to the floor. Shot sat back down next to him with a sigh.

"Where did you go, man?"

"What do you mean?"

"I mean I known you my whole life. You a passionate brother, but you're not violent. I always, *always* got the sense that you in this game because you're good at it, but that you never liked hurting people. I've seen it in your face when you win, and especially when you knocked someone out. When you lost, you looked relieved. I'm saying you're a gentle soul, dude. I've seen you out here with these kids, training them, bringing them up. You coach them like they your own. Shit, you damn near better at it than me. You don't ever raise your voice, even when they being lazy. You ain't got a mean bone in you.

"But what you did out there—I've seen motherfuckers take beatings like that in the street. But in the *street*. Even then, it wasn't nothing like *that*. Nah, man, not in a million years could I believe someone if they told me you were capable of that."

Xavier looked at the ceiling. Tears brimmed then rolled down his cheeks. "I don't know."

"You don't know what?"

"I don't know where I went. Honest to God, Shot, I remember the head kick and then looking at the ceiling. It was that fast. I keep trying to force myself to bring it back." He looked down at Loki and ran an index finger down the bridge of his nose. Loki pushed up into it. "But how do you remember something if it didn't happen?"

"It happened, X."

Xavier tapped his head. "Not here." Another curt laugh to himself.

"What?" Shot asked.

Xavier smiled sadly. "The Scarecrow lost his brains."

Shot's shoulders dropped. The resolve to hold on to his anger melted away. He reached a thick hand out and kneaded the back of Xavier's neck.

"You been to a doctor?"

"No."

"They might help."

"You ever seen this get better, Shot? No, a doctor is going to want to take an MRI, and if it shows something, that's it. I'm done before my suspension is even over. Like you said, if I'm going to be done, it's going to be on my terms."

"You going to stay throwing that in my face, huh?"

"I read somewhere if you repeat things, it makes your argument more convincing."

Shot stared at Xavier, and Xavier held the stare until Shot's pursed lips cracked and a laugh escaped.

"Man, you stupid."

"I know."

The locker room door rattled. A knock followed. Clay called from the other side.

"Shot. They taking him out."

Shot stood. "We're not done with this conversation. Take your ass home. I'll get at you." He headed for the door.

"What are you going to do?"

Shot turned the deadbolt and kept his face to the door. "Same thing I did last time you dumped shit in my lap, X. Clean it up." He left the locker room without a look back, and the door hissed to a close behind him.

"Fuck."

Xavier collected his wraps and blood-stained tape from the floor. He went to throw them in the trash, then stopped. He turned his hand over so the pile rested in his palm, hovering above the can. He retrieved a plastic grocery bag from his gear bag and emptied out the few apples in it, placed the tape and wraps in there, and placed them in his bag. A totem, he told himself. A trigger for his brain to somehow keep from doing what he had done again. He rubbed at the cross around his neck and thought about how many times wearing it had failed to provide him with the salvation promised. The asking was the problem.

He took the wraps out and threw them in the trash.

Changed and showered, he led Loki out of the locker room and back toward the cage to retrieve the headgear he'd forgotten to stow in his gear bag. Clay, rubber gloved, on his hands and knees, scrubbed at the stain on the mat where Lawrence's head rested minutes ago. Xavier rubbed his knuckles again at the sight and swallowed hard, his throat sore from Shot's choke. Clay stood when he saw Xavier. He walked to the fence and hooked his fingers through the chain link.

"You out?"

"Yeah. You shouldn't be cleaning that up."

"I mean, who else is going to do it?" Xavier set his bag down and made for the steps, but Clay waved him off. "Nah, I got it, man. Keeps me training for free. Shit, I'd rather clean up blood than the toilets." Xavier managed a half-hearted laugh. "You all right, Scarecrow?"

"Not me I'm worried about, man."

"I feel you. Like I said, shouldn't have been running his mouth."

"Clay, what I did . . . that's never okay."

"How you figure? He tried to punk you like he always does. You should hear what he says when you ain't here."

"Clay—"

"You ask me, he got what was coming to him."

"Clay!"

Xavier punched the cage. Clay stepped back. Xavier's shout bounced off the exposed warehouse ceiling girders and echoed to the front of the gym. Xavier looked back to see the lunch-break crowd filing in, scanning their membership cards, ties loosened, heels in hand. They looked to the cage where Xavier and Clay stood, an area that was all but forbidden to them, made all the more intriguing for it, necks craned in hopes of catching some whiff of escalating drama in the air. Embarrassed less by the looky-loos and more by his outburst, Xavier turned back to the cage. Clay had taken another step back.

"Man, I'm sorry. I shouldn't have shouted like that." Xavier pressed his fist up against the cage for Clay to bump it. "We cool?"

Clay jerked a thumb over his shoulder, his body stiff. "I got to get this cleaned up before Shot gets back." He fast-walked back to the stain on the mat. Xavier took his fist from the fence.

"Yeah, okay. I'll see you tomorrow?"

Clay waved without looking up and scrubbed with renewed vigor at what Lawrence had left behind.

The whine had returned to his ears, and Xavier wiggled the tip of his pinky in the canal as if to root it out. Xavier noticed the gym patrons watching him as he approached the front door. They made extra room for him and Loki as they came closer. He'd seen people make that same space when sharing the sidewalk with someone walking a pit bull—and sometimes without one—even going so far as to cross the street. Who did they fear more now, he wondered, after what had just happened—the dog or him? The front desk receptionist tossed a goodbye to Xavier as he waved and walked out the door.

Xavier leaned against the hood of the car with all the doors open and the fan turned all the way up. Once the sauna-like heat had vented, he hoisted Loki into the passenger seat, and they drove off. He turned at the bottom of Shurs Lane. The engine shifted and strained as it made the steep climb up the hill through the cattle chute formed by cars parked along the sidewalks in front of the rowhomes and apartments on either side, making it almost impossible for cars to share the two-way street. Once he completed the uphill slalom, Xavier turned at the light at the top of the hill and drove a few short blocks to Roxborough. He pulled into a parking lot and stopped behind a numbered space, occupied by another car.

"What the hell?"

He shook his head and drove further down the lot where visitor spaces sat empty. Once parked, he and Loki walked toward the rear entrance of the building. Loki snuffled the ground, exploring the smells of the environment as if he'd never been here before.

They reached the door. Xavier slid his key home, but the lock wouldn't budge. He pulled then pushed on the door, wiggling the key. When nothing happened, he removed the key and held it up to examine it, then tried another, but with the same result. A middle-aged woman climbed the steps behind them. She was slightly out of breath. Strands of blond hair escaped her tight ponytail in wisps that stuck to her sweaty flushed cheeks. She untied the lace of her jogging shoe, unthreaded her key, and unlocked the door.

"Excuse me."

Xavier stepped aside. "Did they change the locks?"

"Not that I know of."

Xavier reached for the door, but the woman pulled it closed, just shy of pinching Xavier's fingers in the door. "Excuse *me*. Can you let me in?" She pointed at a sign next to the entrance that stated residents should not let non-residents into the building. "Yeah, I know. I live here."

"I've never seen you here before," she said, muffled by the glass.

"How long have you lived here?"

"That's none of your business."

"Lady, it's hot as hell out here. I'd like to get my dog some water. Can you please let me in?"

"Sorry." She shrugged, then jogged up the steps behind her until she was out of sight.

"Unbelievable."

Before he turned away from the door, another pair of feet appeared descending the steps. They belonged to a brother around Xavier's age. His face brightened with recognition when he saw Xavier and he held his hand out for a shake when he pushed open the door.

"What's up, man?" he said, pulling Xavier in for a half hug. "I haven't seen you in a minute. What are you doing standing out here in this heat? You visiting somebody?"

Xavier looked him over. Did he know him? Seemed like he should. Best to act as if.

"What? No. No, I just got back from training and for some reason, my key's not working. I tried to get inside but that woman said she didn't think I lived here and wouldn't let me in."

The man pulled his chin back. "But, I mean, you don't live here."

Xavier laughed in disbelief. "What are you talking about, man?"

"Are you messing with me?"

"Are *you*?"

"I'm saying, you moved out like months ago."

"What? Moved out?"

"My dude, now I know you're messing with me." Xavier watched the man's face collapse with concern. "X, I helped you carry down some of your boxes. You said you were moving into your Pop's house." Xavier heard no lie in his tone. The man put a hand on his shoulder and squeezed. "You all right, man?"

Xavier forced a smile and pointed at the man with both fingers in a "gotcha" pose. The man laughed, though from relief or amusement, Xavier couldn't quite tell.

"Man, of course, I'm just playing with you!"

The man put his hand over his heart. "Whew. You can't do that. I was for real worried there for a minute."

"Nothing to worry about. Just messing around."

There is so much to worry about. I am not messing around in the slightest.

The man side-eyed Xavier. "You sure?"

I am completely unsure of everything. Please help me.

"I'm playing, dude. Of course."

The man laughed. Xavier returned a laugh of his own and hoped the man didn't (did?) hear the despair in it.

"Cool. So, what was that with old girl at the door anyway?"

"You know how it is today. Calling the cops on folks for having a cookout while Black."

"Shit, I know that's right."

"I'm just meeting somebody here. Thought I'd get inside out of this heat is all. She wasn't having it, though."

Don't believe me. Don't believe me.

"Well, damn, I can let you in."

Oh, come on.

"Nah, don't sweat it. I don't want Building Monitor Becky getting you in trouble." The man laughed and Xavier patted Loki's head. "Me and my man will wait out here a little bit longer."

The man appeared unconvinced but acquiesced. He put out his fist and bumped it with Xavier's before walking off to his car and driving out of the parking lot. When he was out of sight, Xavier walked Loki back to the car. Loki jumped in this time, seemingly preferring the inside of the car to the hot asphalt beneath the pads of his paws. Xavier started the car and turned the fan on full blast. Loki blinked against the rushing air. Xavier rested his forehead on the steering wheel. The whine in his ears escalated to a shrill whistle.

Maybe he was just preoccupied. After all, he'd just put a man in the hospital. Perhaps ended his career. No matter how illegitimate that career might have been, ending his livelihood wasn't Xavier's choice to make. That was a lot to carry. With all that on his mind it made sense he'd drive here instinctively. It made sense he'd not recognize what another car parked in his space meant. It made sense he'd not recall he'd moved out when his key didn't work in the door. It made sense it took a nameless someone reminding him that he'd moved out long ago before he actually remembered he had, and it made sense he only remembered where he'd moved to because that same person had told him.

Of course, it made sense. It all made absolute perfect fucking sense.

He lifted his head and turned the ignition again, forgetting he'd already done so. The engine's insides scraped against each other. Loki's wide tongue retracted, and he cocked his head at the sound.

"I think I'm in trouble, Loke," he said. He threw the car into gear and drove off for home.

Out of the car, in his father's house, he went straight to the back of the house and sat on his bed. He gripped the edge and cried. His quiet tears turned to ragged sobs that stole his breath. He pulled at the collar of his T-shirt, desperate for air, ripping the fabric, leaving it to hang loose and shapeless. He howled in a whisper, the muscles of his abdomen contracted and cramped. Loki sat in the doorway, lifted to all fours, then sat once more, as if unsure whether to comfort or to be comforted. As the steam whistle screamed in his ears, Xavier thought of his father's gun, the one he kept tucked in the corner of the bedroom closet. The thought of the gun calmed him. His breathing slowed. He lay back and fell asleep in an instant.

DAMIEN

Y̲ou know what I don't get?

When people get all up in arms about violence. Especially in the cage.

Oh, it's so barbaric.

Oh, it's human cockfighting.

Oh, it's just a blood sport for knuckle draggers and Neanderthals.

Please.

Why is everyone out here denying their true nature? Because, let me tell you, your boy, Clay? He called it right. Lawrence deserved everything you gave him. Talking all that yang about how he's Blacker than you. You just gave him what he was asking for, and you did that shit because, for once, you stopped denying your true nature.

Hell, everybody's got that animal in them.

How many times you been caught in a traffic jam because everybody's slowing down, damn near twisting their heads off to see how bad somebody got fucked up in an accident? They ain't looking to make sure everybody is okay. They want to see heads through windshields. Somebody dead on the asphalt. They want to see something that better be worth making them late to work. They want to see gore. They want to feel that rush.

I'm saying, nobody watches football to see some boring-ass

back and forth tactical game, and if they say that, they're lying. To you. To themselves. They want to see wide receivers in the open field, up in the air, backs turned, get flipped upside down and land on their head, turning their spine into a jack-in-the-box. They want to see those nasty hits when dudes' helmets fly off. They watch with bated breath when the game stops because he isn't moving on the field, and you can't tell me they aren't just a little disappointed when he stands up and walks it off. If that applause they give when he can stand on his own isn't the most half-hearted applause you ever heard, then I don't know what is.

See, violence is in our nature, homeboy. Violence builds empires. Violence destroys tyranny. Violence is the only way forward and it's in our DNA. It's damn sure in yours. But somewhere along the way, we started telling ourselves it wasn't cool. That we couldn't just pick up a club anymore and crush somebody's skull if they were in our way. So, we created all these rules that moved our violence to the ring, the mats, the cage, the field, the ice, and then we created rules, turned it into sport, turned our primal urges into a desire for the most yards, the most points, the most wins in the season, the belt, the trophy.

But people cheer the loudest at a hockey game when the fights break out.

People lose their damn minds when a race car flips end over end at two hundred miles per hour.

People tell themselves they shouldn't get out of the car at the light after someone cut them off in traffic, to pull them out of their car by their hair and bash their head off the hood until their teeth scatter because it's just so *wrong*.

But they want to. Oooh, boy, they all want to visit some violence on that fool. That urge to destroy just claws at them from inside their chest. They're just too soft to do it—to answer that call. And it isn't their fault. It's just how shit is. It's what we turned all this into.

So stop all this hand-wringing and hair-pulling about what you did to Lawrence. You so upset because you think you might could have ruined his career. But so what? You think anybody gives a damn when they see some fighter get knocked out, some football player get concussed, about what happens to them when they turn the damn television off?

Ain't nobody worried about consequences. They just want to be entertained. They want to feel that adrenaline running through their veins like heroin when they see carnage. They can't be bothered to think about what happens outside of their own lives, let alone what happens to *your* ass. They don't care about your headaches, about your memory.

So what are you so upset about?

Be honest with yourself. Because truth be told, it isn't just about the fact that he deserved it, because he damn sure did.

It's about the fact that you liked that shit.

Check that.

You *loved* that shit.

And yeah, yeah, you can go on and on about how you don't remember doing it. Fugue state and all that. Flash knockdown and you forgot where you were. Okay. Tell you what, I'll give you that. I'll let you keep believing that.

Doesn't do a damn thing to change how you felt after.

How was that headache?

That whistling in your ears?

All that went away when you saw him laid out stiff, didn't it?

You know it felt good.

It's because you finally took the leash off.

You finally let the beast out.

See, you spend all this time trying to convince yourself that you've got to stay in this fighting game because fighting is all you know. But that ain't it, and you know it. You were born for violence, my guy. We all are. Just some of us are more attuned to it than others.

I mean, can you imagine what your career—hell, your life would have been like if you had stopped fighting your nature? If you'd just accepted that hurting people is what you do best? But nah, you had to put those chains on yourself. You had to be the face, not the heel. Had to have everybody love you. Had to play the non-threatening Negro so they'd let you in the house. No showboating, no trash talk. Be one of the "good ones." Look where that got you.

That's why you're an old man with no belt.

But now you see what you can do. Don't you? You know what you're capable of.

I don't want to hear this bullshit about, "It'll never happen again." None of this, "That isn't who I am. That wasn't me."

It *was* you. The real you. Because that's all you've ever been.

The toothpaste is out of the tube now, my man.

There's no going back.

PAPA'Z SONG

Xavier opened his eyes.

Had he slept?

The ceiling was his ceiling. Underneath him was his bed.

He was in his father's house.

He lifted his head and blinked away the blur. The clock on the wall across from his bed read just past six, whether in the morning or at night, he couldn't yet tell.

How long had he slept? A few hours? A full day?

Xavier pulled at the corner of the shade. A sliver of light sliced through the gap between the curtains. He rested his head back on the pillow and felt a cool dampness there. He'd been sweating again. The blades of the ceiling fan spun in a blur, threatening to free itself from the drywall with its wobble. His boxers clung cold and wet to the skin of his thighs. Loki had climbed to the foot of the bed. He stirred from Xavier's waking and yawned wide, a high-pitched squeak at the end.

Xavier closed his eyes. The small of his back. The pockets behind his knees. The palms of his hands. All drenched.

Sick, maybe.

A bead of perspiration rolled from his forehead, into his ear where his pulse beat in rhythm with his headache. He recalled the remnants of yet another nightmare, vivid and horrific like the ones that preceded it. The details were often slippery and slid through the creases of his memory like a filmy residue, but they shared a common theme of rage and violence, visited on some nameless, faceless victim. The night terrors had come more frequently with the headaches, more vicious with each occurrence. But this nightmare had been different. Though the face in it was unrecognizable, the details of this dream had friction. He could clearly envision the damage he'd wrought, tinged with such familiarity, such reality, that he'd soaked his sheets with sweat.

He sat up to the smell of urine. Had Loki peed somewhere in the room? He thought it unlikely. In their short relationship, there'd been no accidents, the dog insistent whenever he needed to go outside, nudging his muzzle against Xavier's leg or the back of his hand.

He looked down at his underwear. And he breathed in again.

His boxers were saturated with piss.

Once the vertigo subsided, he stood and steadied himself on the nightstand, knocking his cell phone face down onto the floor. Loki sprung to all fours at the sound of the smack. Xavier was certain the screen had cracked, but he let it lie. Down the hallway, in the bathroom, he peeled off his underwear. Though only Loki had been with him in the room, he felt watched, ashamed of what he'd done. In junior college, when he drank as hard as he trained on the wrestling mat, he'd once gotten so inebriated that he woke in the middle of the night and pissed in a dresser drawer full of clothes. The trickling sound awoke his roommate, a teetotaler who screamed at him in revulsion and snapped Xavier to his senses. Too drunk to stop the stream, Xavier finished. They were, after all, his clothes in the drawer.

Even in such a drunken state, he'd at least retained the muscle memory to get out of bed and relieve himself somewhere, even if it wasn't a proper somewhere. That he'd not had a child's sense to wake up and relieve himself twanged panic along his nerves. A cold palm massaged the skin of his spine and raised a ripple of chill bumps across his wet skin. He held the damp boxers at arm's length and lifted the lid to the hamper. There he saw his fight shorts, balled up in a lump, the white fabric interrupted by faded splotches of red.

It hadn't been a nightmare, but a memory.

That which he had forgotten flat on his back staring at the caged fluorescent lights, that which he'd forgotten staring at Lawrence's ruined face, that which he failed to remember in the aftermath back in the locker room, all came back to him standing there in his bathroom, naked and shivering. Lawrence's matted hair under the palms of Xavier's hands. Lawrence's collar bones under the blades of Xavier's forearms, his clinch clamped vise tight. Lawrence's face smashed into Xavier's rising knee. Xavier flinched at the recall. A bruise throbbed in his thigh. Knuckles ached. His body had recorded the trauma. He remembered the emptiness behind Lawrence's eyes, his face slack just before Xavier brought it to meet his other knee.

His stomach roiled. He stepped away from the hamper until the backs of his legs touched the cold porcelain of the tub and he slid to the floor. The steam whistle moved from the back of his skull to the center. He pressed the heel of one hand into his forehead, and a whisper escaped his dry lips.

"Please, stop."

But the images and the sounds and the sensations would not relent. He was the exposed nerve of a broken tooth, every remembrance like the slightest breeze or change in tempera-ture, all producing exquisite pain. Blood tinged the memory in his taste buds. Maybe Lawrence's blood. Maybe his own. The echo of shouts from those who watched outside the cage played back distorted, a warped record. Louder still was the voice that told him

Harder.

Faster.

Again.

And again.

Until the curtains in the theater of his mind closed.

Seated naked on the tile, Xavier rested his head over the lip of the tub, the edge cool on the back of his neck. He squeezed his temples between his long fingers and tried to push out the mounting pressure, the screeching whistle, but neither would lessen. He succumbed to their insistence and pushed himself off the floor, then pulled back the clear mildewed shower curtain and sat on the edge of the tub. The shower spit to life and filled the bathroom with steam. His head hung low under the weak hot stream, Xavier turned the knob to the left and the steam thickened. He drew a deep breath of wet air and wished for the scalding water to cook his brain, letting the things he wanted to forget drain out of his ears, instead of the near constant disremembering what he needed to retain.

The shower done, he stepped out and wrapped himself in a towel and heard a muffled buzz. He stopped moving and strained to listen. The sound stopped, then started again. He poked his towel into his ear and twisted, drying it out, and listened again. The buzz sounded once more, only slightly louder than the whine in his ears. Was this a new noise in his brain, competing for space? Xavier sneered, disgusted at his inability to trust his own ears. He walked to the bedroom and stood in the doorway. The buzzing resumed. His phone vibrated and shimmied across the laminate floor.

He picked it up to see the nursing home on the caller ID—and they'd already called twice before. He connected. On the other end, a woman muttered under her breath, asking why he wasn't answering.

"Hello?" Xavier said.

"Mr. Wallace," the voice said. "I thought I was going to get your voicemail again."

"You didn't."

"Yes, well." The woman cleared her throat. "This is Mrs. Thomas at Maple Grove."

"Is there something I can do for you?" Xavier asked. "Who is this again?"

"Mrs. Thomas." There was surprise in her tone, yet neither her voice nor her name held any familiarity for Xavier. "The Director of Nursing? We met just a few days ago. With your father's care team. Hello?"

"Yeah, okay. What is it?" There was an unintentional snap in his voice.

"It's your father again, Mr. Wallace. He's been pulling out his nasal cannula for his oxygen and been extremely combative with my nursing staff. Worse than before. He bit an aide on the overnight shift, and this morning he's more agitated than I've ever seen him. This is looking like a clear change in mental status, but he's been asking for you, so we'd like to ask if you can come in to see him. If it calms him down, there's a chance we won't need to send him out to the hospital."

A short buzz sounded in Xavier's ear. He pulled the phone away. A text from Shot.

Come in. ASAP.

Come on.

He tapped the speaker phone icon and spoke as he typed out a return message.

"Has he taken his meds?"

Something up with Pop. Not sure what's going on. Might not make it today.

A response bubble formed, lingered, then disappeared.
Shit.

"Our staff always makes sure our residents get their medications on schedule, Mr. Wallace. Of that I can assure you." Xavier heard the affront in her voice, but his well of patience and understanding sat empty.

"I didn't ask you if you gave them to him. I asked you if he took them. I've caught him hiding them under his tongue before. When he was here."

"Mr. Wallace, all due respect, but I'm not about to ask my staff to go finger sweeping the mouth of a man who nearly took a chunk out of a young woman's arm."

"A chunk of—don't you think that's a little dramatic?"

Another buzz.

Hurry up.

"No, I don't," Mrs. Thomas snapped. Then a pause. Xavier imagined her closing her eyes as she breathed and composed herself. Her well, it seemed, had also run dry. Xavier began a response to Shot when the phone vibrated yet again.

Not asking. Handle your business then get here.

"Well, fuck me," Xavier said.

"Excuse me?" Mrs. Thomas said. Xavier brought his hand to his mouth.

"Ma'am, I'm sorry. I was talking to someone here."

She ignored the apology. "That's not all, Mr. Wallace. Your father has become increasingly verbally abusive to his roommate, to the point where the man has become afraid to go to sleep. Now his family is requesting a new placement, and that's a room we just don't have at the moment."

"Wait, what? Since when does my father have a roommate? He's private pay. We specified that when I brought him in. No roommate."

What was this woman talking about? Had Sam been right all along? Were all these places looking to fleece their clients for every penny?

Not me, lady. I am not *the one.*

"I'm sorry, Mr. Wallace. I'm not sure I understand. We met about this weeks ago."

Uh uh, sure. Commit to that grift. Dig yourself deeper.

"I'm sure I'd remember a meeting like that."

Are you though?

"Your father's funds ran out and his default insurance was Medicaid. We don't offer private rooms to residents on medical assistance. He's had a roommate since then. Mr. Wallace, you signed off on this. I'm happy to show you the documentation . . ."

Xavier held the phone away from his face and stared at the wall in front of him. In preparing Sam's home for sale, Xavier had painted over the wallpaper, not knowing how to remove it. The wall covering was textured, and though the off-white paint obscured any color beneath, the lines and shapes showed through. Xavier relaxed his gaze and watched them disappear, then reappear as he intensified his focus, attempting as he had many times before to make out what might have been underneath. It was a distraction on nights when he couldn't sleep, something to tire his eyes, to numb his mind against its racing and its failings.

"Mr. Wallace?"

Xavier turned off the speaker and brought the phone to his ear. "Yes, I'm here. I remember now. You don't have to show me the paperwork. Thank you for reminding me. I believe you."

He didn't believe her. But he didn't believe himself, either.

Another pause. Xavier heard an alarm bell in the background.

"Are you all right, Mr. Wallace?"

Despite his distrust for her in that moment, the softness in her voice stirred something in his chest. No one had asked him that question in some time. His voice cracked. "I'm good."

Mrs. Thomas breathed out. "If a resident has a change in mental status as significant as your father is appearing to have, we have to send them to the ER. We really don't have a choice."

"No, no, no, please don't do that." Xavier envisioned his father, strapped to a gurney, straining and spitting while they took him to the hospital to be poked and prodded, having no earthly idea why they were doing this to him, only to be sent back because there was nothing that could be done to fix a mind that didn't know itself anymore. "I can calm him down, I promise. I'll get down there as soon as I can. Please don't send him until I've had a chance."

Another breath. "All right, but you'll need to hurry."

"I'm leaving now. Mrs. Thomas?"

"Yes?"

"Thank you."

"See you soon."

Mrs. Thomas disconnected first. Xavier kept the phone at his ear. He craved more of the concern she'd shown. She actually wanted to know if he was okay. He couldn't remember the last time someone asked him that without the flavor of their own self-interest.

He whistled for Loki. The rhythmic click of claws echoed down the hall until he appeared in the doorway. He sat dutifully at Xavier's side. Xavier massaged the top of Loki's muscular head with his fingertips, then pulled up Shot's text thread and tapped out another message. He wasn't ready to face what he'd done yesterday, and the fact that Shot wanted him there immediately made him nervous. Xavier loved his cousin, but he was intimidated by him, and he feared his connections to the hard men he'd mentioned. Xavier had placed

Shot in a precarious position with what he'd done to Lawrence. Blood ran thicker than water, but given a large enough opening, it still ran.

The phone's backlight went dark, and he stared at his face reflected in the blackened screen. It had indeed cracked when it hit the floor. The fissures in the glass etched lines across his forehead. Set his eyes at skewed angles to each other. Sliced through his mouth like a jagged scar. He tilted the phone back and forth, trying to get his features to line up, but the splits in the glass were too severe.

Once dressed, Xavier grabbed his keys from the magnetic hook next to the calendar on the refrigerator. He put a slash through today's date, leaving only the next with a large circle around it.

"One more day, Loke," he said with a smile, twirling his keys around his index finger. Their jangling caused Loki to duck his head and tuck his tail. Xavier looked at him in wonder, then realized that without his leash on, Loki knew what the sound meant. He was going to be left behind.

Xavier pocketed his keys and squatted in front of Loki. He took his jowls in both hands and scratched. "I'm sorry, boy, but I can't take you. You saw how you set Pops off last time, and he's worse now. I'm probably not allowed to take you in, anyway. But look here." Xavier retrieved his phone from his back pocket, pulled up his reminders application, and began typing, then showed the screen to Loki. "See? I've put in a bunch of alarms to remind myself. There's no way I'm going to forget you again. And watch!"

He walked to the pantry and filled Loki's bowl with a mountain of dry dog food. Then he pulled another bowl down from the cabinet and did the same. "Plenty of food and water. Eat and drink yourself silly." He crouched back down and brought his forehead to Loki's. "Don't be scared. I promise I'll be back." With that he stood and walked to the back door. He wouldn't look back over his shoulder but caught Loki's reflection in the window. He sat on his haunches, watching. Xavier took his phone out and double-checked that all his reminders were on.

Outside, the moisture in the air touched Xavier's face like walking into a web. The August sun hung high in the sky, wreathed in a humid haze, and it took a moment for his eyes to adjust to the brightness.

His mother, Evelyn, loved to remark about the darkness of his brown eyes. How they were almost black, darker than hers even, and how she never understood why he was always so sensitive to the light. His father would tease her, tell her there was no science behind that, just an old wives' tale. He'd pinch her behind and tell her that despite her dark skin, he could see her at night just fine with his own baby blues. She laughed, but not in a way that said she found it funny.

She'd chastise Sam for joking "that way" in front of Xavier. His father always apologized, said that his jokes were harmless, explaining away his sense of humor with the notion that "he didn't see color." That always sounded nice to Xavier, still too young to understand the harmful nuance of his father's rationale. That he didn't care if people were Black, yellow, purple, or green meant he was to be lauded for being so "open minded." Considering his wife and child, didn't he have to be?

Xavier found it strange, his remembrance of that moment. Of all the things to recall. Perhaps the impending visit with Sam stirred things he'd pushed to the side, tucked in the recesses of his brain, rarely accessed. As if he'd want to access them. Though he was a grown man, it took little to summon the anxiety he'd felt at thirteen, standing at the doorway of his bedroom, waiting for the next argument between his parents to be *the* argument, where the dreaded "D" word would be invoked.

The word eventually came. It had been an hour or so after dinner. Xavier sat cross-legged in the middle of the living room carpet, rapt before the images of the unrest in Los Angeles flashing on the television screen. While the news anchor spoke of the King verdict, a fireball blossomed from a red brick building. Windows shattered. Evelyn and Sam spoke heatedly behind him, but Xavier had been transfixed. Then his father said something about "thugs and looters" and his parents' conversation ceased. The next sound had been from Evelyn snapping her fingers in Xavier's face, waking him from his trance, telling him it was time to go to bed. Despite the early hour, her tone precluded any desire for protest.

Back in his room, Xavier had strained to hear their resumed discussion. Evelyn's voice, ever even, never rose. Sam's did. Though the words were not always intelligible, his pitch was clear. First came defensiveness, tinged with incredulity. Then the increasingly familiar rationalization. When that failed, desperation took its place. Pleading. Their voices moved closer to his room and the words became clear.

Asking if what he'd said had really been so wrong.

And wasn't she being too sensitive, as usual.

Of course he didn't mean it *that way*.

That he couldn't possibly be what she was accusing him of.

Then just tell him who she wanted him to be and he would be that person if it would make her stay.

Those words Xavier heard clear and true.

Stay? Where was she going? And why wouldn't she want his father to be who he was? Sam Wallace made Xavier laugh and feel safe. What could be wrong with that? Sure, sometimes he said some things to make her mad, but he always,

always said sorry. Didn't that count for something? She didn't have to *leave*.

While his adolescent brain wrangled with the questions, Evelyn's footsteps padded from the living room of their ranch-style home across the hardwood floors, past Xavier's room, toward the main bedroom on the other end of the house. Xavier ducked behind the wall of his room, careful not to close the door all the way, to maintain the illusion that he'd been in bed all along, in case his father's footsteps followed.

They didn't.

Xavier heard drawers slide open and shut. Closet doors creaked on their hinges. Wire hangers clinked. A zipper buzzed around the border of a suitcase. Xavier jumped back into bed, turned on his side, his back to his door. The thin strip of light on the wall from the hallway widened, interrupted by the silhouette of his mother and her natural hair. She whispered his name.

He didn't turn, immobilized by a disconnect between his muscles and his brain. The latter screamed at the former to turn and face his mother or he'd regret it.

But he did not, would not move. Once more Evelyn called to him, almost breathless. He feigned sleep, hoping that he'd have some excuse later on for not turning, that it would somehow make sense to her—and him—that he didn't hear her voice. His father called for her and her outline slid away. The thin strip of light, no longer interrupted by her shadow, slowly disappeared as she closed the door. Then more muffled pleas from his father. The front door to the house opened, the screen door with the broken hydraulic banged shut. And she was gone.

Evelyn and Sam split the week. Mom got four days, he got three. They traded holidays. When they met to hand off Xavier, Sam joked that it was unfair Evelyn got one extra visitation on Kwanza. She didn't laugh at his jokes anymore. When the silence became unbearable, Xavier forced a chuckle, hoping to break the tension.

He failed.

Days and weekends at Evelyn's new apartment passed with little spoken between mother and son. The car rides when she picked him up from school were largely silent. He'd go directly to the room she'd prepared for him, the sheets tucked in tightly under the mattress, though he always pulled them out the minute he was beneath them. The Sega Genesis sung to life and he'd spend hours in his room until dinner was ready.

At the table, Evelyn always seemed to Xavier to be on the cusp of saying something to him, some balm, a remedy for the cloud that hung heavy between them—but she never did. She made small talk, asked about school and sports, though she'd divert from the latter quickly since Sam was involved in his coaching. The words, devoid of substance, gave volume to the cloud, darkened it, obscured mother and son from each other, though they sat only feet away.

Xavier gave one-word answers until she excused him, and he'd return to the glow of the television in his room. She never protested his recalcitrance, never argued that he needed to talk to her more, and that she didn't angered Xavier, though at the time, he didn't know why. Every night, Evelyn's feet would stop for a moment outside of his room, the light beneath the door broken by her presence. He'd pause the game, thinking this was the moment that she'd explain it all. She'd finally make him understand, maybe tell him how he could repair things, as Xavier had come to the conclusion that all this must have somehow, someway, been *his* fault. Maybe, if she'd just told him what he'd done, they could all go back to the way things were, maybe even make them a little bit better. He visualized Evelyn on the other side of the door, fist raised in the air, poised to knock, and he'd will her to do it. He wanted to call out for her to come in, but whatever kept her hand from moving also kept his voice from sounding, and she'd walk on down the hallway to bed. And at that, he'd grow angry with her once more, until he no longer found fault in himself anymore. Until anger was all he had left for her.

His eighteenth birthday heralded the end of the joint custody agreement, and with Sam's blessing, Xavier moved out on his own. Evelyn sent him Christmas and birthday cards with checks that went uncashed. As the years passed, she'd email Xavier about cousins graduating, deaths in the extended family, and eventually her own retirement from teaching. Each time, he typed out short responses, thinking he'd finally bridge the divide, but they inevitably devolved into thousand-word screeds full of misplaced blame and juvenile petulance. He'd delete his replies, and while his mother's missives came less frequently, she never stopped writing to him. Yet he never wrote back.

LOST IN REMINISCENCE, HIS MUSCLES on autopilot, Xavier found himself at the entrance of the Maple Grove nursing home. The red brick building stood nine floors high. The mulch smelled new, the lines between the sidewalks free of weeds. The lawn surrounding the building stayed trim and neat, though devoid of maples anywhere on the property. He remembered how he'd joked with his father when he first brought him here that perhaps they'd torn down the maple grove to make way for Maple Grove and forgot to replant the trees. A certified dad joke, not unlike the countless ones his father had told him growing up, the only thing actually funny about them being his father's ridiculous mugging when Xavier mimed a gag at the punchline. But this joke had brought no joy to his father—only fear, confusion, and anger.

"What is this place?" Sam had asked as Xavier pulled the Volvo into a parking space.

"We talked about this, Pop. They call it a continuous care retirement community. Kind of a mouthful, huh?"

"Yeah, it's a fancy way of saying a graveyard. This is where ungrateful children bring their parents to die when they get tired of them."

"Come on, Pop. Don't be like that."

"Then why are you bringing me here? I can take care of myself. I fell once."

"This month, Pop. You fell once this month. You fell down twice last month."

"Bullshit. I tripped on my oxygen cord."

"And you couldn't get back up. That can't happen again."

"I said I can take care of myself, God damn it. You want to leave me here with strangers to wipe my ass? You want me to die without any dignity, is that it? What did I ever do to you that you want to put me here?"

"Dad, stop. It's not like I'm leaving you in a nursing home. You'll be in assisted living. People here will help you if you need it, that's all. If you fall again, it won't be half a day until someone finds you. They'll make sure you're eating regularly and help you with your medications."

"Why can't you do all that? You're my son. That's what you're supposed to do. Take care of me like I took care of you. And now you're going to leave me just like your mother."

Xavier gripped the steering wheel. His father's passive-aggressive guilt trips had lost all passivity over the last year. Nothing Xavier ever did was enough. Not enough phone calls, not enough visits, not enough trips to the store for groceries, not enough jaunts to the pharmacy for his prescriptions, or to the house to tighten the wheels on his walker which he hardly used anyway. Despite all this time Xavier supposedly didn't spend on him, whenever he pushed back, on the occasions when he truly couldn't make it, either because of work or training, Sam had brought up his mother. The repeated comparisons never lost their sting. He had never numbed to Sam's manipulations. Though he saw them for what they were, the recognition never kept that guilt from finding its way in through his guard.

"You act like I'm going to drop you off like some animal at a shelter."

"You might as well be."

"They can take better care of you than I can right now, Pop. I think you know that."

"Right now? You mean this is only temporary?" Xavier rubbed his forehead, regretting his choice of words. The gesture gave Sam all the answer he needed. "No, I didn't think so. You better make sure you don't let the house go to pot. I worked too hard on that place to let it fall apart."

"I won't. I promise."

"Whatever that's good for. Just get my shit out of the trunk."

Sam opened his door and turned his back to his son. Xavier sighed, popped the trunk, and unloaded his father's things.

THE AUTOMATIC DOORS SLID APART, and Xavier stepped back into the present. The lush burgundy carpet, the bubbling fish tank, the thick cushioned chairs that adorned the foyer, and the pleasant potpourri odor never fully distracted from the faint smell of urine. He signed in at the reception desk. A woman sat in an office chair nearly too narrow to accommodate her hips and faced him. She tucked a wisp of graying red hair behind her ear and pushed her glasses up her nose with a nod and smile that said she's seen Xavier before. He returned the smile, hoping he mirrored her familiarity. She handed him a visitor's badge.

"Who are you here to see?"

"Sam Wallace."

"Thank you. Have a nice day."

That she hadn't responded to his father's name by saying they'd taken him out screaming made Xavier hopeful. Maybe his father had finally calmed down and this would turn out to be just another visit, whatever that meant these days. As Sam's descent into dementia picked up inertia toward the bottom of the hill, each time Xavier came to see him had become a game of chance.

Xavier walked through the cafeteria toward the hallway to the skilled nursing unit. The spiced smell of breakfast sausage and flavored coffee filled the air, as did the gentle murmur of quiet conversations. Glasses and plates clinked as the staff cleaned up plates of soggy toast and half-eaten eggs. Aides wiped at the mouths of residents unable to do so themselves, wheeled them away from their tables. He stepped aside for an aide and grinned as he opened one of the heavy double doors to the unit. She did not return his smile.

Xavier understood why. The open door unleashed a cacophony. The unit teemed with activity. Alarm bells went off in several rooms. Nurses and aides hustled from the station and back again, dodging medicine and janitorial carts as well as one another. In the rehabilitation room, therapists slow-shouted exercise instructions to chair-bound patients. They marched in place, their feet barely clearing the floor.

A train of residents in wheelchairs waiting to be taken back to their rooms lined a wall. Xavier met the gaze of a woman there. She had full brown cheeks and her amorphous body strained the seams of her house dress, the mosaic pattern long since faded. She slumped over the armrest of her chair, her tongue protruding between her dried lips. However, when she saw Xavier looking at her, her dull eyes brightened. Her tongue pulled back. Years fell from her face. She reached her hand out for his, her trunk still bent. Xavier took her hand. The light skin of her palm was warm and soft. Even over the disinfectants and deodorizers, Xavier smelled a hint of honeysuckle on her.

"Good morning, honey," she said.

Xavier crouched down in front of her and smiled. "Good morning, ma'am." She placed her other hand on top of his and patted it. He returned the gesture. Her feet were clad in blue cotton gripper socks, the fleece pilled and dingy. The elastic dug into her edematous legs, the fluid pushing so hard against the skin that it wept through in spots and stained the small gauze pads there a brownish yellow. Xavier cradled the bottom of one foot that had slid to the floor. He lifted her leg back on to the rest, surprised at the heaviness of her short limb.

A wail came from a room down the hall, one with a flashing light over the door, the only alarm now ringing. The voice pleaded for help, asking for someone, anyone to get him out of this place, away from these spooks trying to rob him.

Xavier let out an exasperated breath. He knew the voice. He couldn't believe the words. He stood, wincing at the tightness that settled into his knees in that brief squat, and placed a gentle hand on the woman's shoulder before walking toward his father's room.

A woman in green scrubs held plastic tubing leading from an oxygen cannister next to Sam's bed. She attempted to slip it over Sam's head before yanking it back out of reach of his flailing arms. The fighter in Xavier admired her quickness. Her scrub pants were tight on her hips, yet she had reflexes better than some of the cardio kickboxers at Shot's gym. She shouted as she bobbed and weaved.

"Sam, if you don't put your cannula in, you are going to desat."

Sam yelled back at her. "I don't even know what that means!"

"It means if you don't put it on you *will* pass out, and if you *keep* it off you *will* stop breathing. Is that clear enough for you?"

"You're just trying to gas me up and knock me out so you and that son of a bitch," he said, pointing to his roommate's empty bed, "can steal my things. All you people stick together, don't you? What's your cut for selling my things? Half?"

"*You* people? Which people would those be, huh, Sam?"

His lips pulled away from his yellowed teeth in a sneer. "You know damn well which people."

Xavier shouted from the doorway. "Pop!"

Sam's arm hung in the air. The tightness in his face released and his eyes glistened.

"Xavier." He scowled at the nurse again. "See? My son is here to protect me now from you people."

"Pop, stop that."

"Say 'you people' one more time, Sam," the nurse said, "and I *will* sell your stuff." She looked Xavier up and down, then Sam, then back to Xavier. She scoffed. "'You people.' You do see your son standing here, don't you?" Xavier gave her a wave to say it wasn't worth it.

"You shut up about my son. Get the hell out of my room."

The nurse shook her head. She placed the oxygen tubing in Xavier's hand. "Here. All yours."

"I'm sorry," Xavier said to her. She grunted and walked out of the room. He turned and approached his father, who sat precariously close to the edge of his bed. With a gentle lift, Xavier slid his father back to the center of the bed. He put his hands on Sam's shoulders and held him at arm's length.

Wisps of white hair floated back and forth in the stale breeze from the oscillating fan. Xavier finger combed the strays and patted them down to the top of his father's head. A sheen of sweat held them there. Xavier noted the blue tinge around his father's lips as he slipped the tubing over his head, a medal Sam didn't want, and placed the pipettes in his nose. Sam inhaled deeply, and the tank released a puff of oxygen. He took another breath, then another, and another still, as though drinking water after days of thirst.

"Easy, Pop. You're going to get high."

His father's eyes opened for a moment before disappearing into the folds of his cheeks as he beamed at his son. "My boy." His smile faded. "How did you get here? You didn't ride the bus by yourself, did you?"

"What are you talking about, Pop? You know I can drive."

"Oh, really? When did they change the driving age to fourteen?"

Xavier took a step back. "Fourteen? Pop, look at me. I'm grown."

The once light blue of his father's wet eyes had turned storm cloud gray. They scanned Xavier, seeing who he once was, not him as he was now.

"Don't be in a hurry to grow up, Xavier. Stay a kid. This getting old shit ain't for sissies."

"You got it. No hurry."

"Take me home, son. Please."

"I can't, Pop. You know that. Do me a favor and stop with all this crap. You can't pull your oxygen out and you definitely can't be yelling at people. They want to send you to the hospital."

"Ha!" His father lowered his voice and looked past Xavier's broad shoulders. "Ever since they put me in this room, they've been stealing from me. Every night I go to sleep, that Black—"

"*Pop.*"

"Fine. That rat bastard wakes me up, rifling through my drawers. I press the call button like I'm on some kind of God-damned game show and nobody comes. Even when they do it's one of those damned women, shaking her head like a bobblehead, hands on her hips, telling me I'm imagining things, like I've got no sense. I'm not making this up, Xavier, I swear," he whispered. "I'm not out of my gourd like some of these people here. You know that, right? Just look at them. Can't even take themselves to the bathroom. Shitting in bed-pans. I don't belong here with these dead people. Please just take me home."

Sam's thin cotton robe had come open when Xavier helped him into bed. His once broad chest had sunken in on itself. Drapes of skin hung from his collarbones and rippled over his ribs. Xavier pulled the robe closed.

"Lie back and get some rest, Pop. You got yourself all worked up."

Sam slapped Xavier's hand away. "I don't need a rest. I told you I need to get out of here. If you won't take me home, at least take me to the Goddamned bathroom and then get the hell out of my sight."

Xavier stepped back. He extended his hand to help his father stand, but Sam wouldn't take it. After two false starts, he grabbed Xavier's forearm and stood. Xavier tied Sam's robe tight, then looped his hand behind the belt the way the in-home therapist had taught him when Sam came home from his first hospitalization. Xavier took the tubing with his other hand and bunched it up around the handle of Sam's portable oxygen tank to keep him from tripping. They walked the few short feet to the bathroom. While Sam loosened his robe, Xavier stood in the doorway. Sam glowered when he turned and saw him there.

"What, are you going to wipe my ass for me, too? I'm not

humiliated enough in this dump? Get the hell out of here. I'll call you *if* I need you."

Xavier backed away, hands up in surrender, and let the door close behind him. When it clicked shut, he mimed a gun in his mouth and pulled the trigger, making a gunshot sound effect. Someone let out a laugh behind him. It was the same nurse Sam had berated moments ago.

"I, uh, I thought I was the only one in here," Xavier said.

"I stopped back to make sure you were doing okay."

"For what it's worth, I'm sorry."

"You don't have to be sorry—but I do appreciate that. Hell, that's not even the worst of it."

"From him?"

"Him, the other old white man down the hall, the other white lady the next room down. You name it. It's like they shove down all the stuff they were allowed to say in the 'good old days' but then when they end up here, that filter comes flying off. The things I've had shouted at me? Boy, I tell you what."

Xavier walked to his father's dresser and leaned against it. "How do you deal with that every day? I'd end up slapping somebody."

"What good would it do me? They'd still be racist, and I'd be out of a job. How am I winning? I've been spit on, accused of stealing, bitten—hell, one resident took a dump on the floor right in front of me. Know why?" Xavier shook his head. "Said because he wanted the nigger to clean it up."

"Stop it."

"Hand to God. But this job pays better than ones like it in the city, with the wage tax and what not. It's a long-ass bus ride to get here, but I have health insurance and so do my kids. But besides all that, I'm good at my job. At the end of the day, I'm proud of the job I do. I can go home knowing I did good work. Same as anyone else that works here."

"Damn. Well I appreciate you. For real. Thank you."

She tilted her head toward the bathroom door. "How are you dealing with this? The stuff he's been saying?"

Xavier's spine stiffened in defense. "Him? Oh, he doesn't mean that nonsense. My dad's no racist." He looked himself up and down. "Obviously."

She raised an eyebrow. "Yeah. Obviously." Xavier heard the doubt in her voice, but he couldn't tell her she was wrong about Sam—because he was beginning to wonder if she was. "Well, I'm right down the hall. Shout if you need me."

"What was your name again?"

"Tanya."

"Thanks, Tanya. For real."

She winked and walked out the door. Xavier turned and rested his elbows on top of Sam's dresser. He scanned the framed photographs that sat there. A sepia-toned image of Sam as a young man, shirtless and in boxing trunks, with his arm around another man in similar attire. Both had their hands wrapped, both holding a fist to the camera, both sporting shiners. A post-fight picture of his Navy boxing days. Next to it sat a picture of Sam and Xavier when Xavier was no older than ten. Father and son mean-mugged each other in a fake face-off, fists raised, lower jaws jutted out, their smiles barely contained. Xavier picked it up to look closer when he heard the door to the bathroom open behind him. He turned with the frame in hand to see Sam's face reddened with rage.

"What are you doing with my things? Put that down!"

"Wait, Pop, hold on—"

"Don't you call me that! What are you, blind? I'm no father to some nigger!"

The word stood Xavier straight as an uppercut. He placed the picture on the dresser without looking behind him. The frame sat half-off the edge as Sam shuffled toward him, wagging his finger.

"You people won't be happy until you take everything I have! Nurse!"

Xavier reached out, fearing his father would trip on his oxygen cord, but Sam's hands slapped into his son's chest with far more force than Xavier thought him capable. The shock knocked him back a step and set loose the crucifix that had been hidden under the collar of his T-shirt. Sam's eyes widened at the sight of it.

"You *are* stealing from me, you son of a bitch. Give that necklace back to me now!"

Sam wrapped his fingers around the cross and yanked. The chain links dug into Xavier's skin and burned before breaking free. Tanya appeared at the doorway in a rush.

"What is happening in here?" she shouted. "Sam, what is your problem?"

"My problem is *you* people all trying to steal from me."

"Pop, please."

"I said don't call me that!" Sam swung the necklace like a mace. Xavier dodged, but not quickly enough. The bottom of the cross sliced the corner of his eye. He hissed in pain and backed away. Tanya yelped and called down the hall for more help. Mrs. Thomas and two male aides appeared in the doorway. The aides took Sam by the arms and guided him back to the edge of the bed, but he refused to lie down.

"Please don't hurt him," Xavier pleaded. He dabbed at his eye with two fingers and saw blood on them. He dropped down into the chair next to Sam's dresser. The vibration knocked the photo from its precarious perch. The glass shattered. Xavier kneeled and picked up the shards. He tried to apologize but the words caught in his throat.

"Look what you did!" Sam shouted. A line of spit trailed down his white-stubbled chin. "I want to know which one of you Black bastards let him in and who's going to pay for that frame! Get him out of here!"

Xavier looked with his open eye at Sam in awe. A hand on his shoulder and he turned his head. Mrs. Thomas stood over him.

"The ambulance will be here any minute," she said. "The hospital is just around the corner. I need you out in the hall, please."

"I'm begging you, don't kick him out."

"In the hall, Mr. Wallace. Don't leave. But do *not* come back in the room, even when they get here. Do you understand me?"

Xavier walked out. He leaned against the wall next to the doorway, then slid to the floor, bumping the raw skin where the necklace had cut him against the handrail attached to the wall. Two EMTs appeared at the end of the hall with a gurney.

Xavier pinched his eye shut. The throb there matched the one at the base of his skull. Sam screamed his refusal to go anywhere. Xavier peeked around the corner of the door frame in time to see one of the EMTs slide a needle into his father's arm. Sam calmed in an instant. His body near limp, the EMTs guided him up onto the gurney and laid him back with a gentleness in stark contrast to the violence of the last few minutes. Xavier stood as the EMTs wheeled his father toward the exit, eyes half open. They disappeared behind the doors from where they'd first arrived.

One by one, the aides and Tanya filed out of the room, shaking their heads. Tanya touched Xavier's shoulder as she walked past. She pressed her lips together and her expression apologized. Before Xavier could respond to her silent kindness, Mrs. Thomas appeared behind her.

"Come on with me down to the clinic," she said. "Let me get a look at that eye."

Xavier followed her down a series of hallways. They stopped at a room resembling a school nurse's office. Xavier sat on the examining table. The paper sheet covering the table crinkled, the sound echoing off the white walls. Xavier's headache was in full swing. The fluorescent light above him buzzed. His headache amplified the sound until it felt like a hornet had embedded itself in the center of his skull. Mrs. Thomas brought a footstool over to the table and climbed it to stand face-to-face with him.

"Can you open it?" He fluttered the lids open. She pressed gently at the borders of the cut. "Well, it won't need stitches. I'll put some Steri-Strips on it to keep it together. I'll tell you what, though—you were lucky. Another centimeter in the wrong direction and you'd be at the hospital, too."

"Guess that's my Irish half."

Mrs. Thomas smirked. She stepped down and walked to the desk behind her to retrieve gauze, peroxide, and the strips. She folded the gauze into a smaller square and looked over her shoulder at Xavier before pouring peroxide on the pad. "You all right?"

Xavier held out his hand, palm down. "I get in fist fights for a living and look at this." His hand and fingers trembled. "Shaking like a shitting dog's legs." Mrs. Thomas gave a curt laugh. Xavier did not. "That man back there . . . I don't know that man."

Mrs. Thomas came back to the table and pressed the soaked gauze into the cut. After a few more dabs she applied the Steri-Strips. "I used to work on the old coma ward at the hospital downtown. They kept it on the basement level back then. That should tell you how old I am if the gray hairs didn't already. Anyway, I didn't think I was going to make it. Seeing these families coming in and out all the time, carrying all this hope on their shoulders when most times there wasn't any to hold on to. Having to deliver that kind of news when the younger doctors didn't have the gumption to do it got real hard, real fast. I went home most nights crying. One shift, I met a nurse I hadn't seen yet and, I don't know, I guess she could see the stress in my face. She said, 'Cheer up. It's just another day in the vegetable garden.'"

"That's messed up."

"Yeah, but you know what? I busted out laughing. And the more I tried to stop, the harder I laughed. I thought I would feel bad about it, but I didn't. Matter of fact, I felt better. A lot better. Gallows humor, right? It was the only way I could cope with the hard truths I had to face in that ward—the same truths I had to sometimes dish out to those families. It was either that or quit, and that wasn't an option. Hubby and I had mouths to feed."

She applied the last strip and stepped down from the stool. Xavier's feet swung back and forth like a child on a tall chair, his long legs just clearing the floor.

"What you saw up there. What you heard—you've got a hard truth you need to cope with, too, I'm guessing."

Xavier stared at the floor. "When he first started getting sick, I used to do grocery runs and what not for him. Get his cigarettes and *The Inquirer*. The store was up the hill from his house, so on nicer days, I'd walk. He's got this neighbor. You know the type. I got my hoodie and my basketball shorts on, but I'm just there for my pops, so I don't think twice about it. So, I see this neighbor and I nod at him. What does he do?"

"Asked you if you lived in the neighborhood."

Xavier laughed. "So, you know him?"

"In a manner of speaking."

"Yeah, well, I was politer than I should have been and went inside. I was mad as hell, though. Pop asked me what got me so worked up and I told him what dude said. He said, 'If you came walking through my neighborhood dressed like Trayvon Rice or whatever, I'd ask you, too.'" Mrs. Thomas blew air out between her teeth. "Of course, I jumped all over him about it. Told him how disrespectful it was, how he couldn't even get the names right, and asked him how could he say that to me, of all people. Then he backed down, told me he was kidding, and that I was overreacting. Just like my mother."

"Are they still together?"

Xavier shook his head. "And then this past fucking election . . ."

"Lord, don't I know it."

"The things he said when it was happening. And then after. I just don't get it. He loved my mom. I know he did. He loves me, too. I think. I thought. I don't know."

Mrs. Thomas took a breath. "Is it possible maybe you *do* know?"

"You can't ask me that. Not right now."

"You're right. I'm sorry."

Xavier sniffed. He looked out the window. Fat tears spilled down his cheeks. "I still don't remember talking to you about his roommate. His money. Any of that."

"I gathered. Something to do with what you do for a living?"

Xavier kept his gaze trained outside. "Yes."

"Do you think maybe you have a hard truth you need to tell yourself?"

"Yes."

"Do you want to quit?"

"Sometimes."

She dipped her head and looked up at him from under her brow. "I don't mean fighting."

"I don't either."

"You're seeing your future in him."

"It's like looking in a mirror with the lights off."

She took a deep breath and sat in the sole chair in the room. The window looked out onto the grounds behind the facility. Beyond the manicured lawn stood a line of trees. The sky had grayed. Swollen clouds passed behind the trees at a rapid clip. A thunderhead rose on the horizon. The large leaves strained to maintain their hold on the branches against the wind of an oncoming storm. Xavier tilted his chin toward the window.

"What kind of trees are those?"

"Maples. They were planted there after they tore down the originals from the grove this facility was built on."

Xavier half-smiled. "How about that. They didn't forget after all."

IT'S A FIGHT

After Mrs. Thomas cleaned the abrasion at the back of Xavier's neck, she assured him that she would call as soon as she had information about Sam's condition. Xavier fought the urge to embrace her. She squeezed his arm before she left to return to her duties on the nursing floor. Xavier lingered and gazed at the tree line for a moment longer. Thunder rumbled. He shoved his hands in the pockets of his hoodie and made his way to the exit.

The rain beat rhythmically on the roof of the Volvo. The passenger seat looked emptier than usual without Loki. He retrieved his phone to check the time, the dash clock broken since he'd punched it after a frustrating training session. He was astonished to see a little less than half an hour had passed since he'd arrived. Funny how the worst things always moved the slowest, he thought, though his father's decline seemed faster than ever.

He knew he should feel sympathy for Sam's situation. He didn't. He knew he should feel guilty for ever bringing him to Maple Grove. He didn't. Instead, what welled and brimmed over was anger. And for once, the fury was not unwelcome.

That's right. Fuck that old man. Old racist deserves whatever he gets.

The things Sam had said to that nurse. To those aides. To *him*. How could he? How *dare* he? And he *meant* that shit.

There was venom in his voice. Those were not the words of a man who hadn't said those things before.

Tears welled once more, and Xavier's frustration with himself mounted. His emotions switched as easily as a television channel. Unable to redirect them, he cried tears of confusion and betrayal. He cried for a mistake he'd made that he might never be able to remedy—though maybe now was the time to try.

His phone buzzed. Shot.

Where u at?

Xavier rested his head back on the headrest. It had to be about Lawrence, and it couldn't be good. The television channel changed once more. Guilt plucked at his nerves. Lawrence was a piece of shit, top to bottom, but Xavier regretted what he'd done. Lying on the mat, his career draining from openings in his face, ones that Xavier had taken joy in creating. He could admit that now—that he'd enjoyed it—but that enjoyment scared the shit out of him. Or so he told himself.

His phone buzzed again.

U got ur read notification on nigga. I know you seen this.

Xavier cursed, changed his settings, and looked at the time again. He could make it to Shot's before going home. Loki had plenty of food and water. He'd be fine.

On my way.

Xavier turned the ignition and the Volvo chugged to life. The car was stifling, but the rain continued to pour so the windows stayed up. The whine in his ears returned. He turned the fan on full blast and cranked the radio up as loud as he could stand it to drown out the tinnitus. The Scarecrow was off to see the Wizard.

THE RAIN SOAKED XAVIER'S SWEATSHIRT in the brief run from the parking lot to the lobby, and the hoodie hung heavy on his shoulders. He gave the front desk attendant a nod, one the man barely returned. His odd look didn't escape Xavier's notice. It was the same look he noted on the face of one of Shot's protégés as they stopped short when they saw him. Xavier's paranoia escalated. He walked toward the boxing side of the gym.

Shot and Clay trained in the ring. Shot held weathered focus mitts and wore a body pad. He circled Clay, throwing looping outside shots, admonishing the youngster to keep his hands up but his elbows low.

Protect the body *and* the head.

Get that lead hand up in front of your face.

Stop with that Mayweather shit. You ain't him and you fitting to get knocked out.

Now counter.

Clay shot out sharp ones and twos. He feinted high then dropped to the body. His skinny arms delivered hooks to the ribs that, when he dug deep, caused Shot to wince; hooks that mirrored those of the man who trained him. And Clay knew it. He spent too much time admiring those punches and Shot made him pay. He brought a powerful uppercut underneath Clay's lazy guard, a toll for staying in the pocket too long, not hitting him with the flat side, but the hard edge of the focus mitt. Clay stumbled backward.

Xavier cupped his hands around his mouth and shouted. "Stop watching your punches, Clay. They ain't that pretty."

Clay looked up and over to Xavier for less than a moment and caught a looping focus mitt from Shot for his trouble. Flat side this time, to the ear. Xavier cringed and mouthed "my bad." Clay tightened his lips over his mouthguard.

"That timer go off yet?" Shot asked. Clay shook his head. "Then mind your motherfucking business in here." Clay reset.

Xavier loved watching Clay work. He had rough edges but possessed incredible talent for his age. He'd voiced some interest in mixed martial arts and moved effortlessly on the mat when Xavier showed him some of the ground game. Absent were the wild movements of someone new to jiu jitsu. The two of them had a solid rapport as trainer and student, one Xavier feared might have been damaged by his behavior the day before.

The ring timer chimed. Clay returned to his corner, threw off his gloves, and unwrapped his hands. Xavier walked over to him. Clay glanced at him, then looked away.

"You're still staying inside too long on those body shots. Keep it short, make him drop his hands so you can bring that big left hook over the top."

"Uh huh," Clay said. He looked anywhere but at Xavier as he collected his gear, stepped through the ropes, and jumped down off the apron. Xavier went to call after him when Shot gripped his shoulder and spun him around.

"The hell you wearing a hoodie in this heat for?" He peered at Xavier's face. "And what the *fuck* happened to your eye?" He then called past Xavier to Clay. "Did I tell you to unwrap your hands? Go practice them body shots on the bag. Keep going until I tell you to stop." He turned back to Xavier with a look that asked why he hadn't received an answer yet.

"The eye, cuz, is one long-ass story."

"That need stitches? It better not. Man, if you messed around and got cut—"

"Nah, no stitches. Why, what's the deal, man?"

"My office."

Shot unstrapped the body pad and dropped it and the focus mitts to the floor. He turned and made for his office. Xavier followed, anxious. He looked back over his shoulder for Clay, and saw him absentmindedly hitting the bag, watching him.

Once caught staring, Clay went back to unleashing combinations as he'd been told. Xavier frowned and looked forward again as he followed Shot, who asked him to close the door behind them.

"This day couldn't possibly get any worse, so just tell me how bad it is."

"Huh?" Xavier asked.

"Isn't this about Lawrence?"

"That chump. Yeah, you messed him up real bad. Quarter inch separation in his jaw. They had to plate and wire that shut. Going to be drinking his food for a while. Which honestly don't much matter since he won't be able to taste it, because his nose is all packed up from the surgery to move it back to the middle of his face."

Xavier ran his hands over his head. "Christ."

"Plus, they had to put plates around his eye socket to hold it together. I'm saying, why couldn't you do this in some of your other fights? You'd have motherfuckers ducking you left and right. Would have gotten that title shot with the quickness."

"Is he going to fight again?"

"Who?"

"*Who?* Lawrence, man."

"Hell nah, he ain't fighting anymore. Not for me, anyway. He's no use to me broken like that. I can't have somebody in there afraid to pull the trigger."

"Fuck, Shot."

"Nigga, what do you care? Why we still talking about this, anyway?"

Xavier's eyelids narrowed to slits. "Are you out your natural born mind? 'What do I care?' The guy that did all that to him?"

"You *should* be in here upset over the fact that you have, yet again, put me in a fucked-up position that I *still* ain't figured out yet, and while you crying for someone who ain't earned one of your tears, what I don't hear is solutions as to how I'm supposed to fix this shit."

Xavier sat quiet. Shot let the silence hang heavy, staring at his cousin. Xavier looked at Shot's mouth, his hair, his ear, anything to keep from looking down while also not looking him in the eye. He was a scolded child, one who knew good and well that he'd done wrong and was fresh out of excuses.

"You're right," Xavier said.

"I know."

"It's just these past couple of days, man. They've been rough. And what happened with Pop today. You wouldn't believe."

"Yeah, well, I don't really care about all that, neither."

"What?"

"That man's no kin to me."

Xavier blinked in disbelief. "He's your uncle."

"By marriage, which don't mean a thing. You know good and well I ain't ever been treated like family in your house by anyone but you. Not by Auntie Evelyn and damn sure not by your pops."

"No, that's not true."

"You know it is." Shot sat back and folded his arms. "In fact, I think you know more now than you did then."

Xavier couldn't settle the tremor in his voice. "He didn't know me today. He came out of the bathroom and thought I was stealing his stuff." He breathed deep. "He called me a nigger."

The hard lines around Shot's mouth softened. "I forget how old I was. Seven or eight, maybe. Moms had dropped me off at your house for the afternoon and Auntie Ev had gone out for groceries or some such. We was tearing ass all over the house like the knuckleheads we were." Xavier smiled weakly. "At one point, you were hiding somewhere, and I was running all over looking for you. Your pops was watching the Eagles' game, and when I ran past him, he stuck his foot out. Tripped me."

"What?"

"Yeah. I went ass out. Fell right on my face. Funny thing was, I laughed. I thought he was playing with me, but when I stood up, wasn't no smile on his face. I won't ever forget what he said. 'Stop running around my house like a Goddamned monkey.'"

Xavier winced. "Come on."

"No bullshit, X. I just stood there at first. I mean, I was a kid, right? What was I going to say? I couldn't even process it. I'm not even sure I really knew what he meant at the time. I remember that look on his face, though. Dead serious. I was straight up scared. I just said, 'Yes, sir,' and then went to find you. And I walked. I damn sure didn't run.

"I thought about that day a lot. When I got old enough to understand what it meant, that shit pissed me off so bad. I couldn't get my head around it. Here he was married to your mama, had you, a Black son, but he was fitting to trip my ass and say some shit like that to me."

"That's why you stopped coming around when we were in high school."

"Yessir."

"Why didn't you tell me?"

"Because we had so much damn fun together, man. We weren't just cousins, we was *boys*. And it just didn't make sense to me, you know? I saw the way he was with you and the way you were with him. Y'all two were tight. I couldn't understand how he could be racist *and* still show you all that love. So, I left it alone. I didn't want to mess that up because I didn't want to mess up *our* thing. I guess I felt like if it came down to a choice for you, if it had to be me or him, I was losing that one every time. I figured if he was really like that, he'd show that to you eventually. Then y'all would have to work all that out on your own."

Xavier shook his head. "I'm sorry, man."

"For what?"

"That he did that to you."

"Did you tell him to trip me? To say that to me?" Xavier wiped at an eye. "No, you didn't. Don't apologize for things you ain't got be sorry for. Go cry on your own time." Xavier lifted his eyebrows and Shot smirked. "I didn't bring you in here to talk all this sad stuff, anyway."

Xavier smiled back. "Well you the one running your mouth. What did you bring me in for then?"

Shot laughed and picked up his cell phone from the table. He wiggled it in the air, then tapped at it and pressed the speaker function on the screen. Xavier leaned forward as the phone rang. When the voice on the other end answered, Xavier sat back in his chair and covered his mouth with his hand. He hadn't heard Carson Davis's voice since the day he'd told him the commission had suspended him for a year. And that year was up. Xavier stared wide eyed at Shot.

"What's up, Shot? You got the Scarecrow there?"

"Sitting right across from me."

"Xavier, how are you, kid?"

Xavier bit his lip. The last time they'd spoken, Carson had told Xavier in no uncertain terms that a yearlong suspension at his age meant his career was over and asked how dare he embarrass the organization at a time when they were working to convince the public that the sport was clean.

The tone of that conversation was gone now. Xavier knew too well what he heard now in Carson's voice. Need. Carson *needed* him. Knowing that, Xavier pumped his legs up and down like an overeager child. He pressed his hands against his knees, as much to stop his frenetic motion as to dry his palms.

"I'm good, Carson." His voice was nearly an octave higher, he cleared his throat and stepped it down. "What's up?"

"I won't beat around the bush, I'm sure you're a busy man." Xavier rolled his eyes at the patronization. "Here's the deal—we got this guy who's got some heat behind him. He strung together some wins on the regional circuit, and he had a big knockout in his debut with us. Still a prelim fighter, but I've got a feeling he's going places. Anyway, we had a pretty exciting fight lined up for him and the guy dropped out."

"How come?" Shot asked.

"As far as the press knows, it's an undisclosed injury. Let's leave it at that."

"And?" Xavier said.

"*And?* What do you think? You want the fight?"

"When?"

"Saturday."

"As in *this* Saturday?"

"As in this Saturday."

"Carson, it's Tuesday, man," Shot said.

"Yeah, my phone has a fucking calendar on it, too, Shot. Congratulations."

Shot gave the phone the finger.

"What's the upside?" Xavier asked.

"The upside is you're back in *The Show* after not having fought anywhere for a year, that's the fucking upside." Carson took a deep breath. "Look, there's a redemption arc in this for you, right? Aging fighter, disgraced for pissing hot, takes a last-minute fight against some brash up and comer right after his suspension is up. You can't write that shit. Is he good? Yeah, he's got some raw talent, but he doesn't have your experience. This is a tune-up fight for you, at best."

"And I'm a steppingstone at worst," Xavier said.

"Minimal chance at that, kid. Minimal. Plus, the guy said

he'd meet in the middle for a catchweight. A hundred ninety-five pounds."

"Fuck that," Shot said. Xavier furrowed his brow and made the sign for Shot to stop but he ignored it. "One eighty-five or nothing. I don't want your guy having any excuses for a loss."

Carson's grin was audible. "That's what I like to hear."

"What's the terms?" Shot asked.

"Fifteen to show, fifteen to win."

"Bullshit," Xavier said.

"You're crazy, Carson," Shot said. "We was getting thirty and thirty before the suspension."

"Key word is *before*, Shot."

"It's a last-minute fight, no catchweight," Xavier said. "Come on, Carson."

"Hey, your manager there is the one turning down the catchweight, kid. Look, at best this guy's got a puncher's chance. KO him or submit him and there's a good chance of a bonus coming your way, though we both know your chances are a lot better if you knock him out. Or hell, create some heat at the weigh-ins, get more people to tune in, maybe your prelim gets televised, and then I'll see what I can do. Bottom line, I shouldn't have to sell you boys on this shit. Opportunity of a lifetime, here, fellas. Maybe your last one, X. Take it or leave it. I've got like six thousand other calls to make."

"He's in."

Xavier's eyes widened.

Carson clapped once. "Beautiful. Soon as our guy signs, I'll shoot the paperwork over to your email, Shot. Smart move, kid. See you in Atlantic City."

Shot tapped the "end" button. He put his hands behind his head with a self-satisfied smile. Xavier did not smile back.

"What was that?"

"X, you been talking about nothing else for the last year except getting back in there. No, the deal ain't great, but we know that cat. He was about to pull that deal. Now you got the chance to fight again, and not on one of these janky regional jawns. We both know those smokers don't feel the same once you been under the big lights. So, you asking me what that was? You're welcome, that's what that was."

"Fifteen and fifteen, Shot. That's insulting. You know after expenses that doesn't amount to jack. That's *if* I win."

"You act like you going to see one red cent of that money, anyway."

"What?"

"What you mean, 'what?' Do I really got to explain this to you? Is your brain that scrambled?"

"Fuck you, Shot."

"I think I've made it clear you already done that."

Xavier's cheeks flushed. "I told you that wasn't my fault."

Shot's jaw muscles pulsed. "Not your fault. *Not your fault?* Okay, so how about the 'tainted supplements' bullshit you spouted off when you pissed hot? Was that your fault, or were you all messed up in the head then, too? I sure as hell hope so because, otherwise, I would love to know what you thought was going to happen. Who did you think they were going to look at when you said your supplements had steroids in them?"

"I said I was sorry for that."

"You stay thinking 'sorry' fixes everything, huh? X apologized and he feels better, so everything's copacetic. Do you know how much I had to go through to handle that?" Xavier opened his mouth but Shot cut him off. "No, you don't. Know why? Because I saw how it crushed you to lose your license for a year. So, I took care of my business even though it was *your* mistake, even if it meant *your* shit rolled downhill into *my* open mouth. And then just when I thought I was out from under *that*, you go ahead and put Lawrence in the hospital. Now I—check that, *we*—are in the deepest shit imaginable with people who do not play, X. Do you feel me? But I'm keeping you out of the deep end the best I can because you're my boy. So, if doing that means every dollar of this fight purse goes to keeping you and me out of the ground, then you best believe I'm going to give it to them."

Xavier rested his forearms on his legs. His ears rung. Shot had laid bare Xavier's selfishness in a way no one else in his life ever had. It surprised him to find that as much as all that truth hurt, he was grateful to his cousin for delivering it.

"I'm sorry, Shot. I know the more I say it the more meaningless it sounds, but I don't know what else to say." Xavier stood and walked around the front of Shot's desk to stand in front of him. He extended his hand for a shake but Shot kept his gaze toward the door to his office.

"For real, you need to get out my sight. I can't even look at you right now." Xavier dropped his hand and nodded, defeated, then headed toward the door. Shot called out to him. "Seven in the morning tomorrow. Don't be one minute late."

The distance from the gym to his car felt longer than any he'd ever traveled to the cage. For every one of those fight walks, he'd been as prepared as he could be, whether he'd taken a fight on short notice or if he'd had a full training camp. No matter the circumstance, he knew he'd done everything possible. Primed himself for every combat scenario, every battle permutation in the time permitted to ready himself.

But nothing had, nor could have, prepared him for what had happened in the span of just a few hours. The truths that caromed inside his skull made his head heavy, his neck weary, and his legs leaden. He was weighed down, dragging a training sled loaded not with iron plates, but with the realities brought to bear in the space of less than a day. The truth about his father, what he'd done to Lawrence, and to Shot, all compounded by his own deteriorating mind—he hadn't the first clue how to reconcile them. And now he had a fight.

In the car once more, he gripped the steering wheel. Rain pelted the rear windshield as another gust tore through the parking lot. The sky flashed white. He'd been terrified of storms as a child, and though he now found a certain beauty in their ferocity, he still felt a mild jolt of adrenaline in anticipation of the loud crack that followed the white veins running through the clouds.

During storms like these, his father had sat him on his lap and when the lightning lit up their living room, he told Xavier to count.

One-one thousand, two-one thousand, three-one thousand.

Rumble.

How many seconds did you get? That's how far away the storm is. The longer you count means it's almost gone. Then you won't have to be afraid anymore.

He remembered the moment often, during storms both real and imagined. While Xavier loved the fight, he'd never been blessed with the steely resolve other fighters seemed to possess, or at least claimed to. In the locker room, he was anxiety personified. He made multiple trips to the stall to empty his stomach, his throat strained and burned by bile. His fear began a dialogue within him. Told him to quit. Told him nothing was worth this overwhelming dread that made him feel as though he might actually die from it. Rather than answer his fear, he'd wait for the voice to stop. And then he'd count. The longer it took for the voice to come back, for the thunder to roll, the less fearful he'd become. By the time they called his name, he could make the walk to the cage without hesitation.

Seated in his car now, Xavier counted the seconds between the strike and the rumble. He only made it to one.

SOUND OF DA POLICE

When Sam signed him up for his first Silver Gloves competition, roadwork became a part of Xavier's daily routine, a routine he quickly despised. Already long-limbed at fourteen years old, his stride had all the grace of a newborn giraffe. The effort to keep his legs coordinated beneath him made them burn as intensely as his lungs. After every run, he'd complain to his father that running had nothing to do with fighting, that no skills developed from these long, boring-ass runs. Time on the asphalt was time wasted when he could be in the gym hitting the bag or jumping rope for footwork.

"You're training the most important thing." He'd tap Xavier on the forehead. "Right here. You could run sprints, sure. But here's the thing about sprints or long runs on the treadmill, or even bag and focus mitts. You can stop doing any of those at any time and you're exactly where you want to be. You can walk to the locker room and towel off or over to the water fountain for a drink. You can go home.

"You can't do that on the road. If you get tired before the halfway point, so what? Wherever you stop? That's halfway. It's that strength of mind, that force of will that powers the return. Knowing that you have to run the same distance back with less than what you started with, toward a finish line you can't see until you're within strides of crossing it. *That's* mental toughness. That's knowing you can finish the fight when the other guy can't. Because you face down that challenge every day."

The explanation never satisfied Xavier. His only contentment in training came when he could feel the pop of the pads at the ends of his punches. When he heard the whip and crack of the rope skating across the cement floor while doing double unders. When he saw how his father, holding the heavy bag, had to adjust his footing when Xavier hit with the right amount of power.

Sam would laugh in amused exasperation at his son's lack of appreciation for the run. "Think about it this way, then. You have to build up your cardio because you'll blow half your gas tank before you ever set foot in the ring."

"What? How?"

"In those moments leading up to a fight, your heart rate goes way up. You start thinking about how you're going to move and what the outcome might be. How your opponent is going to react and how you're going to react to his reaction. Before you know it, your heart has been pumping so fast and for so long and you've already dumped a bunch of adrenaline in your system. When you actually step through those ropes, you've already fought at *least* one round."

"Maybe that's what *you* think about. I'm thinking about that pizza I'm going to get when it's all over."

Sam tousled Xavier's loose curls. "And that is exactly why you need to get your ass on the road. You won't have that metabolism forever."

XAVIER PULLED THE VOLVO INTO the driveway and rested his head against the back of the seat. He was exhausted, despite the fact he hadn't physically exerted himself all day—just like his father had told him decades ago. There was no way to train his psychological cardio.

Still, once he'd left the gym, one thought prevailed over all the others. Shot was right. He had a fight. Not the circumstances he'd like, but a fight, nonetheless. Not a smoker where a veterinarian was the only doctor on staff, and they weighed in on a bathroom scale. Far from it. He was back in *The Show*. All was forgiven, as long as he gave Carson what he needed. All Xavier had to do was lose a limb to make the weight and give up his entire purse.

For the moment, his excitement outweighed the stress of the brutal weight cut looming. The nervous anticipation before a fight was an old friend, one who rolled into town and asked to crash on your couch and eat all your food. A friend he knew was trouble, one who would probably get him in over his head, but whom he couldn't help but spend time with. Never mind the inevitable pit in the stomach, the fretful, sleepless nights, the times he went to bed hungry and thirsty. Though all of it bordered on maddening, the fight never made Xavier feel beholden to anyone, and the fear and anxiety that accompanied it paled in comparison to the sense of relief and accomplishment, the near orgasmic sense of elation and fatigue that, win or lose, he knew awaited him on the other side.

As his longest year had drawn on, Xavier had been an apparition, in between this plane and the next, on a search for shape and form, unsure he'd feel that anticipation ever again. He'd convinced himself that was a good thing. The memory loss wasn't improving despite his time away. But nothing had made him happier in the past year than imagining how he'd welcome that gorgeous misery back into his life today.

Then he felt it. More remarkably, he heard it.

Nothing.

His headache, the whine in his ears, the rage and frustration—all of it gone. He smiled what felt like the most genuine smile he'd had in some time. He grabbed his groceries (he'd kept them in the passenger seat this time) and walked up the back steps to the house.

He slipped on his first step in the door. Something cold and wet crept onto his slides and under the sole of his foot. He looked down and saw a puddle, and a trail down the hallway into the kitchen that was either the fluid's origin or its end. Some of the liquid had seeped into the seams of the laminate where it bubbled up in the center of the pool.

Then the smell hit him. Not unlike the car the morning he found Loki in the back seat. He called out for the dog and heard the slow telltale click of paws on the floor. Loki's head peeked from behind the doorjamb and moved not an inch further.

"What did you do?" Xavier said in a low whisper.

Xavier straddled the line of urine as he walked down the hall to the kitchen. There he saw two large piles of formless feces and two more urine puddles. Both the food and water bowls were empty. The corner of a wooden bench that sat on one side of the kitchen table had been chewed into mush, the shavings collected in a small anthill on the floor. Xavier shook his head. His father had made that bench in the basement when Xavier was just a boy.

Xavier set his groceries on the counter and walked the floor, an investigator taking inventory of a crime scene. Loki followed slowly, his tail tucked, maintaining a constant distance. When Xavier stepped into the living room, he drew a sharp breath. The foam innards of two of the cushions and one of the arms of the couch had been strewn about the living room, the ripped fabric a gaping wound. Sam once told Xavier that he and Evelyn had playfully argued for months about the green plaid monstrosity, a holdover from Sam's first bachelor pad, about where it would go when they moved into a real home. Xavier turned in a slow circle and surveyed the damage done to things irreplaceable. The steam whistle in his ears returned. Xavier screamed.

"What the fuck did you do, you stupid fucking dog?"

Loki skittered across the kitchen floor. He lost his footing and bumped his hind legs on the back of the table as he scrambled to hide underneath it. Xavier picked up the chewed upon bench and slammed it seat side down. Loki flinched at the resounding crack and retreated further. Xavier leaned on the table and peered underneath.

"Come out of there right now!" he growled. "Look what you did!"

He swiped and grabbed at Loki's scruff. Loki bared his teeth, pressed as far back against the wall as he could go, his back in a feline arch. Xavier had visions of closing his hands around Loki's thick neck and squeezing or sticking his hands into his maw and pulling apart until the jaws of his bones cracked like shellfish. His second swing brushed Loki's muzzle and the dog loosed a protective snap that caught the edge of Xavier's hand. Xavier leapt back. He kicked the food and water bowl stand, sending them skating across the kitchen. The bite throbbed. Xavier's rage needle pinned.

Xavier pushed the drying rack off the counter and onto the floor. Plates shattered. Silverware bounced and chimed. Xavier held his hand under hot water and watched the blood from the puncture wounds turn into tiny tributaries and snake down the drain. He ripped off a stream of paper towels and held them to his hand in a bunch. When he pulled it away, he saw only two small spots of red. The bleeding had already slowed to a near stop. The fog of his rage parted just enough for him to see that Loki had only meant to warn him, to tell him he was afraid. His furious haze further dissipated. Xavier leaned against the sink and took in the tumult.

"What am I doing?"

He sunk down to the floor across from Loki, who panted, eyes fearful and trained on Xavier with desperate intensity. Xavier checked the paper towel again. The bleeding had all but stopped. He moved on his hands and knees across the floor to the table where Loki hid, but stopped short when Loki showed his teeth again. Though his throat could not produce a bark, a strained growl rumbled from within.

Xavier put a defensive hand up. "Okay, okay. You're right." He sat back. Loki covered his teeth but did not move. "It's just, that stuff is—was—*is* special. One of a kind. I don't . . . it's been a complicated day, man. And then I come home to all this shit and piss, and then *this*?" He felt the rage summit again, a geyser ready to erupt, but this time it came with a surge of panic at its irrationality and terror at the violence he envisioned visiting on Loki. The combination vented the building pressure and kept the explosion at bay. "You deserve better than this, pup. I'm sorry."

Xavier picked himself up off the floor. Then he cleaned. He wiped up the puddles of urine. He emptied the groceries from the doubled-up plastic grocery bags and used them to scoop the stools. All the while, Loki watched him from underneath the table. The whites of his eyes relayed his fear and mistrust. Once Xavier cleaned the floor with bleach wipes, he stuffed all the trash into a garbage bag and moved into the living room. He placed the shredded foam in the bag and tied it off, then tucked the damaged cushions under his arm and headed for the front door. Before he opened it, he looked back to see if Loki had ventured out from his cave. He hadn't. Xavier stepped outside and walked to the trash bins on the side of the house.

A police cruiser slowed to a stop at the end of the short walkway. Two officers exited the vehicle. The older of the two sported a pair of reflective sunglasses and wore his graying blond hair close cropped, save a half inch or so on top of his head. Xavier couldn't help but laugh to himself at the notion the officer would look like police in or out of uniform. His younger partner hadn't yet subscribed to the official hairstyle or eyewear, his brown hair moussed up and away from his black wraparound shades. Both, however, put their hands on their belts as they ambled up the driveway.

"How you doing today?" the older officer asked. The cheeriness and familiarity in his question irritated Xavier instantly.

Xavier loaded the trash into the dumpster. "I'm good."

"You sure about that?"

Xavier looked at the officer's stance. Feet wide, arms tense, shoulders up, belying the relaxation his words were meant to convey. Xavier looked past him to his partner, who had moved his sunglasses down his nose to peer at Xavier through tight eyelids. Xavier caught movement in his periphery. He turned his head quickly enough to see Ray replace the blind to his window. Xavier remembered the open windows in the kitchen and cursed. The noise of his outburst had given Ray all the rationale he needed to finally call the police.

"Mind if we see some identification?" the older officer asked.

Xavier shielded his eyes from the sun to get a better look at his badge. "Yes, Officer Wilson, I do mind. I don't carry my ID to take out my trash."

"Well, it seems you've got some neighbors concerned about what's going on in your house," Wilson said. "This is *your* house, isn't it?"

"Neighbors? You mean Ray, right? I mean I don't see anyone else peeking out their windows. Are you sure Ray's house is *his* house? Why don't you knock on his door and ask for his identification?"

"I know Ray. I don't know you."

The younger partner stepped closer to Wilson. He eyed Xavier, but his look lacked the disdain of his partner's. Xavier wiggled a pinky in his ear in a failed attempt to stifle the whistling. He turned to face Ray's house and shouted at the window.

"This what you wanted, Ray? Enjoying the show? Fuck you, Ray. Fuck. You."

"Why don't you settle down, son, and show me that identification," Wilson said.

"Son?" Xavier turned back and saw Wilson gesture with one hand while the other stayed by the gun side of his belt. Xavier put his hands in his pockets and Wilson's hand moved to hover over his gun. He knew he should be afraid, but all he felt was anger. And he couldn't change the channel. "Like I said, I don't have my wallet on me. It's inside."

"Well, why don't the three of us step inside and you can show me."

"No, I'm not going to do that."

"Sir, are you refusing us entry into the home?"

"First it's 'son' and now it's 'sir'?"

Xavier took his hands out of his pockets and Wilson's gun hand twitched. Xavier slowed his movement, then held his hands up and wiggled his fingers before crossing his arms over his stomach. "That's exactly what I'm doing. You're here pressing me for ID, assuming I don't live here, and you didn't even ask me my name."

"Okay, so what is your name?" the younger partner asked from behind Wilson.

"Xavier Wallace. This is my father's—"

"Ha! I knew it!" the second officer said, whipping off his

shades. "I knew I knew that face! Wilson, you know who this is?"

Wilson kept his stance and eyed Xavier, unmoved by his partner's sudden enthusiasm. "Who?"

The young officer clapped his hands. "Man, this is the Scarecrow!"

"*Who?*"

"Xavier 'Scarecrow' Wallace! This dude is a pro MMA fighter."

"Never heard of him."

"What? Man, he fights in *The Show*."

"That right? That's the big time, isn't it? You a big-timer, Xavier?"

"Not lately, no."

"Yeah, I mean he's not a household name or anything," the younger partner said. Xavier jerked his chin back. The officer saw Xavier's body language and turned sheepish. "No disrespect intended, Mr. Wallace. Wilson here's a casual. I'm more of a hardcore fan. That suspension should be up soon, right?"

Xavier and Wilson continued their stare down. "Today, actually."

"No shit? Nice! You getting back in there?"

"This Saturday, yeah. That might be up to Officer Wilson here, though."

"Oh, shit, forget about all that. Chill out, Wilson. He's cool."

Wilson did not relax. With the residue of rage still clouding his judgment, Xavier had forgotten himself. He'd forgotten that his lighter skin only got him so far where the police were concerned. Maybe they'd looked at him twice when he'd been pulled over, sure, but they never seemed to approach him with the same bravado he'd seen them display when Shot was in the driver's seat. Instead of that kind of aggressive posturing, they showed Xavier a cautious disdain. It was a privilege he was well aware of, but now he'd taken it too far.

Being the only Black man in front of Wilson meant he was as Black as Wilson needed him to be. He was in a neighborhood in which he'd already been told he didn't belong, with a cop in front of him who had been called by the same man who told him he didn't belong, and this was a cop who knew that same man well.

Xavier stood in his sliders, baggy basketball shorts, and oversized Sixers jersey, as much a uniform to Wilson as the cop was to Xavier. Though the officer's partner might have believed he'd defused the situation by revealing his status as a professional fighter, he'd only made things worse. Now Xavier was even more dangerous, a threat that provided additional justification for whatever came next. Wilson had doubled down on his ready stance, and it became clear to Xavier that he was in very real, very mortal danger.

He tried hard to maintain the casual cool he'd conveyed just moments before, but the channel had finally changed. He was terrified, and he saw that Wilson saw it. Xavier knew his next physical movement might see him bleeding in his own driveway from a hole in his chest. Only one, if he was lucky. He could see Wilson had been doing this long enough, had had enough Black men in this position to see the fear behind Xavier's suspect swagger, and he looked like he was enjoying it. Xavier wouldn't have put it past Wilson to move his hand toward his gun just to see Xavier flinch, to see one solitary bead of sweat trace a line down his face, to tell him who was truly in charge.

"Wilson, seriously," the younger officer said, patting his partner on the shoulder. "It's cool. Let the man get ready for his fight."

The corner of Wilson's mouth twitched a subtle smirk. Then he finally relaxed, moving his hand away from his holster. He hooked his thumbs in his belt and walked backward toward the cruiser. His partner followed suit.

"Do Ray a favor and keep it down with whatever it is you're doing in there, huh?" Wilson said. "He's an old man, you know? Big scary guy like you makes him a little edgy."

Xavier's heart thumped. "Mmm-hmm," he said, lips tight.

"Hey, uh, I know this is weird," the partner said, "but would you mind if we took a selfie?"

His throat dry, Xavier whispered. "What?"

"Ah, you're right. It's gross. You know what, forget I asked."

"Oh, come on, take a picture with the kid," Wilson said. "We drove all this way and now our coffee's cold. I mean, he *is* the reason we're letting you off with only a warning. Reed, go over and get your picture."

Only a warning? For taking out your own trash? Man, don't you do a damn thing for this piece of pork.

"Yeah, all right," Xavier said.

Reed's face brightened. "Really?"

Xavier waved him over. Wilson crossed his arms, a self-satisfied grin on his face. Reed bounded back up the walkway and pulled his cell phone from his front pocket. Xavier leaned into the frame and made a fist but did not smile. Reed extended his hand and Xavier took it in his wet palm and shook it. Reed thanked him, wiped his hand on his leg, and jogged back down the driveway to the passenger side of the patrol car. Wilson gave Xavier a salute as he opened the driver's side door. "Stay out of trouble now. Maybe start keeping that ID on you, huh? You just never know."

Xavier gave a nonchalant nod. Satisfied, Wilson sat down into the cruiser and drove off with a solitary whoop of the siren. Xavier noticed a curtain pull back in a window of the house across the street. He turned back toward Ray's house, where he once more saw Ray peek through the blinds before letting them snap shut.

"They didn't shoot me, Ray," Xavier called out. "Sorry to disappoint. I'll be here whenever you want to come over and apologize." He returned to the house and muttered under his breath, "Fucking asshole." Once back inside, Xavier dropped down onto the remaining couch cushion and put his head in his hands. "They didn't shoot me, Ray," he said again.

He laughed. A solitary snort. Then another, until he couldn't stop laughing. The more he tried, the harder he laughed. He laughed until his face ached, and his stomach muscles burned. That he couldn't stop alarmed him, and as if downshifting his car, his laughter veered into crying, tearless at first, until he understood that whatever was going on with him, whatever was happening inside his brain, was as far beyond his control as whatever Wilson had decided he would do with the nigger in the driveway.

Was this how Shot felt the night the police beat his career out of him? Xavier had always felt righteous in his anger toward police, but part of him knew he never really understood what his cousin had gone through. His tears fell unfettered at the thought. He reined them in with gulps of air like a skinned-kneed child. Then he felt a cold dampness at his leg.

He pulled his hands from his face to see Loki at his feet. The dog pressed his cool wet nose against Xavier's knee again. The gesture of selfless love in the face of what Xavier had made him endure moved him to further tears. Xavier moved to stroke the top of his head, but Loki withdrew. Xavier reached again and Loki took a full step backward, so he brought his hands to his lap. Loki stepped forward again and sat by his side. Xavier took a deep breath and stood, which sent Loki bounding backward and skidding across the kitchen floor to his refuge under the table. Xavier sat back down. Soon after,

Loki peeked his head around the door jamb separating the kitchen from the living room. Xavier slid from the couch to the floor and held out his hand as he had done when they first met. Loki reappeared fully in the doorway and sat on his haunches. He gave no signs of moving any further.

"Smart. I'd stay there, too."

Xavier picked up his cell phone. No texts from Shot. No missed calls from Maple Grove. He unlocked his phone and scrolled his contacts, hoping to find a number he didn't remember putting there, while also hoping it wasn't there.

It was. He called.

AN HOUR PASSED. XAVIER STAYED seated on the floor, back against the couch. His ass ached from the pressure, but with each passing minute, Loki's posture had relaxed. He went from sitting in the doorway to stretched across it. From there he began a slow and deliberate commando crawl across the floor, a trust game of inches. With each shuffle, he reassessed. Xavier's only movement came from his eyes, establishing contact in spurts, then looking away. He kept his arms by his sides, hands upturned, welcoming Loki to sniff them, hoping he'd smell the comfort he'd found there just the day before.

Sixty minutes later, Loki had covered almost the entire distance, but stopped short of Xavier's reach. He looked up at Xavier, his massive head between his paws, arching one side of his brow, then the other, the inquisitiveness of his expression all too human. Xavier laughed in spite of himself. Loki's head popped up. Xavier looked down at his lap. "Sorry, sorry."

Loki rose to all fours and sat next to Xavier. His thick torso leaned against Xavier's arm. The pair looked straight ahead at the blank television screen. Loki's warmth had the power of an embrace that Xavier hadn't known he missed or wanted. He slowly raised his hand. Loki side-eyed him and licked his chops but stayed in place. Xavier placed his palm on the velvet softness on the flat of Loki's head. Two thumps sounded from his rear before he stretched out to lie alongside Xavier's long legs. Xavier patted his back. His tail swooshed then stopped, swooshed then stopped, as if he were unsure of the safety in displaying his happiness.

"Good boy, Loke. Good boy."

Another thirty minutes went by. His legs and ass numb, Xavier finally stood. At ease once more, Loki wagged his tail freely. Xavier went to his pantry, where an unopened bag of treats sat on a shelf. He grabbed them, as well as what was left of the opened bag of dog food. The rustling brought Loki trotting into the kitchen. Xavier picked up a leash and collar, which sent Loki bouncing.

Xavier snapped the collar around Loki's neck and led him down the back hallway. He made a quick stop in his room to pack his bag with his jiu jitsu gear. He then changed into a pair of running shorts, pulled on his cross trainers, and laced them up. Loki watched and cocked his head curiously. Xavier threw his bag over his shoulder, collected the food and treats, and walked Loki down the back steps to the Volvo. Loki jumped so quickly into the passenger seat with the lure of a treat that Xavier cursed himself for not thinking of the tactic sooner. He pulled out of the driveway and drove to the 309 expressway, toward Germantown Pike, until they reached the entrance to Forbidden Drive.

THE STIFLING HEAT HADN'T DETERRED the after-work bikers, runners, and walkers from taking their rides, runs, and constitutionals on the canopied gravel trail. Xavier pulled into the first available space he could find, closer to Germantown Pike than the trail itself, and re-leashed Loki. With four paws on the ground, Loki pulled like a Clydesdale toward the trail entrance, so hard he panted, until he was hoarse and strained. Each time Xavier matched his pace, attempting to put slack in the lead, Loki broke into a brief run, until the tension in the leash pulled him off his front paws. Xavier smiled wistfully at his enthusiasm.

At the beginning of the trail, Xavier stood on one leg as he stretched one quad, then the other. Loki sat, but only just. With every movement Xavier made, he lifted off his haunches, ready to take off down the path. "You think you can keep up?" Loki's large tongue unfurled and lolled, his jaws wide open in a smiling pant. His paws danced back and forth in anticipation. "Okay. Let's do this then."

Xavier ran. Loki took off sprinting out of the blocks, nearly pulling Xavier off his feet. Once Loki felt the initial tug of the lead, he fell into a rhythm with Xavier's pace, the cadence of his four legs in almost perfect rhythm with Xavier's two.

Xavier rarely ran without headphones in his ears. His playlists ran the gamut from "Clair de lune" to DMX to the chunkiest power chord hard rock and metal, all organized in a fashion to hit the highs and lows of his distance runs, to drown out the sounds of his own labored breathing telling him how tired he was, how alone he was in the struggle to find his halfway to the journey back home.

Today was different. Today's run was one of a kind. Today he wanted to hear the crunch of the gravel under his feet. Today he wanted to hear beyond the brush that bordered the trail, the burbling of the Wissahickon as the water smoothed and reshaped the rocks it had run over before he'd ever set foot in these woods and would continue to do so long after. Today he wanted to hear children beg their parents for triple scoops piled high on homemade waffle cones as they climbed the steps to the ice cream shop. Today he wanted to hear the musical cacophony of birds in the trees on either side of the trail, trees whose branches reached across and intertwined like the laced fingers of hands holding. Today he wanted to hear the hellos that accompanied the nods of fellow travelers on the trail as they passed in opposite directions. Today he wanted to hear Loki pant and trot, the closest sounds to joy the dog was capable of producing, as their legs propelled them through the woods.

When tension let up in the leash, Xavier slowed his pace, believing Loki needed relief from the heat and effort. Loki rewarded Xavier's attention with a faster trot and pulled Xavier back into a run, as though the reprieve was for Xavier and not him. Before Xavier knew it, they'd reached the turn-around at Kelly Drive and Loki seemed even more energized. He looked at Xavier with eagerness, his tongue at a length that seemed impossible for his head to contain. They turned back and ran on.

As they approached the last quarter mile, Xavier felt tight-ness in his chest, though not from the effort of the miles. The inevitable awaited them at the entrance to the trail. There was no way to explain to Loki that what was to come was neces-sary, that it would hurt Xavier no less. That while better things were on the other side, there would be pain and loss, and all those other things impossible to see past in the moment.

"Not yet."

Just past the covered bridge, he pulled Loki off the trail and onto a footpath that led down to the creek. The rocks were algae covered and slick. He took off his running shoes and socks and left them on the bank. Three young Black boys were knee high in the water a hundred feet away. One had created a makeshift rod with fishing line and a branch. Two of them kicked and splashed at each other. Water beaded in their hair and glinted like diamonds as it caught the sunlight peeking through the trees. The young fisherman admonished them for scaring away his quarry. The two splashers caught sight of Loki and Xavier cooling their feet in the water and stopped for a moment.

"Is he friendly?" one of them asked.

"As friendly as they get."

"Can we pet him?"

Xavier looked down at Loki, who looked up at him. His rear swayed side to side with the whip of his tail. Xavier reached down and unclipped his lead. "Go on."

Loki bounded off, breaching and sinking in the creek water. When it was deep enough, he paddled his way over to the boys. His paws found ground again and he stood and shook the water off from head to tail, spraying the boys to their delight. Loki reveled in their jowl rubs and butt scratches, their head pats, and "good boys." Xavier smiled and walked along the bank to join them. One of the boys pulled a stick from the mud and tossed it out into the water. It landed with a splash and floated across the surface. Loki sprung after it. His large head wiggled above the water as he swam back holding his muzzle high with pride. After a few more minutes of fetch, Xavier felt a text buzz in his back pocket. He retrieved his phone. His smile faded and he chewed at the inside of his cheek.

"Okay, Loke. Time to go."

The boys voiced their disappointed protest. Loki played sprinkler again, shaking loose a hail of droplets all over his playmates, lingered for a few more pets and scratches before trotting back to Xavier. The pair made their way back up to the main path. Xavier waved to the boys and left them to their fishing once more.

They approached the entrance to the trail. Loki's tail vanished in a speedy blur. His paws pranced back and forth. Zoey, the head of the rescue Xavier had met at Maple Grove, stood at the path's end. She turned and saw Xavier and Loki and smiled, though not happily. Xavier let him off the leash. Loki galloped and threw himself at the crouched Zoey, sending her onto her rear with a giggle. Loki wiggled and squirmed in her embrace until he was on his back. She obliged him with furious belly rubs. Xavier stood over them, hands in his pockets.

"Thanks so much for meeting me here," he said. "I hope it wasn't too much of a drive."

"To see this guy again? Worth it." Zoey looked down at Loki and got a tongue to the cheek for her trouble. She pointed her chin up to avoid a second lick and looked at Xavier. "Are you sure about this?"

"He won't be put down, right? I mean if no one else takes him."

"We're a no-kill, so no. Honestly, if you hadn't taken him, I probably would have kept him myself at some point. I just wanted to give him a chance somewhere else. Did you?"

"Did I what?"

"Give him a chance."

"He's not the one who messed up." Xavier poked himself in the chest. Creases lined Zoey's forehead. She inspected Loki, her affection turned examination. She held his face in her hands and checked his paws. "No, no, he's fine. It was nothing like that. I'd never hurt him."

"You're about to, though. Doing this will hurt."

"I know. But time heals all wounds, right? He'll forget about me soon enough. Look how happy he is to see you."

"That means he doesn't forget." Xavier had no response. Zoey shook her head. "You know, I get so tired of people treating dogs like accessories. They don't understand that they're responsible for another life. It's not like you can just keep the receipt and return it if the fit's not quite right. It takes work."

"You're absolutely right. But this isn't that."

"Yeah. God, I don't want to, but I believe you, actually. I wouldn't have let him go home with you if I didn't think it would have worked out. I never saw him react to someone like he did with you. That's why I came. I had to hear from you what went wrong. And maybe see if I could talk you out of it."

Xavier crouched down and joined in the belly rubs. "You probably could. But it would be a mistake."

"Hey. *Hey.*"

Xavier kept at his scratching. Meeting her eyes meant explaining. Saying it out loud would only affirm his decision. But he knew she'd let him change his mind. He knew she wanted him to. But he couldn't. It wasn't fair. He looked up at her.

"What happened?"

He wanted to let it all out, to tell her everything, no matter how horrific and embarrassing and terrible and irresponsible. He wanted her to hate him, so she'd snatch Loki up without another word, take him to her car and drive off as fast as possible, to keep him away from the awful man who treated this gentle soul so, no matter how good his intentions were. It would be best for all of them. But he couldn't. He was afraid of what saying it all out loud would mean. Telling her what happened meant speaking it into reality, and he feared it might sear all he'd done into his brain when all he wanted to do was forget. Forget he had forgotten, forget the rage, and forget Loki the way he hoped Loki would forget him. "I couldn't take care of him the way he needed it." And as soon as he said it, he realized he didn't know if Loki was the only one he couldn't take care of.

"Maybe I can help? It just seems like you two were supposed to be together."

The words left her mouth, but none registered with Xavier. He'd been rocked by the epiphany harder than any punch he'd taken. Loki had been a subconscious test for him to see if he was meant to take care of anything since he had failed his father. Now he'd failed Loki. Xavier wasn't fit to take care of Xavier.

He stood. "I've got a bag of food in my trunk and some treats, but I'm parked all the way up by Germantown Pike. I can bring it down if you want. Donate it to the rescue or whatever."

"Just like that?"

"It has to be."

She pursed her lips, her disappointment clear. "Then no. If you're going to go to your car, then you should just go. Bring the food to our drop-off box outside the shelter if you want. But do me a favor and don't come inside. I don't want to take the chance that he might see you. It won't be fair to let him see you leave twice."

Xavier's mind went to his mother's silhouette on his wall, replaced by light as her shadow slid out of frame before she walked out. He'd lost track of the number of times he'd imagined that night, somehow different each time. Sometimes her outline would reappear, and he'd turn over. She'd come in and sit on the edge of his bed, loop her fingers through his curls and tell him she'd stay if he asked her to. And he'd ask her to. And she'd stay.

Yet as often as he'd conjured that happy ending, he'd recreated another experience as well, one where he called his mother's name to have her stay in the doorway, only to have her leave despite his pleas. A recollection as fictional as the other, but one that hurt in equal measure. He'd imagined these scenarios so many times as of late that he began to question which of them was the untruth.

Zoey was right. If he left, he'd have to leave for good. Her resigned look made it clear she'd hoped she'd pulled off some feat of reverse psychology. Xavier reached down and gave the top of Loki's head a tousle. His panting ceased and he pressed his head into the caress. Xavier tucked in his lips and took a step back. Loki's tongue stayed in his head and his posture tightened, visibly confused as Zoey wrapped an arm around his thick chest with a hold meant to contain and console. Xavier turned away from the trail. Behind him Zoey asked Loki to sit, then to stay. Her voice sounded strained, and Xavier knew Loki pulled at her to follow. He considered a last look back. And then he walked on.

BREATHE EASY

Heat filled the Volvo by the time Xavier reached the top of the hill. The smell of death from that first fateful afternoon with Loki was gone. In its place was Loki's scent, the one Xavier had already come to relish when he buried his nose in the top of the dog's head. He rolled down the windows on both sides, pulled out of the space and onto Germantown Pike. At a stoplight, he checked his cell. Still no texts from Shot. Still no call from the nursing home. His anticipation for the former was surprisingly greater than the latter. Before the light turned green, he scrolled his contacts and made a call.

"Deep Water Jiu Jitsu. This is Mike."

"Hey, Mike. Franklin in?"

"Scarecrow! Yeah, he's here."

"Tell him I'm heading in for some flow rolling, will you?"

"Sounds good."

Xavier hung up. His stomach growled. After a year of eating unrestricted, he'd grown unaccustomed to the tightness cutting produced in his belly. With the luxury of an eight-week training camp, he'd down ice water to see if it was thirst and not hunger that called to him. Weigh-ins now just days away, he could afford no more fluids than absolutely necessary. Though he'd stayed active in the gym during his suspension, he'd given in to his cravings—the salts, the breads, the sugar-laden sauces.

With every bump and pothole, he felt a wobble, an unrestrained jiggle around his middle that sounded an alarm bell in his brain. Though he'd taken short notice fights before, he'd been on the active roster and kept a reasonable walking-around weight. He'd never had to cut this much this quickly. But Shot didn't want him to start his training today. Did he really have that much confidence in him? Or was he that angry with him for his perceived ingratitude? Maybe he wanted him to miss the weight and lose out on the fight, but odds were the promotion would only penalize him by reducing the purse if his opponent agreed. The fight would still be on.

That he might have angered his cousin to the point of irrationality was disquieting. Shot was intimidating when he was happy. Xavier had never meant to anger him, and now that he had, he wondered if he'd traveled the proverbial bridge too far. The whistle in his ears returned. Whether from the anxiety over Shot or the sadness of abandoning Loki, he didn't know or care. Loki deserved better, a home where he'd be loved and safe. He'd had to surrender him. Didn't he? By the time he pulled into the parking lot behind the jiu jitsu academy, he'd had just about enough of himself. He scolded his reflection in the rearview.

"Man up."

"Get your head right."

Another member of the academy sat in the car next to Xavier's. He looked away when Xavier glanced up at him. It was obvious he'd been watching Xavier's argument with himself and had been caught staring. Embarrassed, Xavier took a deep breath, puffed out his cheeks, and breathed out. He waited until the man drove off, then grabbed his gear bag and headed inside.

The jiu jitsu academy felt decidedly different from Shot's place. Not better. Not worse. Just different. No cracks of leather against leather as glove struck pad, no shins thudding curves in the densely packed bottoms of heavy bags. The smacks heard here were hands slapping before players bumped fists, signaling the start of a roll. Palms hit the mats as students drilled break falls. Thuds sounded as hip tosses and double-leg takedowns sent bodies to the ground in a heap. The smell of sweat lingered heavy here, too, but tinged with the astringent smell of antiseptic used in the never-ending battle against staph.

Xavier walked in during a *gi* fundamentals class. While he waited for Franklin he leaned on the front desk and watched. The enthusiastic but jerky movements of the white belts paired with each other brought a smile to his face almost as big as theirs. He envied their feeling, that first-time euphoria of the first class. They'd unwrapped a new toy, except the toy was themselves. They did things they never thought they'd be doing, things they never thought they'd be comfortable doing, and things they certainly never thought they'd be happy doing. Rolling on the floor in a pair of pajamas, often with a complete stranger, dodging sweat dripping onto their face, into their mouths, their partner's hot breath just inches from their face as they looked for an opportunity to lock a limb or choke a neck. And yet, when the round timer chimed, they'd shake hands and embrace, cheeks flushed, grinning ear to ear. They might not have thrived, but they undoubtedly survived. The chance to thrive came again tomorrow.

Franklin appeared from the back and called out to Xavier as he padded barefoot across the mat. Franklin was a walking fire hydrant, short and stocky with one of his legs equaling two of Xavier's in width. He wore spats under a pair of bright board shorts and a rash guard with brown sleeves signifying his rank. A middle-aged man trailed behind him, face flushed, toweling off the top of his bald head. His shoulders slouched and he shuffled across the mat. Xavier chuckled. It seemed Franklin had had his way with another hapless private lesson participant.

Franklin stopped at the edge of the mat while the man passed. "See you Friday," he called to him. The gentleman waved over his shoulder at Franklin and walked out the front door. Franklin shook hands with Xavier and pulled him in for a half hug.

"Another victim, huh?" Xavier said.

Franklin scratched at his salt and pepper beard. "I keep telling him to come in and take some of the regular classes, but he insists on getting his ass kicked by the one and only. He pays my fee on time, so what am I going to do? Say no?"

"Got to get that paper."

Franklin laughed. "So, flow rolls, huh?"

"Got a fight."

"No shit? When?"

"Saturday."

"*This* Saturday?"

"This Saturday."

"Damn. How's your weight?"

"My sauna suit's in my bag."

"That bad?"

"That bad. You got time?"

"For you, champ? Always."

"My man."

Franklin led Xavier across the mat to the back room where he held private lessons. Once there, Xavier dug into his gear bag for a pair of plastic pants and pulled them on over his shorts. Then he donned his rash guard and put on a plastic shirt over top, wiggled himself into a pair of sweatpants, and put on his hoodie. He pulled up the hood and yanked the drawstrings tight. Franklin linked his phone to a small

Bluetooth speaker in the corner of the room and bass from a hip-hop track thumped in the tiny subwoofer. Both men dropped to their knees in the middle of the mat. Xavier put in his mouthpiece.

"Ready?" Franklin said. Xavier gave the thumbs up. They slapped hands, bumped fists, and the timer sounded. They locked up in a collar tie and Xavier sat back to pull Franklin into his guard, but Franklin shifted from his knees to a crouch and made a smooth move to pass Xavier's legs. Xavier pivoted on his back, shifted his hips, and got his legs back in between himself and Franklin. Franklin sliced his knee through the middle, but Xavier underhooked his arm and sat up, following Franklin's momentum in an attempt to gain control of Franklin's back. Franklin reacted by rolling and pulled Xavier into his own guard. The two smiled at the fluidity and rhythm they found within seconds of beginning the roll. They both caught submissions but let them go, continuing the flow, moving from one position, one attack, one counter to the next, always at half speed, engaged in a choreographed fight.

Heat prickled Xavier's skin under the layers of fabric and plastic, and the first blessed drop of sweat trickled down the bridge of his nose. Each bead that streamed down his cheeks carried with it the stress and worry that had crested throughout the day until it loomed like a tsunami, on the precipice of folding in on itself and washing everything away in a violent crash. The more he sweated, the more easily his limbs moved, the more uncluttered his mind. There was no whistling, no headache, or if there was, there was no time to pay it heed. There was only the roll, the strategy, the escapes that converted to attacks, the thinking three moves ahead to make Franklin fall for the fourth. Despite the fatigue and rising temperature in his self-contained sauna, there was relief bordering on euphoria. He felt as though he could do this forever. Until he couldn't.

Franklin shifted to his side and caught Xavier with a well-timed sweep. The move turned Xavier in mid-air. Before he could extend his arm to break his fall, the back of his head smacked off the mat. Though it was an impact he'd taken while training many times before, those days were not this one. The whistle in his ears returned in an instant, accompanied by a familiar throb in his temples. He lay on his back and raised one hand in the air, signaling Franklin to stop.

"Shit, man, you all right?"

"Just give me a minute." The fluorescent lights above turned slowly on an axis. Xavier closed his eyes. The self-imposed darkness only worsened the sensation of the ground moving beneath him. He placed both hands palm down on the mat and clawed his fingers to keep either himself or the floor from rotating. The spinning wouldn't stop. He sat up and pulled is knees into his chest.

"You're looking a little green, man."

Xavier sat up too quickly and a vertigo twister touched down. He went to stand, but before he could, he turned his head to the side and emptied what little contents occupied his stomach.

"Whoa," Franklin said. He sprung up from his squat next to Xavier and stepped back. "I'll grab some wipes." He took off toward the front of the gym.

Xavier wiped his mouth with the back of his sleeve. Franklin bounded back in with paper towels, a trash can, and a container of bleach wipes. Xavier looked up at him, contrite and embarrassed. "Fuck, man, I'm sorry." He took the roll of towels from Franklin and sopped up the vomit.

"No worries, my dude. It happens. So, you got a concussion?"

Xavier dropped a wet wad into the trash bin and pulled a wipe from the cannister. "Something like that."

"And they're going to let you fight?"

A jolt of panic stopped Xavier's scrubbing. Franklin was right—he was going to have to pass medicals for the fight. How had he not thought of this already? He'd told Shot no doctors, no MRIs, but taking the fight removed that option. If this thing in his brain showed up on a scan, it wouldn't matter how willing he was to take this short-notice bout, nor any others, because the results could mean there might not *be* any others. The dam broke and unleashed a flood of fear all over again. He scrubbed harder at the mat.

"It's all good. It's not really even a concussion. A mild one, if anything. I'm fine."

Franklin crossed his arms. "Uh huh."

Xavier recognized that look. That tone. Franklin had seen a number of fighters come through the doors of his academy. He'd seen plenty of men and women downplay, even outright hide their injuries, anything to ensure they walked up those metal steps come fight night. Xavier knew that, and he knew Franklin knew that he knew it.

"Seriously, man. I'm good." He tossed the wipe into the waste bin. With his clean hand, he offered a fist for Franklin to bump. Franklin's arms remained crossed for a moment. He looked at Xavier's outstretched hand and gave him the once over. There was no disdain in his countenance, only concern. Xavier held his fist out and met Franklin's earnest gaze with one of his own. *I need you to believe me, because if you don't, I'm not sure I can believe it myself.* As if the thought crossed the air between them, Franklin touched knuckles with him.

"Sorry again about the mess, and thanks for the roll. I'll get changed and get out of your way."

Franklin picked up the trash can and walked away. "See you up front."

Xavier dipped into the locker room adjoining the private training area and stripped off his wet clothes. He shook his head at what had just happened. *Nothing like puking to make weight.* He laughed to himself at the thought, but panic returned quickly as his thoughts shifted again to his medicals. *Shot will know what to do. He's probably already thought about it. Stop worrying. He's always got your back.*

Does he now?

Xavier toweled off and got dressed. His empty stomach growled in protest and he gave it a calming pat. Even boiled chicken, brown rice, and broccoli sounded like a feast of kings at this point.

Did he have any?

Of course. He'd bought some on the way home from Shot's. Hadn't he?

He did. He had to have.

Maybe another run to the grocery store. Just in case.

Xavier shook hands with Franklin once more as he left and walked back out to the car. He fished his phone out of his gear bag and saw he'd missed a call from Maple Grove. They'd left a message asking him to call at his earliest convenience. He pinched the bridge of his nose and leaned on the trunk of the car.

The phone rang. The front desk connected him to Mrs. Thomas. He steeled himself for the worst but was surprised at the sense of ease he felt when he heard her voice, even with the knowledge the news she had to deliver was unlikely the good kind.

"Good to talk to you again, Mrs. Thomas."

"Likewise. How is the eye?"

He'd forgotten about the cut and brought two fingers to check, relieved when they came back dry.

"Doing fine, thanks to you."

"I'm glad."

"So, how is he?"

"The hospital stabilized him. He had some mild dehydration and oxygen desaturation from constantly pulling out his nasal cannula. It may have been what led to his excitability this morning."

"Wait, how would he become dehydrated? Aren't you supposed to make sure he gets fluids?"

"We can't force him to drink if he doesn't want to, Mr. Wallace. Some days he won't eat even when he tells us he's hungry."

"Well, maybe you need to try harder. He's wasting away and you're just giving up on him." The goodwill well was low and quickly emptied.

Mrs. Thomas took a deep breath. "Mr. Wallace, I know this is difficult to process."

"Do you? Do you know that?"

"I've seen it day in and day out, with families like yours. And my own."

Xavier looked skyward, exasperated at his defensiveness toward a woman who had shown him kindness just hours ago. His emotions turned on a dime, worse than the usual irritability that came with a weight cut. The oscillations embarrassed him, but they could not be caged. "I'm sorry, Mrs. Thomas."

"Don't be. It's just that this is the way it is with dementia. His mind is betraying him in so many ways. I wish I could tell you otherwise, but I'd be lying to you. The last thing I wanted when my mother went through this was for her caregivers to give me false hope."

"After what happened today. Is he allowed back at your facility?"

A pause. "The hospital wants to keep him overnight for observation. Make sure his fluids stay up and his oxygen remains level."

"Right, okay. What about tomorrow?"

"Yes, we'll allow him back. But conditionally. The verbal abuse is one thing, but I won't put my staff at physical risk. If there is another outburst like the one earlier today, we're going to have a different conversation."

"Understood. You've been more than flexible and under-standing."

"No more for you than for anyone else, Mr. Wallace."

"I appreciate you, anyway."

"You're welcome. Have a good evening."

Xavier returned the sentiment and ended the call. He opened the driver's side door and tossed the phone onto the passenger seat and his bag in the back. The news should have been welcome. That Maple Grove would allow him back should have been a respite. Sam returning meant not having to find a home that could accommodate his needs and that also took medical assistance insurance. That conversation still loomed, but he'd bought another day.

That stay of execution should have flooded him with sweet relief, no matter how temporary. But it didn't. He almost wished Mrs. Thomas had told him his father was dead. Then he might finally have felt that weight come off his shoulders, because in those moments, when Sam screamed racial epithets at his first and only born, when he threatened and then committed violence against him like a stranger, Xavier lost the capacity to care for him anymore. Any concern for his father's condition had gone swirling like so much waste. Wasted time, wasted effort, wasted love. How much he had given up for him. How many he had pushed away to care for him. How much more deeply he had connected with his father, because as his mind deteriorated, so did Xavier's. All this only to discover that to his father, for all his professions of paternal love, for all the coaching, for all the matches he'd attended, for the consolations in defeat and the hugs in victory, for all the supposed challenges professed by this white man raising a Black son alone—that to him, his son was just another nigger.

He ran two red lights as he crossed the peaks and valleys of Joshua Road as it led him away from Lafayette Hill and back toward his father's house. In the grocery store, he hardly noticed when the cashier welcomed him back for the second time that day. He gave his usual polite nod, hearing without listening, and walked out the sliding doors in a trance.

Back at his father's home, he ascended the back stairs to the porch. He felt a sense of déjà vu, the playlist of his life stuck on repeat. He pushed the back door open and was struck by the faint smell of feces and urine.

"Loki! What did you do?" He listened for the rhythmic click that accompanied Loki's trot across the laminate floor, but the only sound that answered his call was his voice as it echoed off the walls of the hallway. "Loki?"

He stepped into the kitchen and set the groceries on the counter. He saw the chewed wooden bench and table. He saw the missing couch cushion, the foam innards of the arm stuffed back in under the upholstery like a packed wound. And he remembered.

He was angry all over again. Not at Loki. At himself. He couldn't be so far gone as to have forgotten it so quickly. Yet there he stood. Calling out to no one. He swiped the groceries from the counter and stood in front of the refrigerator. When he opened the door, he saw the exact same contents of the bags in his hand occupying the glass shelves. He'd already bought them. He flung the bags across the room.

"Fuck!"

He crouched down in front of the open fridge and lifted his face to meet the cool air. In his mind's eye, his father screamed at him again. Lips curled under. Teeth bared. Drops of spit on his chin. Then Loki cowering under the table. Cowering. Inches from his fingers grasping at the empty air. Then his mother's shadow sliding away from the wall.

He stood. Automaton-like, he pulled the chicken and broccoli from the fridge. He grabbed the rice from the pantry and boiled water in separate pots. He placed his plate on an old aluminum tray table. He consumed the flavorless meal seated on the couch's sole remaining cushion. He stared at his opaque reflection on the blank television screen. He leaned back on the couch when his meal was finished. He dared not close his eyes again, lest he bear witness to another horror show. He rinsed his dishes in the sink and walked down the hall to lie down in his room.

The silence amplified the steam whistle's insistent scream. He sat up and checked the time. Shot would have gone home from the gym by now, along with most of his protégés. The boxing side of the gym would be empty. He repacked a bag and walked back to the Volvo.

Halos ringed the headlights from the opposing traffic on Lincoln Drive. The lights shone in his eyes and turned the ring in his ears to a piercing peal, the chime of a blade pulled from its sheath. He took each sharp bend and blind corner and imagined releasing the steering wheel. For years, the old car had pulled to the left. All he had to do was let go and he'd cross the center line.

No more forgetting.

No more remembering.

He loosened his grip. The wheel slowly slid between his fingers.

Another car rounded the bend and he tightened his grasp. He moved his car to the right, out of the passing lane, away from temptation. The sun lowered in the sky and painted the clouds orange as he drove beneath the Wissahickon bridge. Looking up at it as he passed underneath produced a sense of unsteadiness, and he drifted into the left, much to the irritation of the driver occupying the lane just inches behind him. At the sound of the horn, he jerked the wheel and took a deep breath to slow his heart. Not moments ago, he'd considered intentionally putting himself in harm's way. He laughed at his own ridiculousness.

At the gym, Shot's office sat locked and darkened. The kickboxing class wound down their final session of the night. The front desk attendant moved from weight machine to treadmill with a spray bottle and dingy towel wiping down the equipment. They exchanged half-hearted hellos as Xavier headed over to the boxing side of the gym.

A lone gym member had found the courage to train the heavy bag with the real fighters. Xavier watched his clumsy hooks. The way his opposite hand fell from his face as he threw all he had into every strike. The way the bag swayed with the push of his sloppy punches. Seeing Xavier approach, the man stopped, straightened up, and hugged the bag to stop its swing. He pulled a hand out of its glove and pushed his wet hair out of his eyes.

"Sorry, there was no one here, and I was just finishing up my workout and—"

Xavier signaled for him to pump the brakes, putting a stop to the man's nervous rambling. "Don't push the bag. Pull your hand back like the bag is hot. It should bounce up and down, not swing."

The man cautiously stepped back into his fighting stance and eyed Xavier, searching for permission. Xavier gave it with a nod. The man threw a solid right cross and whipped his hand back as soon as it made contact. The bag bobbed up and down. He smiled big and looked to Xavier for approval.

Xavier brought his fist to his own cheek. "Good, just keep that other hand up." The man smiled again and returned to punching. His first cross and hook were solid, but the bag began to sway again as he continued his combinations. "You'll get it," Xavier said. He walked off toward the mini cage in the far corner of the gym.

He stepped into the cage and set his bag on the mat. The red stain where Lawrence had lain in a pool of himself had since turned brown. Xavier groaned as he lowered himself down to the mat. He lay supine, his bag under his head like a pillow. In the earliest days of his fight career, he'd slept in the cage the nights before the fight. If he trained there and slept there, come fight day, there was nothing about the cage to fear. The cage was home. As his career progressed, he'd discarded the habit. He convinced himself the strategy was a weakness, that he had moved beyond such mental gymnastics. Xavier folded his hands over his stomach and stared at the extinguished lights overhead. He closed his eyes. And within seconds, he fell asleep.

HERE WE GO AGAIN

I've got to be honest with you, my guy. I don't get you.

It's like you're determined to be this sad sack all the time when, the way I see it, things are finally lined up the way you've always wanted.

Look, I understand why you wanted the dog. I do. I didn't before, but it's clear now. You couldn't take care of your old man and him not knowing who you were, it made that little boy inside go all fetal and weepy. You needed your teddy bear, so hey, a dog will do.

But it's time to stop holding on to all these things you think you're supposed to be. Acting the way you think people want you to. Thinking you've got to be this model son for your poor old suffering daddy.

Fuck people. Fuck them all. Not one of them has been there for you the way you needed. As long as I can remember, it's always been about us—you and me against the world, baby. But you've *got* to stop all this whining about every little thing. I can't take it.

Hard truth time, homeboy. You never wanted that dog, and now that he's gone, you're relieved, and you know it. That dog wasn't going to do anything but hold you back—just like your old man. You can get mad at me all you want, but you know I'm right, especially about your pops.

You know why you don't feel anything about him being

sent back to the home? It isn't because of what he said to you, I can tell you that. Act all surprised about him dropping the n-bomb on you if you want, but you know as well as I do that that's no surprise to you. Lying about it to me is the same as lying to yourself. You wanted to believe different because that let you be mad at your mama. Gave you an excuse. Truth is truth whether you want to face it or not.

What, you thought you could just go on denying it up until the day he died, and you wouldn't never have to confront it?

For real?

I thought you were supposed to be the cat that runs toward a fight, not away from one.

I'm saying, dude—embrace this shit.

You couldn't take care of the dog and you didn't want to anyway. Fuck him, he's gone. Boo hoo.

You can finally admit your pops is a racist piece of shit. He's dead to you now, at least until he up and kicks the bucket for real. Fuck him. He's gone. Boo hoo.

Your Mama walked out on you because she couldn't hang? Fuck her. She's gone. Boo hoo.

Except—did she walk out on you? Or did she walk out on him?

Is there a difference?

Are you sure?

Ah, but that's not important right now. Forget I said anything.

You don't need nothing or nobody but the fight.

We all we got, baby!

There's *nothing* standing in your way anymore. You can be the "you" you always wanted to be. The one you always knew you were. The one that put Lawrence in the hospital. The one who would rip a dog's jaws apart with his bare hands for shitting on his floor and tearing up his daddy's couch.

Time to throw that shit you heard about being too emotional out the damn window. Time to stop pretending and be who you really are.

By the way, you ever entertain thoughts of pulling into oncoming traffic again, and I'll steer you into the cars my damn self. We're done with that fake whiny shit. Man up.

This fight you got is going to be your coming out party. We're about to let people see the real you. Open the door to the basement and let us out. Your pops gave you the keys.

THINGS FALL APART

Buzzing sounded overhead. Light shone orange behind Xavier's eyelids. The fluorescent lights over the cage flickered. Pain stabbed at the base of his neck as he lifted his head. His gear bag made for an ineffective pillow. He cupped the back of his head with his hand and sat up in the center of the cage. Legs splayed out in front of him, he stretched. Bubble wrap pops ran up his spine. He wriggled his fingers just short of his toes. His teeth were covered in a pasty, dehydrated film. He rubbed the sleep from his eyes. Clay approached the rear corner of the gym, switching on the lights as he opened up.

"Morning, Clay."

Clay flinched. He peered through the chain link and saw it was Xavier. Xavier watched a mix of disappointment and trepidation come over his face. He couldn't blame the kid. He'd smashed Lawrence right in front of him, then left him to clean up the aftermath. Then he'd snapped at him for no good reason. Things between them had changed.

"What time's Shot getting in?"

Clay shrugged. "Whenever he gets here, I guess. Y'all training today?"

"You heard about the fight?"

"Uh huh."

"Cool. You going to give me some rounds today or

what? Don't put it on me too bad if you do. I'm old and brittle."

"Nah, I got some stuff I got to do today."

"What you got to do you can't help out your boy?"

"I don't know. Stuff Shot wants me to do."

Xavier grabbed the top of the cage and leaned his face toward the fence. "Clay, I'm sorry I snapped at you the other day. For real, I didn't mean that. I was just all messed up after what happened, you know?" Clay put his hands in his pockets and traced patterns on the tile floor with his feet. "I know what I did to Lawrence probably scared you—"

Clay's head jerked up. "What you mean, scared?"

"Maybe that was the wrong word—"

"Ain't nobody scared. I'm not scared of you."

"Okay, you're right, I'm just saying—"

"Look, man, I got to go finish opening up before Shot gets here."

Before Xavier could utter another word, Clay walked off. Xavier chewed at the inside of his cheek again.

Whatever. That's another one you ain't got to worry about. Fuck him, too. Boo hoo.

"Damn," Xavier whispered. He turned to retrieve his gear bag when he heard Shot's voice boom across the gym.

"Is that motherfucker here?"

Xavier saw Clay near the front of the gym gesture with his head toward the cage. Shot walked toward Xavier with intention, absent the usual swagger in his strut. "Wrap your hands and meet me in the ring. Time to go to work."

Minutes later, Shot stood in the center of the boxing ring. Body pad slung over his shoulders. Hands sheathed in focus mitts. Xavier emerged from the locker room and Shot clapped the mitts, sending a crack echoing throughout the gym, turning heads. The sound sliced through Xavier to a part of him he'd

almost forgotten existed in the past year. The skin on his arms
turned to gooseflesh. Heat radiated up the front of his neck and
into his cheeks. On his walk to the ring steps, he tapped his
gloves together, a meditative tic he'd adopted in his earliest days
of fighting. Ignoring the whistling, he imagined his walkout music
in his ears and the way the white noise roar of the crowd nearly
drowned it out. He'd never done drugs, but the first time he heard
thousands of people shouting and stomping their feet, he knew
he'd been hooked on a narcotic he'd never kick. He felt a fraction
of that rush as he ascended the steps to meet Shot in the middle.
Fire lit in his chest. He had but to breathe it out. Shot must have
seen something of the old look in his cousin's eye, for as Xavier
bounced from foot to foot and shadowboxed, Shot smirked.

"Shoeshine," Shot said. "Get them long arms warmed up.
With your old ass."

Xavier dipped his chin and threw loose ones and twos at
the mitts. Shot fed them into his punches. After ninety seconds, Shot dropped the mitts. Xavier shook out his arms.
They burned with lactic acid. He had missed the comfort of
the discomfort. Shot stepped forward and called out a three-
punch combo. Xavier's arms snapped from hips to pads. On
the last punch, Shot caught him in the ear hard with the flat of
the focus mitt. The blow made Xavier take a step to his right.

"What, your punches so pretty, you going to watch them
now, too? Move your head, nigga."

Xavier tapped his forehead with his glove and put his hands
back up. Lost in the moment, he'd forgotten the basics, despite
coaching Clay and the other kids against those exact mistakes.
He stepped back in the pocket and unleashed the same combination. Each punch cracked. He ducked and weaved under
the swinging hooks Shot threw after the last hit landed. Shot
missed them all. Xavier backed out and reset. Xavier saw
Shot wiggle his fingers inside the focus mitts. Those punches

had hurt. Xavier tightened his lips to keep from smiling. Shot raised the pads for another go. Xavier moved in.

Fifteen minutes later, Xavier's arms glistened with sweat. His shoulder muscles adapted to the burn. He felt more energized with each round of strikes. Shot failed to find Xavier's head with counters since that first lapse in focus. More than once, Xavier slipped, pivoted, and faked a follow-up punch fast and real enough to make Shot flinch.

"Keep grinning. I'm about to put my gloves on."

"Come on with it, then. If you want to get pieced up, I got something for you."

"Yeah, okay. Ain't no takedowns in my game, son. You going to stand with me until you can't."

"Okay, you got that. You the man."

"Fucking right."

"Shot!" Clay called out from the door of his office.

"What?"

"Phone!"

"You don't see I'm busy?"

Clay jogged across the gym and stood at the edge of the ring. "You said to get you if your mama called. That's what it says on the caller ID. She been blowing your phone up the last couple of minutes."

Xavier cocked his head. "Your mama?"

Shot ignored Xavier and leaned over the top rope to take his phone from Clay. He cursed under his breath and motioned for Clay to come into the ring.

"Hold pads for him. I'll be back."

Xavier saw Clay's hesitation. Clay climbed the steps and held the ropes open for Shot, who walked off toward his office. Clay stepped in, but Xavier waved him off.

"It's cool. Don't worry about it. I'll go hit the bag."

"Shot'll have my ass, I don't do what he said."

"I'll tell him I didn't want no chump holding pads for me."
Clay made a face. Xavier gave him a playful punch on the
shoulder. Clay relaxed. Xavier sat on the ring ropes and Clay
stepped back out through the gap. Xavier followed. Almost as
soon as he'd disappeared behind it, Shot threw open his office
door. It banged off the wall and rattled the blinds.

"That was fast," Xavier said.

Shot looked at Clay and Xavier. "The fuck you two doing
out here? Didn't I say run drills?"

Clay blanched and opened his mouth. Xavier stepped up.

"Come on, now. You know he can't hold pads for me. Shit,
you can barely hold them for me." Xavier winked but Shot's
mood had darkened. The sense of play was gone, replaced by
something Xavier couldn't discern. "You all right?"

"Back in the ring."

"Okay, cool. Whatever you say."

Xavier trailed behind Shot and looked back over his
shoulder at Clay. Xavier shrugged, as did Clay. Back in the
ring, Shot set the round timer and called out combinations
again, but it was clear his mind was elsewhere. He stayed
rooted in one spot, calling the same two combinations over
and over. He missed a pad feed on a cross and Xavier swore
when his elbow hyperextended. Shot took no notice. He called
out another combination. Xavier stopped.

"What's going on, man?"

"What do you mean?"

"You're distracted all of a sudden. And we both know that
wasn't auntie calling you, unless she figured out a way to do
it from the afterlife."

"You always got jokes, huh? Something's always funny to
you. Shut up and hit the pads."

"I would if you'd pay attention and feed them right. You
going to have me dislocate something with that weak shit."

"What'd you say?"

"Come on, Shot. What's the deal? It's all over your face. Something's up. Who was on the phone?"

His hands still tucked inside the focus mitts, Shot put his wrists on his hips. He looked down at his feet, then back up. But not at Xavier.

"They announced the fight. The odds are already out. You're a heavy favorite over this kid."

"Yeah? That's what's up. Finally getting some respect. Is that why you're all in your feelings? What, you don't think they got it right? Where's the love? I'm feeling like my old self in here." Xavier shadowboxed for effect, moving his feet back and forth in an Ali-like shuffle. Shot was not entertained. The muted anger he had leaving his office gave way to a look of regret. Xavier saw the change and stopped dancing. His punches slowed until his arms dropped to his sides.

"No."

"A two to one favorite."

"Hell no, Shot. Are you kidding me right now? No. After everything I've been through? You know what this fight means to me. I can't *believe* you would ask me to do that."

Shot pushed his tongue into the side of his cheek. "I'm not asking, cuz."

"Oh, so you're *telling* me? I got no say in whether or not I throw a fight for you?"

Shot closed the distance between them and spoke with quiet menace. "Keep your fucking voice down."

Xavier stepped to Shot. Inches separated their faces. "I don't care who you are or who you know. Don't get up in my face telling me to keep my voice down when you the one out here doing dirt. Who the fuck do you think—"

Shot popped his shoulders and Xavier's hands went up to protect his face from the feint. Shot leaned to the side and

threw a sharp shot to Xavier's liver with the hard edge of
the focus mitt. Air left Xavier's lungs in a rush. The pain in
his flank removed the bones in his legs and he dropped to all
fours on the canvas, begging for air like food. Shot crouched
down in front of him. He looked over Xavier at the onlookers
and whispered.

"If you even thinking about getting up and swinging, tell
me now and I'll get my gloves so we can handle our business.
Or, you can get your shit together, stand up, and you can
talk to me about this in my office like a man. What do you
say?" Xavier gasped and clutched his side. "Oh, you can't
talk? Well then just nod or shake your biscuit head before you
cause a bigger scene than you already did." Xavier nodded.
"All right then." Shot tossed the focus mitts off his hands
and lifted Xavier from the mat by one of his arms. "That's
why you can't bring them hands up too high to protect your
head," he said loud enough for others to hear. "One of these
days he's going to learn. Not today, I guess."

Some of the spectators laughed nervously and went back to
minding their business. Shot took off the body pad and flung
it to the side, then stepped through the ropes, not bothering
to hold them for his cousin. Xavier followed behind. He kept
his arm splinted against his ribs as if to keep his insides inside.
Shot held the door to the office open for him, then slammed it
shut behind him. Xavier flinched at the crack and sat down.

"Why?"

"You were being a bitch."

"No, why are you doing this to me? You're supposed to be
family. How could you put me in this situation?"

Shot sat. He leaned forward, arms on the desk, hands
folded. "You got your nerve asking me how *I* can do this to
you. For the last year and change I been clawing my way
up out the pile of shit you dropped on me, and just when

I made it to the surface, when I could stop breathing and eating it, you go ahead and take another dump on me. Well, no more."

"Unbelievable, man. Everything Mom and Pops used to warn me about when it came to you. Here it is. I just couldn't see it."

Shot leaned back. "Oh, please, do tell me what it is they used to say about me that you now see so clearly."

Xavier waved him off. "Whatever, man. Forget it."

"Oh, no, you put them cards on the table. You best ante up."

High-pitched pings rang in Xavier's ears. While one voice told him to shut his mouth, a louder one abandoned reason.

"They said you were nothing but a leech. That because you and your mama didn't have any money, she would drop you off at our house all the time thinking we'd take pity on her and help her out. That you never really liked me. That you used me for my toys and video games and what not. I didn't believe it, though. I always stood up for you, always convinced them to let you come by, to sleep over, because I knew that could never be true. And now here you are. I trust you to be my trainer and my manager—my friend—and you dumped me in a snake pit for a dollar."

Shot ran his hand over his face. "You trifling nigga. I'm a leech. *I'm* a leech? I've been looking out for you almost your entire life. When we were in middle and high school and the brothers was making fun of you, picking on you for being too white, calling you Oreo and zebra and shit, nobody else had your back *but* me. Matter of fact, I don't recall your scrawny ass having but one friend. Again—me. The one who taught you how to fight because I couldn't be in the bathroom every time you needed to piss. I couldn't be in the hall every time someone knocked the books out your hands or pushed you around in gym class, could I?"

"Hold up—"

"Uh uh, no. You *done* talking now." Xavier pressed his lips together and stayed silent. Shot scoffed. "You know, I'm almost jealous of this shit you got going on with your brain. It must be nice to get to remember things the way you want to remember them instead of the way they really was. I mean, you're actually rewriting history. That's a Goddamn super-power."

This no-account motherfucker. Man, jump out of your seat and show him what's up. This is *your* fight. You aren't throwing anything for this broke-down, punch-drunk hanger-on. When he was champ, did you come sniffing around his pockets, looking for handouts, trying to get into the clubs? Hell no. But the minute you got even a taste of success, the minute you got called to *The Show* the first time, there he was. "Let me be your trainer. Let me manage you. I'll take care of you." You don't need this parasite.

Xavier squeezed his fingers into fists. His toes clawed at the soles of his boxing shoes. Tension in his feet and calves climbed up his thighs, knotted in his gut, spread up his neck and into his jaw, tense from gritting his teeth. Xavier saw Shot receive the message his body language sent.

"Don't like what I have to say? You feeling froggy? Jump then. Come on with it. You might even whoop my ass. But you ain't walking away from it intact, I'll tell you that much right now. And if that happens, then we both got bigger problems than our history, you feel me?"

Xavier understood—but he didn't want to. "Wait, what are you saying?"

"You know what I'm saying. You don't throw this, we are both in a world of hurt."

"I thought you were supposed to be the cat nobody fucked with."

"If I'm that cat, then these dudes are wild dogs."

Xavier put his head in his hands and groaned. "Jesus, Shot. What did you get me into?"

"That's the question of the year for both of us, ain't it?" Shot stood and came around to lean against the front of the desk. "X, listen to me. Hate me all you want right now. But you do this and you can walk away. These guys have the kind of money that a fix on two-to-one odds makes everyone fat stacks. You could retire. Leave your gloves in the cage and all that shit. Make a show of it. Then get out. Do something else. Anything that doesn't involve getting your head knocked off your shoulders no more."

"Bullshit. There's no way."

"How you think Lawrence afforded reconstructive surgery and a hospital stay with no insurance? You think I was covering his expenses? You see me matching 401ks in here? That dude *stayed* paid with those fights. And you a bigger name than he ever was. These guys know this, and they have the cash to make this happen. But here's the thing, X. All that cash they have? They like making it too. They like it so much that most times they'll do more than fuck somebody up for messing with that money. You hear what I'm telling you? And you took out one of their most reliable dudes. You lucky they're going to pay you out anything at all."

"So why are they?" He regretted the question the minute he uttered it. There was no answer that improved his situation.

"Just looking that gift horse right in his mouth, huh? Because if they pay, you don't talk. If you don't talk, they don't have to take you out. Everything is cleaner that way."

"And if I retire? Then who are they going to use?"

"That's not your problem."

"Is it yours?"

"It's not yours."

This is all bullshit. There's no *they*. He's playing you to up his cut. This is payback for last year. Don't buy this nonsense. You know you can't trust this fool.

Xavier squeezed his head between his hands and groaned. "Who are these guys, Shot? Really?"

"Who do you think, X? Gangsters. Hard motherfuckers. If you knew who they were, they wouldn't be too good at being gangsters, would they? They are not dudes to be messed with. You satisfied with that? You scared enough now? Maybe you'll stop asking questions you don't really want answers to?"

He'd been so close. So close to having what he wanted. Called back home. Back in the fight game. Back to *The Show*. But Shot was right—he owed him. He owed him for the humiliation and aggravation that followed the tainted supplement controversy. And the debt for his assault on Lawrence defied valuation. It was one thing to be in Shot's pocket for these things. To be on the hook with some shadow league, some faceless, unseen villains pulling the strings of a man like Shot was something else entirely. His back was up against the cage. He was stuck in the opposing corner, punches sneaking through his guard, and his coach had no means of throwing in the towel.

"Okay. What do I have to do?

Shot's eyebrows rose. For a moment, he looked as if he might cry. He didn't. "You have to win the first two rounds. Make it look good, but if you see the knockout opportunity, do not take it. Light him up, take him down, dominate from the top, but don't cut him. If he's got no answer from the bottom, stall until they stand you up. If you're on the bottom, don't look to submit. If you catch him in a submission, it's going to look suspect if you let him out. Just ride out whatever he throws at you from the top."

"Jesus, Shot."

"I know. But it's got to go three. The more the odds move in your favor from round to round, the bigger the payoff."

"This is too much."

"We'll watch all the tape on him we can find the next few days, look for his tells. He's a big puncher, so chances are he's going to telegraph by loading up. In that third round, when you see he's looking for that haymaker to steal the fight, drop your hand enough to give him an opening. I can't count on whether or not you can sell a knockout. You're just going to have to take it on the chin."

"Shot, I can't do this."

"I told you, it's done."

"No, I mean, I literally don't know if I can do this. How am I supposed to keep all this straight? With my head?"

"Between rounds I'll tell you where we're at."

"You might be miked up for television. No way you get away with that."

Shot snorted. "You talking like I never done this before. You think I can have the rest of the corner knowing what's going on in there? You think I can afford to pay the cutman to keep his mouth shut? There is a code to all this. I'll say some shit that actually means some other shit." He shook his head and waved his hands. "Look, stop worrying. I'll explain it to you. Trust me, if that idiot Lawrence could understand it, you won't have no trouble."

Xavier gripped the torn pleather of the armrests and dug his fingers into the yellowed foam stuffing. This couldn't be happening. For a year he'd given up the only thing he'd ever felt he'd done well in his life. Worked to repair the rift in his relationship with Shot. As quickly as his opportunity to return to *The Show* was given, it was taken away, and there was no way out. If he pulled this off, he'd have done something he swore he'd never do, and were they to get caught, he'd never fight again. But if he didn't do this, then he and Shot were in very real trouble. The worst kind, the way Shot told it. He stood.

"I have to get out of here."

"When's the last time you ate? You a little paler than usual."

"I need air."

"All right. Go take a walk or something, then get back here for drills. No sparring. We just doing pads and footwork to get that weight off, but we're still doing three a days. Do what you got to do and then be ready to put in that work."

Xavier waved over his shoulder as Shot's voice trailed off behind him. He took his gear bag back to the locker room, where he donned his running shoes. He fast-walked to the gym's front door keeping his gaze straight ahead, not wanting to see or hear anyone. His pulse peaked and valleyed. Shot's office, the locker room, even the gym itself, felt as if it had all the space and air of a shoebox, and he was desperate to push off the lid. He'd never had a panic attack before, but he was sure one was on its way.

Outside, he breathed deep. Then again. When his respirations slowed, he leaned on a wall and stretched his quads. Once finished, he bounded up and down on the balls of his feet, then broke into a jog down the sidewalk and turned onto Main Street.

The smells of restaurants preparing food for their lunchtime openings mingled with the exhaust in the air as cars inched along the thoroughfare, traffic traveling only a car's length before the light changed once more. Pedestrians sidestepped and gave him a wide berth. His forefeet thudded against the concrete, a look of resolve that told them *they* were in *his* path, not the other way around. He narrowed his shoulders to squeeze between women in tights and tank tops, mats slung over their shoulders as they padded in their flip flops to their morning hot yoga. He yelled "on your left" to worker drones walking to the train station, heads down on their phones, ear buds implanted. He took slight pleasure in their startled jumps before they nearly leapt into the street.

He reached where the Schuylkill dumped into the Manayunk canal. The rushing water grew louder as he approached the turn across from the SEPTA rails that took him into the trails along Lincoln and Kelly Drives. As he made the left, a gust of warm wind blew across his sweat-dampened face. The torrential rain from the previous day had stopped, but the wind that accompanied the storms remained. Thin trees that lined the path and filled the woods swayed and bowed to the wind. Larger trees moved as well, the ground soft from the soaking.

The first hill into the woods was steep. His legs burned as he summited. The lack of food and water stoked a flame in his thighs and calves. He did not stop at the top of the trail. Instead pushed harder when the ground leveled out. His feet dug into the muck where rainwater had pooled. The ground squelched as it released its grip on the sole of his sneakers. The trail was slick in spots. Though he pushed the pace, he stepped carefully. He realized he'd forgotten his cell phone in his locker. The path was not far from civilization, but a turned ankle or a fall off the side of an incline into a ditch could leave him alone and without help for hours, maybe even days. Death from starvation or exposure was not a remote possibility if he wasn't careful.

As if to put an exclamation point on the thought, a strong gust smacked against his back and propelled him faster than he intended. His foot hit a loose rock and his ankle rolled. He recovered quickly enough to avoid a sprain, but the mild throb he felt there slowed his cadence. Wouldn't it be poetic? The journeyman fighter, running through the woods, reconnecting with nature in preparation for his cinematic return, ready to climb again the ladder toward glory when it was kicked out from under him, breaking his ankle and starving to death in a ravine. That was one way to cut weight.

Xavier snickered at the ridiculous morbidity of his mental melodrama. He told himself the situation was terrible, but temporary. If he did as he was told, he'd live. Maybe not to fight another day, but live, nonetheless. So would his cousin.

Xavier resented Shot's reprimands back at the gym, but he had no choice but to acknowledge his own complicity. Xavier hadn't refused the steroids when Shot had offered them. He'd told himself he was leveling the playing field. It wasn't cheating if everyone else was doing it. In fact, he owed it to himself. He had to be *as* strong and *as* fast—not stronger and faster. *That* was an exercise in futility. There wasn't enough juice in the world for him to level up on the young fighters looking to make their name on the back of a veteran. He needed something to keep him in the gym just a little bit longer than them, something to dial his cardio back to his early twenties instead of his late thirties, something that got him out of bed with a little less pain. It was just common sense. Just making things square.

He'd been blindsided by the news of the positive test. Shot had promised him they'd timed the cycle correctly, that these were designer PEDs, so good they could have missed the cycle and still have been fine.

A reporter from one of the plethora of MMA news sites had wrangled the news before the athletic commission or even *The Show* had had the opportunity to inform Xavier of the violation. He'd recognized the journalist's number and answered his phone, thinking the call was to congratulate him on his latest win bringing him the closest to title contention he'd ever come. The reporter did mention that fact—and he used it to lull Xavier into a false sense of security before he dropped the axe and cut off Xavier's legs.

"Did you willfully take performance enhancing drugs?"

"Does this explain your unprecedented run?"

"How can you justify putting your opponents at risk for more physical damage in an already dangerous sport?"

"Tainted supplements" tumbled out of Xavier's stammering mouth before he'd processed what had happened. He hung up the phone, shell-shocked.

Then his vision went white.

He imagined finding this so-called columnist, typing away at his keyboard in judgmental bliss in the apartment above his parents' garage, fingertips greasy from bag after bag of potato chips. He'd yoke him out of his chair by the collar of his shirt, throw him to the ground, and pummel his face until he punched all the way to the back of it, striking nothing but the wet floor underneath. All the while, he'd ask him his own questions.

"Have you ever been on a mat, or even stepped foot in a gym, let alone stood across from another man in a locked cage?"

"Who are you to judge me when you've never thrown or taken a punch in your life?"

Angered by the remembrance, he quickened his pace again. The wind shoved him back and forth along the trail. Large branches had broken off and fallen across the path. He leapt over them. His legs pumped and propelled him until his foot plunged deep into a waterlogged patch of mud and clay. The wet ground held his running shoe and his foot pulled free. He skipped on one foot until he slowed his momentum enough to stop. Then he hopped back to retrieve the sneaker.

As he crouched down, a crack loud as a gunshot sounded behind him and he spun around. Twenty feet down the path, a tree had given up the fight between the ground it was rooted in and the wind beating against its sides. It splintered at its trunk and fell with a thud across the trail where Xavier would have been had he not lost his shoe in the muck. Had he kept running, he would have been crushed. The realization hit Xavier with the force of the felled tree.

His hands searched his bare neck for his father's crucifix. He felt frantic when his fingers found only the divot in his skin where his collarbones met his sternum. The corner of his eye twitched, a reminder of where he'd seen the pendant last. He touched the healed-over cut and frowned.

The cross was only a talisman to him, a reminder of his father, never a symbol of faith, for Xavier had none. Before the wrestling meets and the Silver Gloves competitions, Sam used to take Xavier's hands in his and tell him to bow his head in prayer. Xavier would wait until his father lowered his head and closed his eyes before he rolled his own.

Xavier never subscribed to either of his parents' love for the church. He never understood why sitting once a week in an ornate building far more expensive than any home they'd ever hope to own was the key to their salvation and life after death. He couldn't comprehend how people believed that a man in a robe turned bread and wine into flesh and blood. Why no one was creeped out by the idea of eating it. He never understood how his father could drink and smoke and swear and eventually divorce yet know for certain that as long as he showed up on Sunday and asked for forgiveness that someone would hold open the gates to paradise when that day arrived.

The pre-competition prayer, though, had been important to his father. Even more so, it seemed, after Evelyn left. Xavier had humored Sam. The cross had given Xavier some comfort in his mother's absence, though he never quite figured why.

Crouched on the ground, looking at the broken tree across the path, he understood. The crucifix made him feel less alone, but not because of the presence of God. The cross reminded him of the family he had once had. There on the trail he missed that comfort and thought to recite the passage his father so loved. But the words wouldn't come. They were a signpost, off in the distance, too far to read. He thumped his forehead with the heel of his hand and willed himself to remember. But he couldn't.

The struggle to recall left him irritated. First at his unreliable mind, then because he had just reminisced with some fondness about the father who'd called him a nigger. But before irritation gave way to rage, another thought intervened.

He pulled his laces tight, stood, and turned back on the trail toward Main Street, back toward the gym. He ran fast and hard, taking to the street instead of the sidewalk, avoiding the slalom between pedestrians.

"Shot's looking for you," the desk attendant said, eyes on her cell phone.

"I told him I'd be back."

"Said there was a bunch of calls for you."

"He say who?"

The receptionist said no and resumed her texting. Xavier went to Shot's office.

"What's up?"

"You don't take your phone?"

"I forgot it in my locker. I said, what's up?"

Shot's look was grave. "The nursing home called here looking for you. Said you put this number down as your work contact. Guessing they tried your cell a bunch of times."

Xavier ran to the locker room. He rifled through his gear bag to find his cell. Three missed calls. He hit redial and gave his name to the receptionist. There was a brief pause before Mrs. Thomas's voice came through the line.

"Mr. Wallace."

A crack in his voice stripped away the façade of feigned annoyance. "What did he do now?"

"Not a thing."

"Okay, well, you called my cell three times and then my job. Let's not leave me in suspense, please."

"Your father has taken a turn since he came back from the hospital."

"I think we're past euphemisms at this point, Mrs. Thomas."

"Your father is dying, Mr. Wallace."

"He has been, hasn't he? That's not news."

"He's *actively* dying, Mr. Wallace. Our physician says it could be a matter of days."

His stoic resolve drained from him as quickly as the blood from his face. He sat on the bench. "What happened?"

"We see this pretty frequently, Mr.—"

"Xavier."

She paused. "Xavier. We see this pretty frequently. A resident goes out to the hospital, and they get them tuned up, so to speak. Rehydrate them, adjust their meds. Everything seems back to status quo. But then they send them back here and . . . sometimes people just fail. I've seen it countless times, and especially with patients suffering with dementia. They're out of the nursing home and maybe feeling clearer than they've felt in a long time. And they get back here and somehow, they know that this is their last stop. I think when they realize that they just give up. Their body starts quitting on them. There's no infections. No real cause that we can ever really see as to why they're failing. They're just . . . done."

Xavier opened his mouth to speak but his throat seized. He cleared it and tried again. "Is he in pain?"

"His breathing is very labored, even with the oxygen. Do you know about hospice?" Xavier said he did. "The physician here can write an order for it if that's what you want. I've already called the service we use to check on their availability. They say they can be here within the hour. They'll make him comfortable for as long as he needs. And don't worry, his insurance will cover it. Is that something you want to do? I don't want to talk you into anything. If you do want it, I just need your approval as his power of attorney."

Xavier nodded.

"Mr. Wallace? Xavier."

"I'm sorry. Yes. Please."

"Okay, I'll get it working as soon as we're off the phone."

"Thank you."

"You're welcome. We don't have visiting hours per se, so you're welcome to come in to see him anytime."

"Yeah, okay."

"There will be some paperwork to sign."

Xavier recalled his father's frailty the last time he saw him. When he'd helped him stand, the creak in his joints reverberated through his bones. His skin slid like tissue paper over his deflated muscles. Xavier imagined him now, in his bed, tucked tightly under a blanket, suffocating to death. Despite his anger with Sam, it was not something Xavier was prepared to see.

"I can't get there right now. Can't you just tell whoever that I said yes?"

"I can note a verbal agreement in his chart, but I'll need you to come in and sign off in the next few hours. I'm sorry, but my hands are tied as far as that's concerned."

"That's fine. I'll be there. Thank you."

She hadn't finished responding before he hung up. He looked up and saw Shot leaning against the door jamb of the locker room. At the sight of him, Xavier lifted his chest and caught a tear with his finger before it fell.

"What's the deal? Your pops all right?"

Xavier stood and walked toward the door. Shot sidestepped to give him room to leave.

"Let's train," Xavier said.

XAVIER PUSHED THROUGH EVERY DRILL Shot threw at him. He threw in extra repetitions, extra punches, extra seconds and minutes to each round. One more length of sled pulls. One more set of truck tire flips in the parking lot under the high late afternoon sun. Thirty more seconds of sledge-hammer swings. Five more minutes on the Airdyne. Two extra rounds on the heavy bag. The round timer chimed and Shot took off his mitts. Xavier danced around Shot, shadow-boxing.

"What are you doing? I need to cut this weight."

"What you need to do is take a break. You going to push yourself too damn hard and make yourself sick. You making *me* tired. Get some rest. Go handle your business with your pops before it's too late."

Xavier looked off to the clock hanging above the mirrors and the dumbbell racks. Just shy of 4 P.M. "Ah, man, I got time. Someone will be there."

Shot stood at the edge of the ring with one leg between the ropes. "That's not what I meant." Xavier's hands dropped to his sides. He tongued the inside of his cheek and nodded. Shot returned the gesture and stepped out through the ropes. He walked back to his office while Xavier stood alone in the center of the ring.

AFTER A SHOWER AND A change of clothes, Xavier drove back to Maple Grove. He'd lingered under the hot streams of water until his skin felt raw. He took his time rubbing cocoa butter into his bruised shins and chafed elbows. Leaving the gym, he had started a conversation with just about anyone who made eye contact. Eventually, he'd caught Shot's gaze. His cousin tapped his watch and tilted his head toward the door. Xavier complied, then cursed when he looked at his phone and saw just how little time had passed.

Once again through the sliding doors to the front of Maple Grove, the smell of food wafted from the dining hall to the lobby. Aides rolled and walked the residents back from dinner to their rooms. Xavier's hopes lifted. If dinner had ended, maybe Mrs. Thomas had gone home for the evening and he could put all this off, at least until tomorrow. He leaned his elbows on the reception desk.

"I don't suppose Mrs. Thomas is still here, is she?"

"I believe she's left for the day but let me ring her office."

Xavier thanked her and backed away from the desk. After the third ring he turned to leave. Then he heard the receptionist behind him.

"Mrs. Thomas? There's someone to see you at the front desk." She called out to Xavier. "Sir, what was your name?"

"Wallace," he said, his jaw tight. "Xavier Wallace."

She repeated his name into the receiver. "Have a seat over there," she said, motioning to chairs against the wall. "She'll be right out."

"Terrific." He took a seat. Mrs. Thomas rounded the corner moments later.

"Xavier." She extended her hand. Xavier stood and took it in his.

"Mrs. Thomas. I thought you might have gone home for the day."

"Thought? Or hoped?"

"Maybe a little of both."

"At least you're honest. Follow me. This won't take long."

Xavier took a seat in the plush chair across from Mrs. Thomas. She opened the manila folder she'd been holding when she came out to meet him and turned it toward him. She spread out the various forms, explaining what each section meant, pointing where he needed to sign. His hands were sore from the striking drills. The right one cramped and shook with each scrawl of his name. He opened and closed his fingers, shaking off the discomfort, but unable to stop the trembling. He noticed Mrs. Thomas noticing him. He put his hands in his lap and waited for her to direct him to the next document.

"A lot of training today. Hands hurt."

She kept her head down and reviewed the forms. "Have you seen a physician, Xavier?"

"I'm sorry?"

She tilted her head toward his hands resting on his legs. He looked down. His fingers moved on the keys of an invisible piano. He quickly covered that hand with the other.

"For this? No, this doesn't have anything to do with the other thing. Like I said, I had a hard day of training."

"And have you seen anyone . . . for the other thing?"

"No, but I have to—" He stopped. He remembered once more that he *was* going to have to see a physician to be cleared for the fight. An icy bucket of panic dumped over his head and raised the hairs on his arms. He hugged himself and rubbed the chill away. If Xavier couldn't fight, Shot could end up deeper in debt with whoever was pulling his strings, which meant Xavier would be too. Or worse. But it could also be a way out. If the doctor said he couldn't fight, he'd be free of that obligation. He'd move heaven and earth to help Shot find another fighter. To find a way to make up for what he'd done. Of course he would.

But not clearing his medicals would also mean that the last fight he'd had more than a year ago would have been just that— his last. No redemption tale. No storybook ending retiring in the cage. He'd finish out his days holding pads, cleaning locker rooms, and shutting off the lights before closing the gym for the night.

"Yes, I agree, you should." Mrs. Thomas mistook Xavier's words for a complete thought and he felt no compulsion to correct the notion. The papers signed and collected, she stood, as did Xavier. He followed her out of the office. She made a right toward the nursing unit while Xavier took a left back toward the entrance.

"Xavier." He turned. "Where are you going?"

"I have to go."

"You don't—don't you want to see your father?"

"Is hospice in there?"

"Yes."

"And they've made him comfortable?"

"Yes, but—"

"And there's nothing else for me to sign? He's taken care of from here on out?"

"Xavier—"

"Then I've done my part. The answer is no. I don't want to see him."

He turned to leave but Mrs. Thomas placed her hand on his shoulder. Where once her touch and demeanor created comfort, they now produced annoyance. He turned to face her.

"I know he said some hurtful things to you the other day. Lord knows, he's said them to me and my staff. I'm in no way trying to excuse any of that. I don't know your story together. But I've seen people change into a person their sons and daughters and husbands and wives don't recognize. And I've seen it eat those family members from the inside out, especially when their loved one's body stays strong while their mind continues to fall apart. Those families just want it to be over, and they feel so guilty for thinking it, so they run. They stay away, even when the person they once loved more than anything in the world is dying. I can't tell you how many of those people I've seen burdened with regret because they let their last memory be colored by the awfulness that drove them away. They've cried in my office. But almost every one of them told me the same thing. That despite all that had happened, they'd wished they'd been there for them at the end so that they didn't die alone in a strange place. I don't know you, but I know you don't want that. There's no fixing that. Once it's done, it's done. Maybe selfishly I don't want to watch another person go through that all again. Not if there was something I could do to stop it."

"You're right," Xavier said. Mrs. Thomas smiled slightly. "You are being selfish."

Her smile disappeared. "I'm sorry?"

"Don't pretend you know me just because we share this." Xavier rubbed the skin of his hands and face. "You stand here acting like you understand what I'm going through because you think we've got some kind of shared experience? You don't know a thing about me, so don't pretend that me going back there to see that man has anything to do with me. You want to feel good about the job you did bringing two people together, because most of your day is made up of cleaning up other people's piss and shit. I got news for you—I am *not* the one. You feel me? You are not going to guilt me into seeing that hateful son of a bitch wither away so you can say you did something meaningful with your life for the day."

Mrs. Thomas looked around the lobby. Xavier's raised voice had drawn the attention of others. "Xavier, can you please keep your voice down?"

"You opened this door. Now you don't want to walk through it?"

She looked down. "You're right. It wasn't my place to assume."

Don't you patronize me. "You're Goddamned right it wasn't."

"I'm going to need you to calm down, Xavier."

"Stop calling me that. It's Mr. Wallace."

She put her hands up in surrender. "Mr. Wallace. If you're not coming back to see him, then please excuse me. I'm going to see if anyone else needs me to clean up their piss and shit so I can go home to feel good about myself."

"No, I'm not going back to see him. Fuck him." He sneered. "And for that matter, fuck you, too."

Mrs. Thomas jutted out her jaw. Xavier tensed his. He wanted the fight. He wanted her to react, to lose her cool, and engage him. Her face relaxed and the tension in her shoulders eased. She turned and walked away.

"That's right. Walk away from the situation. That's what you do when things get too tough, right? You leave. People need your help, and you head for the hills. Well, that's just great. Good for you."

She stopped. "Who are you talking to, Mr. Wallace? Because I think we both know it's not me."

Xavier's stomach tightened as if he'd been punched. His eyes watered. He shook off her words, then gave her a round of sarcastic applause as she strode toward the nursing unit. When she reached the door, she pulled it open and let it close behind her without a look back. Xavier stood and watched the door with his hands on his hips while staff, residents, and visitors walked around him. Some looked away. Others outright stared. Xavier's ears went hot.

"Shit," he whispered.

XAVIER RETURNED TO THE GYM. Shot sat in his office, his face lit by his laptop screen. He looked up and saw Xavier hovering, then signaled for him to pull up a seat. Xavier dragged the chair around to the other side of the desk. Shot sucked his teeth.

"Watch my floors, man."

"Are you serious? These asbestos tiles are probably giving everyone in here cancer."

"That's what I'm saying. Don't kick up that dust."

The joke was a welcome reprieve for Xavier. "Porn at work again?"

"You wish. Tape on our boy. Egan Finn."

"How's he looking?"

"Any other time, I'd say he looks like a pushover, at least compared to you. He fights real flat-flooted, always looking to uncork a big power shot. Most of his *L*s came from him getting taken down and pounded out or submitted. He'd have been nothing but a tune-up for you, all things being equal."

"But?"

"But things being what they are, that makes him dangerous for what we got to do. You get sloppy in your defense for a minute, you let that left hand come over the top and put you to sleep too early, we're both going to be looking at the roof of the church."

Xavier groaned. "He's a southpaw."

"And he got a bomb in that left hand." He sat back and slid the computer closer to Xavier just when the video showed his future opponent score a one-punch walk-off knockout.

"A little cocky, too, huh?"

"Look at what he did to homeboy. Knocked stiff. His feet ain't touching the ground. I'd walk away with my chest puffed out, too."

Xavier watched Finn stroll toward his corner, hands raised. He watched the referee wave in the ringside physician, who then waved in others. They surrounded the downed fighter, his heels hovering inches above the mat, knees locked in extension. Xavier had left more than one fighter in his wake in a similar condition. Though he always felt some remorse and concern for their well-being, he knew it was part of the price of the contract they'd agreed to. Not the one they signed their names to, but the one they entered into when they met in the center of the cage and touched gloves.

The normal human sentiments of fear and dread at seeing someone rigor mortis stiff, their breathing labored, their eyes open but vacant, had to be pushed to the side. Filed away in some recess of his brain he wouldn't—and eventually couldn't—access, even when the fight was over. Giving in to those feelings meant thinking too much, an affliction that had plagued Xavier's career. He'd overanalyze in the weeks leading up to a fight. Countless were the nights he'd spent envisioning everything going wrong in a fight, every possible way that he could lose, instead of conceiving scenarios where his hand was raised, until his imaginary losses became self-fulfilling prophecies. So, he'd taken the short notice fights whenever they'd become available. Doing so left him little time to think, resulting in the win streak he'd amassed before the suspension.

As he watched the referee raise Finn's hand, the drawers of the cabinet in which Xavier filed those feelings flew open, shot into the air as if manipulated by a poltergeist. His heart rate spiked. Hot needles jabbed at his neck and under his arms. He paused the playback and pushed the laptop away.

"Shot, what are we going to do about the doctor?"

"What do you mean?"

"I mean if they put me in the tube and find something on the films, they're not going to let me fight."

"Yeah, you ain't got to worry about that, cuz." Shot opened a drawer in his desk and tossed a manila folder on the desk. "You already been to the doctor. Clean work up. In fact, you got the brain scan of a man ten years younger. Pretty crazy considering your career, huh?"

Xavier grabbed the folder and shuffled through the

documents. Though he knew he wouldn't understand the terminology, he understood the doctor's recommendation at the end of the report: cleared to fight. "How?"

"That's one of those rhetorical questions, right? Because I'm pretty sure you don't really want the answer."

"No. I guess I don't."

"Plausible deniability, my man. The less you know, the less you can say if it comes to that. You do this right, and it *won't* come to that."

The steam whistle returned. Xavier looked back to the frozen image on the screen of Finn with his hand raised. Worried bodies surrounding his felled opponent. His feet still stuck out between them as though those tending to him were the house that crushed the wicked witch. Xavier blew air out through his pursed lips and scrolled the playback bar to the beginning of the fight. He clicked the "play" arrow and turned the volume all the way down. Shot took the cue.

"All right, well, I'ma get up out of here. Study up on this cat and get a little something to eat. We'll weigh in and get back at it tomorrow." He slapped Xavier on the shoulder and gave it an extra squeeze as he walked around him and toward the door.

Xavier stared blades into his back, resentful of the sincerity that Shot intended that squeeze to convey. He told himself when this was over, family or no, he and Shemar Tracy were done. He'd lose the fight, get the money squared, then he'd throw in the towel. Walk away from the sport and away from Shot, from all his bullshit, all his tough talk and bad decisions and guilt trips about the situation Xavier had supposedly put him into. As if Shot were to be pitied in all this, because life had dealt him a raw hand, like he'd had no part in that, either. Xavier had had enough. He didn't need Shot. He didn't need anyone.

Yeah, right.

Disbelieving his own bullshit, Xavier leaned into the laptop screen. He watched fight after fight. He hunted Finn's name on different search engines, looking for amateur fights, grappling tournament footage, interviews, anything he could find. It struck him that he was studying Finn harder than he had any opponent before him. But then never had so much been at stake. Fighters, fans of fighters, commentators, and the like often stated that men and women like Xavier put their lives on the line each time they stepped into that cage. They had no idea how right they were.

Minutes slid into hours. The sun had set outside, but Xavier hadn't moved from Shot's desk. The overhead fluorescents were off, the only illumination coming from the laptop screen. He looked up at a tapping on the office door. Clay poked his head through a slim opening.

"Cool if I head home? Nobody's in the gym and we're closing up soon anyway."

"Shit, I hadn't even noticed the time. Yeah, go on ahead home, man." Clay lingered in the doorway. "Something else?"

"Watching film for your fight?"

"You heard?"

Clay cocked his head. "We talked about it earlier."

Of course they had. "I'm just messing with you, man. You, uh, you hear anything else?"

Clay tilted his head to the side. "What do you mean?"

"Come on, man. Don't play me."

"You mean it being a last-minute fight?"

"Clay."

"Straight up, X. I don't know what you're talking about. Just heard you had a fight this weekend is all and that Shot only wanted you doing cardio and drills so you don't get hurt. Is that what you mean?"

Xavier leaned back in the chair. When he'd learned Shot had been fixing fights, Xavier felt betrayed, not just by his cousin's indiscretion, but also by the idea that he didn't trust him enough to tell him. Maybe he didn't want Xavier's judgment. Whatever it was, Xavier felt the fool. The last to know. He wondered if it had been common knowledge to everyone else in Shot's orbit all along. Clay had to have known about Lawrence. Maybe Shot thought Xavier's fight was too big to risk word getting out. After all, this fight wasn't in some regional feeder promotion. This was *The Show*. Loose lips would get people hurt.

But maybe there was something else. Maybe Shot wanted to let his cousin go out with his dignity intact, to let his redemption arc transcend the moment in the cage. Even with the loss, Xavier could walk back into the gym with the young men he'd helped train and keep his head high. Though he wanted so badly to be angry at his cousin for what they had come to, there was a smaller, quieter voice saying Shot would at least try to give him the exit he so badly wanted.

"Yeah, that's what I meant," Xavier said. "I couldn't have y'all walking around here saying I was a pussy behind my back because I wasn't sparring."

"I mean, we'd say that even if you *was* sparring, so . . . you know."

"Oh, it's like that?"

"It's like that."

Xavier welcomed the familiar banter between them. He'd feared it lost. Clay's trepidation seemed to have vanished. The protective slouch in his shoulders gone.

"Get on up out of here, then. I'll lock up."

"Cool. Catch you tomorrow?"

"Where else am I going to go?"

"True. Peace." Clay closed the door behind him.

The thought of returning to his father's house brought Xavier back to the lobby of the nursing home, watching Mrs. Thomas walk away from him. He opened a new window on the laptop and typed in a different search. Once he'd found what he was looking for, he set a reminder for himself in his phone, then collected his gear bag and made his bed in the center of the cage once more. Though he was physically spent and emotionally exhausted, his eyes didn't stay shut for long. He shifted from his side to his back to his other side, folding and bending his gear bag. But the lack of physical comfort was not the reason for his restlessness.

Tomorrow, he'd go and see her—and he was frightened more than he'd been for any fight on any mat or in any ring or cage.

DEAR MAMA

Xavier leaned back on a bench in the center of the sprawling community college campus. The morning sun was high and bright, unencumbered by the haze of the oppressive humidity of the last several days. He spread his long arms across the back of the bench, tilted his head back, and let the rays massage his skin. Just when it felt as though he'd stayed there too long, a breeze breathed through the quad. The soft wind brushed across his face and billowed through his loose tank top, carrying with it the perfume of lilac trees that dotted the grounds. Xavier breathed in the pleasant aroma and held it in his chest. The scent was soothing, yet he felt every thump of his heart in its cage as he at once hoped for and dreaded her appearance.

His phone buzzed in his pocket. He released his breath. Shot.

Where u at?

Xavier typed out a response and let it linger before deleting it, a page from his cousin's playbook. He shoved the phone back in his pocket. Across the courtyard, people filed out of one of the educational buildings. He sat up straight and squinted to bring their faces into focus, recognizing none. When the last of them walked through the doors, he breathed out, disappointed, but also more than a little relieved. He'd taken a guess as to what time he might see her based on the scheduling information he'd gleaned from the college website. Still, he knew he could sit on that bench all day and never see her.

Go inside then, you want to see her so bad. Ask around. Find her office. This passive crap isn't going to do it and you know it. You're playing the odds, hoping you'll lose so you can tell yourself you tried. If that's what you really want, then just leave and go train.

"This is so fucking stupid."

He stood. This wasn't the time. No matter how much he'd convinced himself the night before, he wasn't ready. He'd lain awake in the center of the cage, rehearsing their conversation as he would any professional fight. She wielded words better than he ever did his feet or fists. In the ring of his mind, he played rope-a-dope. Covered up while he weathered her verbal storm. Restrained himself from throwing counter shots of his own. Taking all that she had without resistance, defending until she'd released enough anger to let calm overtake her. Maybe then an actual conversation could take place.

He hadn't trained enough for this. He took a last look at the doors, then turned to leave. Then movement flashed in his periphery. He turned back. And he saw her.

She wore her natural hair cropped close to her head now. Silver and white wove in and out of her curls, but the black retained its shine. If it weren't for the telltale graying, he might have mistaken her for a student. He couldn't believe she was the same age as his father. She had not grown old gracefully—because it appeared that she had not grown old at all. Her posture, the one she'd always failed to impart to Xavier, was still impeccable. Chin up, shoulders back, chest high, in stark contrast to the students who walked out behind her, necks slumped over their phones, backpacks rounding their shoulders and bowing their backs. She carried a thin leather satchel slung over one shoulder.

He went to call out to her, but fear strangled the words in his throat, even as she walked toward him. She almost passed by when her gaze lingered on his face. She stopped short.

"Xavier?"

The sound of his name released the fingers wrapped around his voice box. His heart pounded so hard, he thought he might faint, so hard he heard the beat shake his voice when he answered.

"Hi, Mom."

Evelyn brought her hand to her mouth. Her eyes glistened as they darted back and forth, scanning his face, her eyebrows raised in disbelief. Xavier plunged his hands deep into his pockets and he kicked at nothing on the ground. He was a boy again, unable to look his mother in the face when he'd done wrong.

"I'm sorry for just showing up like this. I hope it's okay." He looked up and watched her wide eyes narrow, skin crinkled at the corners, her cheeks rising as she smiled big beneath her hand. Xavier went to speak again, but she stepped forward, went up on her toes, and wrapped her arms around his neck, pulling him in for a fierce hug. Xavier bent his knees to accommodate and squeezed around her waist.

The emptiness filled. He took a sharp inhale. Though her embrace was strong, she trembled. His tears fell and he joined Evelyn in a mixture of sobs and laughter. They stood in front of the bench for almost a minute, crying and laughing, until Evelyn released Xavier's neck. She grasped his shoulders and held him at arm's length. His limbs hung by his side. He hadn't wanted her to let go. She pulled him in again as though she sensed his need, pinning his arms to his side. She rested her head against his chest and squeezed. Xavier dropped his head and filled his nose with the familiar sweet fragrance of her hair oil, which he'd once smelled every time she kissed him good night. His tears fell faster, grateful for the remembrance the scent evoked, remorseful of the time lost. Time he'd chosen to lose.

Evelyn gave him a final hug and stepped away once more. She pulled a packet of tissues from her shoulder bag and dabbed at her eyelids with one. Xavier wiped at his cheeks with the heel of his hand.

"We're a mess, aren't we?" Evelyn said.

"Somehow you still look classy. Even with snot coming out of your nose."

"Stop it. My nose is not running."

"Whatever you say."

She brought the tissue to her nose for good measure. Xavier laughed.

"It's good to see you, baby."

"You, too, Mom." She hadn't called him "baby" in years. Maybe this would be okay.

Her face tightened. "I'd be lying, though, if I didn't wonder out loud why you're here."

Maybe not. Straightforward as ever. "Is there somewhere we can go to talk?"

She tilted her back toward the building she exited moments ago. "The department head lets me use her office in the summer hours. Come on."

Xavier put his hands in his pockets again and fell in step with the click of Evelyn's heels, shortening his long strides to stay alongside her.

"You look good," he said.

"You look too thin. You're cutting weight?"

"Fight Saturday."

"Your suspension is up?"

He stopped walking. "You knew about that?"

She continued on. "I do know how the internet works, Xavier."

He took two quick steps to catch up to her. "I know that. I didn't think you followed fighting, though."

"I don't follow fighting. I follow you. Was it Shot?"

"Was what Shot?"

"Do you think just because you're grown means I can't see in your face when you're lying? I saw the videos. 'Tainted supplements?' When you said that, you had the same expression on your face as when I asked you if you broke that ceramic figure my mother gave me."

"That obvious, huh?"

"So, was it Shot?"

Xavier laced his fingers on top of his head. "Yes and no."

She shook her head. "Xavier."

They drew closer to the building. He took two large steps ahead and opened the door for her. Eager for her approval, he hoped the gesture would counter her disappointment in him. She walked in without acknowledging the act.

Maybe if she'd been around, if she hadn't taken off running, you wouldn't have done some stupid shit Shot told you to do. With her judgmental ass.

No. That is not *why you're here. Stop it right now.*

"Are you coming?"

Xavier hadn't noticed that he'd stayed holding the door open. He released the handle and followed her inside. Evelyn led Xavier to a set of stairs that took them down to the lowest level of the building. They walked down a narrow hall, the walls lined with corkboards, covered with overlapping flyers for apartments, music lessons, tutoring, and the like, the bottoms fringed like party favors with tear-away phone numbers. Evelyn greeted everyone they encountered, from faculty tucked behind their desks in their offices to the janitor squeezing his cart by them going in the opposite direction. All spoke to her as if they were old acquaintances reunited after a long absence without a hint of insincerity. The absence of her warmth in his life, both past and present, saddened him.

They reached an empty office at the end of the hall and Evelyn unlocked the door. The room was larger than a broom closet, though only just, with space enough for a prefabricated bookcase. Its shelves bowed at the middle, stuffed to capacity. Light fought to enter the room through a small window that opened to sidewalk level. The sill doubled as yet another bookshelf. Another stack of books towered precariously on the floor, reaching the height of the small but elegant cherry wood desk behind which Evelyn sat in a high-backed burgundy leather office chair. A candle on the desk, though extinguished, filled the room with its advertised scent of vanilla and lime. Evelyn gestured to a plush sage green velour chair. Low to the floor, Xavier sunk into the seat and looked up at his mother.

"Well, that looks uncomfortable. I can try to find another office if you'd like. Most of the full-time faculty are gone for the summer."

Xavier waved her off. "I'll manage. Looks like retirement lasted about as long as I thought it might."

"So you did get my emails," she said with no small measure of sarcasm. Xavier looked at the ground and nodded. "I stayed away longer than I thought I would. I could only go to so many brunches and book clubs. I had to *do* something. Besides, it's only adjunct work. Just enough to keep me busy."

"You've never been one to stay put." Evelyn's brightness dimmed, and Xavier understood how she interpreted the unintended implication. "I'm sorry. You know that's not what I meant."

"It's okay, Xavier."

"I mean it. I didn't come here to fight, Mom."

"Baby, I know. It's all right."

Xavier's knees bounced. Evelyn sat forward and leaned on the desk, watching his frenetic motion. He pushed down on his thighs and slowed the jumping.

"So . . . is this about your father?"

"He went into hospice yesterday."

Evelyn blinked as if she'd been slapped. She leaned back. Xavier leaned forward.

"I didn't know he was sick. What is it?"

"Emphysema. He went out to the hospital and when he came back his body just quit on him. Didn't help that he was constantly pulling out his oxygen."

"Why would he do that?"

"Bad dementia. Like really bad. Lately, there have been days where he doesn't know me at all." He paused. "Other days he hates me."

"He doesn't hate you."

Xavier's eyes stung again. "Mom, I know why you left."

Evelyn brought both hands to her mouth this time and tears streamed down both cheeks. When she spoke, her words came out hushed. "What did he say to you?" Xavier's own tears fell as he looked down. "Not that. Please tell me not that."

"That."

"Oh, God. Xavier."

"The night you left I was standing in the door of my bedroom. You two were fighting. After the Rodney King verdict. You'd already been fighting a lot at that point. I couldn't hear what you guys were saying, but I knew it wasn't good. I still remember—at least I think I do—him saying something about looters and asking what he'd said that was so wrong."

"And then he asked me who I wanted him to be."

"You remember."

"I remember everything about that night."

"I have this other memory of that night, too. I dream about it sometimes, if you can believe that. I heard you coming down the hall and jumped into bed. Heard you going through drawers in your room, packing your stuff. Then I saw your shadow on my wall. Looking in on me. And then you were gone. Why didn't you ask me to go with you, Mama?"

She pulled her chin back. "What?"

Her confused look frightened him, and he looked away.

Don't say it. Please don't say it.

"Xavier, I *did* ask you to come with me."

He looked about the room, anywhere but at her. She craned her neck to catch his gaze.

"No, you didn't. I would have remembered."

"Yes, baby, I did. You said no."

"No." The whistle screamed in his ears. "No, I wouldn't have done that."

"Xavier. You did." Her eyes widened. "Do you mean to tell me—all this time . . . you thought I just left?"

"Yes."

She blew out. "Wow."

A bubble caught in his throat. "Then why didn't you just make me come with you? I was a kid. I didn't know any better."

Evelyn dropped her shoulders. "I thought about it. But I was angry. At your father for what he'd said. At you for not coming, even though you were just a kid. In that moment, it felt like you'd chosen a side. There were so many times, Xavier, *so* many times before that night where I came close to telling you *everything*. How your father had managed to hide that side of himself from me for so many years. But it wasn't until after I'd left that I realized in some ways he'd been hiding that side from himself. He never thought he was prejudiced or racist. In fact, he believed so deeply he wasn't that I couldn't help but believe it, too. That and I loved him. I really did. In college, we had so many of the same friends, people I cared about and trusted. He was safe. And he was so funny. Here was this edgy, hip white guy, right? The kind who only told racial jokes to point out how ridiculous racism was." She paused. "Saying it out loud makes me realize how how blind I was—scratch that—how I chose to blind myself to it."

"You can't blame yourself for that, Mom. That was so long ago. Times have changed."

"No. That's an excuse, Xavier. To think otherwise is irresponsible. I made my choice then the same way I made the choice to leave that night. By that time, we'd moved well beyond troubling jokes. He stopped being funny. He started being cruel. His demeanor. His politics."

Xavier scoffed. "One guess who he voted for."

Evelyn pursed her lips, then relaxed them. "That would have surprised me once. It doesn't now."

"That makes one of us."

"That was the amazing thing, Xavier. He somehow managed to reign all of that in when you two were together. I think he knew he'd been your hero and he knew well enough not to mess that up."

"You were my hero, too, Mom."

Evelyn folded her hands in front of her. "I'll be real with you, Xavier—not that I could tell. You two had your sports, which don't get me wrong, I was glad for. But you spent almost every waking moment with your dad. So, if you want to know why I didn't try to make you come with me—that's why. Back then, I couldn't compete. I knew that telling you those things about him would have made you resent me, and I couldn't live with that. I was having a hard enough time living with myself living with him. I couldn't stay. I *wouldn't*. I deserved better, and truthfully, I put up with all that a lot longer than I should have, whether we had a child together or not."

Xavier's teenage guilt resurfaced. "You're right. This is my fault."

"Stop that. You were a child. Was I angry you didn't want to go with me? For a moment, yes. Not my best moment. But it only lasted the walk to the car. I never blamed you, Xavier. To be honest with you, I don't blame myself, either. There's no need to."

"I blame him."

She leaned back in her chair. "I get that. I do. I had some hard days when things got bad. I asked myself, with everything my parents had ever been through, the things they fought for, the things *I'd* fought for—how I could have been so blind. The unrest in Los Angeles was the last of many straws. As you'd said, we'd been fighting quite a bit up to that point. But they didn't always start as fights. I tried so hard to make him understand the things he was saying were hurtful. That having a Black wife and child didn't make it impossible for him to be prejudiced, even racist. He didn't take to having his blind spots called out, either. He denied to the moon and back, and when his denials didn't have their desired effect, he became more and more withdrawn. Got more defensive. And eventually—naturally—so did I. That only seemed to make him double down on his rhetoric to the point we simply didn't know each other anymore. The years and distance brought me enough clarity to say I don't think we ever did."

Xavier looked at Evelyn. She sat in her chair more upright than before, as though the confession had left her unburdened. Though he was glad she was finally free of that weight, he wondered how long she'd carried it silently—if she'd had no one else in her life with whom to share it out loud. He felt shame at not knowing. He was emabarassed, for her and for himself, that it was the first time he'd heard any of it—he, the person he knew she felt needed to hear it the most. And he'd denied her that.

She took a deep breath and let it out in a relieved huff. "I told myself I got you out of the bargain. I told myself every visitation that we'd have the breakthrough that let us cross that ravine between us, and that if it wasn't that week, then it'd be the next. Then I turned around and you were eighteen. I never thought when you came of age, *you'd* be the one to leave. I don't know what I expected. I hadn't trusted you enough to understand why I had gone. Considering how you thought things went down, I guess you felt you didn't owe me that trust in return."

At that, Xavier looked up. "I owe you everything, Mama. I'm sorry."

She wrinkled her chin. "Thank you, baby. I'm sorry, too." She stood, circled behind her chair, and gripped the headrest. "Now, how about we promise that's the last time either of us says that word again. We're here now. No more apologies."

"I'm with that."

"Good." She looked out the small window. "Dementia. Lord. You know, it makes sense, Xavier. It probably started a long time ago. All the boxing he did in the service. The way he started to reveal himself. All those filters he'd put up just started to fall away."

Xavier bit his lip, but a short, sharp sob escaped. Another attempt to hold it back failed, and he collapsed over his knees, his face in his hands. His body trembled and he gulped air. Evelyn circled around to the front of the desk and squatted down in front of him in the small space between his chair and her desk.

"Xavier, what is it, baby?" She took his cheek in her palm and he pressed into it. "Tell me."

He told her everything. The forgotten groceries. Loki. His father's house. Showing up to his old apartment. His interactions with Mrs. Thomas. Lawrence. He let it all go, drawing out rambling sentences until he ran out of air, his breath stuttered. Evelyn patted his knees and told him to slow down and breathe. He watched her try to mask the horror at hearing her son, not yet forty, suffering so. Hearing that he was capable of such violence, brain injured or no. Her face was tight, jaw clenched and pulsing. Still her look held softness and warmth, a mother's love that had not been dulled by time or distance or words. Love that could not be diminished by all he'd done.

She removed her hands from his knees, stood by his side, and pulled his head to her stomach. He leaned in as she stroked his head. Her breath and her touch had the same effect on him as it did when he was a boy. She shushed him until his crying stopped. When it did, he looked up at her. She smiled at him, eyes red, but absent tears. He knew she'd stopped crying not because she wasn't sad, but to remove his fear at the sake of her own. Just as she had always done.

"I'm scared," he said. "Seeing Pops like that. I know what's coming. For me."

"Drop out of this fight, Xavier. Don't do yourself any worse than you already have."

He pulled away. "I can't do that."

"What do you mean, 'can't'?"

"I can't, Mom."

"You're in trouble?"

"The worst kind."

Lines of concern in her forehead deepened into furrows of anger. "Did Shot get you into this, too?"

"Does it matter?"

"To me, it does."

Xavier breathed deep. He took account of himself and all the things that had led to her question. If he'd asked for help when his mind gave its first indications of abandonment, how different his present situation might have been. And yet those circumstances brought him here to this moment, to his mother. For that, he'd trade nothing. Not even the erasure of the misery that came before. "It wasn't all Shot, Mom. He did his dirt, too, but you said it yourself. If I put it all on him, it's an excuse. To think otherwise is irresponsible. This is on me, too."

"Okay, then." She sat on the edge of her desk. "You do this fight. And then you're done?"

"I'm out of trouble, if that's what you mean."

"No, that's not what I mean, Xavier. Are you done fighting after this one?"

"That might not be up to me."

She folded her arms. "I realize you're being cryptic because you think you're protecting me, and that's fine. It's probably better I don't know. But trouble comes in different forms, Xavier, and you and I both know the other kind of trouble you're in will get worse if you keep this up. You have to stop."

"Maybe. But Mom, when I even think about stopping, I remember I'm alive under those lights. I've got no one and nothing without it."

"Yes, you *do* have someone else. And I'm going to see to it that you have something else, too." She went back to her chair. Once there, she awakened her desktop and clacked away at the keyboard.

"What are you doing?"

"I'm friends with the athletic director here," she said, scanning her monitor. "Ah. There it is. He mentioned that they were searching for a wrestling coach, as well as someone to teach their fitness boxing elective. It's one of their most pop-ular classes and the teacher took another job somewhere."

"Mom, I have a job. I work at Shot's."

"This is real work, Xavier. Good work. You don't have to be connected with whatever it is that cousin of yours is into anymore. You can come here and feel good about what you're doing. I know my friend would give you these jobs if you wanted them." Evelyn chewed at the inside of her cheek, as did Xavier. *So that's where I got that.* "Tell me you'll think about it."

"I'll think about it." His phone buzzed in his pocket again. Shot was getting impatient. "I should probably go."

"Already? You just got here. We could drive into the city, maybe get some lunch?"

Xavier smacked at his stomach. "Got to make that weight."

"So how about after?"

"That's a date."

"I'll walk out with you."

Back down the hall, up the steps, and into the main lobby of the building, they were quiet. They exchanged glances more than once, always breaking away from the look with a smile, as if to say they couldn't believe they were in each other's presence but were overjoyed to be so. Xavier didn't want to leave. He wanted to spend the entire day with her, uttering as many apologies as she needed to hear, even though she'd told him no more. He gripped her wrist as she reached for the door and she turned with a surprised look.

"Mom. Again. I'm sorry."

"What did I just say about no more?" He bit his lip. "I know, Xavier. I am, too." They huffed simultaneously. "Okay. *Now* we're done with that word. Deal?"

"Deal." He stepped to the side and held the door open again. This time, she placed her palm against his cheek again before stepping out the door. They walked in step toward the lot where he'd parked the Volvo. She stopped when she saw the car.

"I can't believe you still have it."

"She's a fighter."

"That she is." A grave look replaced the mirth. "About your father, Xavier."

"Yeah?"

"Take him home."

"What? No. Mom, I can't go back there. I told you what happened the last time I went. Hell, they might not even let me back in the building."

"Is that what you think or is that what you hope?"

Xavier looked away. The years had not dulled her ability to slice through his bullshit. "Seriously, why do you care? I mean look at you. You look like you got younger since you left. I can't imagine how you carried all that for so long. Won't you be—" He stopped himself.

"Say it."

"Won't you be relieved? When it's over?"

"I don't wish him ill, baby, despite everything that happened. How could I? He gave me you. It's because of you that I won't feel relieved or happy or any of those things when he's—when that time comes. For you, I can put aside all the hurt I felt at finding out the person he was, because I know what he meant and what he still means to you, whether you believe that right now or not. I don't want him to die alone in some nursing home surrounded by strangers because I know it's not what *you* want. I know that as justifiably angry with him as you are, how much you might hate him for what he said, you can't just shut off caring about him. You don't want him to die that way. You've had enough regret in your life, baby, either of your own making or someone else's. I just don't want any more of that for you. Not if I can help it."

Xavier folded his arms over his stomach. "Damn. Always teaching. You know I can't say no to you when you drop science like that."

"It's what I do." She held out her arms. "I love you, Xavier."

He walked into her embrace and hugged her back. "I love you, too, Mom."

She rocked him side to side in her arms and then let him go. "You're too damn skinny."

"We'll make up for it after the fight."

"I'll be watching. Take it to him. Might hurt the job offer here if you lose." She winked.

"I said I'd think about it," he said, lowering into the car. He started the engine and shut the door. She blew him a kiss and waved to him all the way out of the parking lot, the way she used to when he was a teenager, going back home to his father. This time, he waved back.

I AIN'T MAD AT CHA

as blind, but now I see.

Xavier rolled down the window and hung his arm down the side. As he picked up speed from the traffic light, he made waves with his hand, slicing through the wind resistance like he'd done when he rode in the back-seat of the same car as a boy.

The first time he'd heard his mother hum the tune to "Amazing Grace" was when the family had returned from church one morning. It had been like any number of Sundays he'd been forced to go, boring and overly long. He never knew when to sit, stand, or kneel. He liked the tune, though, and asked his mother what it was. She told him the name and sung out loud the line: *was blind, but now I see.*

"That don't make—" Xavier had started.

"Doesn't," Evelyn said.

"Huh?"

"Don't say 'huh.' You can say 'what' or 'excuse me,' but not 'huh.' And you say, 'That *doesn't* make'—not 'that don't.'"

Xavier rolled his eyes. "That *doesn't* make any sense."

She winked. "What *doesn't*?"

"You can't get better from blindness. That part of the song is dumb."

Sam had laughed sharply.

"What?"

Evelyn batted Sam playfully on the shoulder. "Don't mind him. It's a figure of speech, honey. It means that the person's eyes are open to something they couldn't see before."

"Yeah, but what does it matter if their eyes are open if they're blind? They can't see if they're open or closed."

"Boy's got a point, Ev," Sam said.

She laughed. "Don't *you* start. Xavier, it means that the person was saved by God. They were lost without him, but he helped them find their way. They were blind to what life was like without him, and he let them see. Does that make more sense?"

"Through him who gives me strength," Sam said softly. Evelyn hummed in agreement.

Xavier sat back. "Not really. But the song is pretty. You can keep singing it if you want." Evelyn patted his knee, turned back to face the front, and sang it again.

ALL THE WAY BACK TO Shot's gym, Xavier smiled. He hadn't realized he was smiling until at a stoplight. Another car pulled up next to him, driven by an older Black woman. He turned to look, and she grinned and tipped her head at him. Maybe she recognized him. Maybe it was that nod of familiarity he'd noticed more often from other Black folks since the election. That look of recognition and camaraderie that said, "We're in this together, because we're all we've got." She drove off first when the light changed. He kept smiling. It felt good to keep that grin and he relished the mild ache in his cheeks.

Was blind, but now I see.

It hadn't been too late. Evelyn held no ill will for him for the decision he'd made to stay with his father, for barely maintaining contact with her. But she was only human, after all. There must have been times when she thought him ungrateful, times when she felt betrayed. Those feelings had to have been there, tucked away in her gut, a cancer that ate away at anything she might have felt for him. They must have been there, because it's what he would have felt. But she wasn't him.

In an instant, no longer than it took for her to recognize his face, she had excised any malignancy that might have grown inside her. There was no falsehood in her embrace, nothing reptilian about her tears. Her son had come back to her. She was ready to receive his love, but not to forgive him, because she made it clear there was nothing to forgive.

Xavier understood that for all the opponents he'd faced on the mats, in the ring, or in the cage, his mother was the strongest person he'd ever known. Though his father had been his coach, everything he learned about fighting came from her. Her capacity for love was boundless, despite the very human cost of that love. If she had that in her, he told himself, then maybe he did, too.

He pulled into a shopping center lot and parked. He'd missed more texts from Shot inquiring insistently about his whereabouts. Xavier went to clear the texts and accidentally dialed. He hung up quickly, but Shot returned the call immediately. Xavier sent him to voicemail. If he didn't act on this feeling now, he might lose his nerve, or worse yet, he might forget that he felt it at all. He pulled up his contacts and pressed send.

"Maple Grove, how may I direct your call?" the receptionist answered.

"Mrs. Thomas, please."

Classical music carried across the connection as he waited, though not for long.

"Nursing."

"Mrs. Thomas?"

"Yes?"

"Xavier Wallace."

A pause, then a slow inhale. A clearing of the throat. "Mr. Wallace. Good to hear from you."

"It is?"

"I'm sorry?"

"No, I am. I owe you an apology for yesterday, Mrs. Thomas. I could give you a bunch of excuses as to why I acted that way, but they'd be just that. Excuses."

She exhaled. "Thank you, Mr. Wallace. I appreciate that."

"Thank you for not hanging up on me."

Another pause. "Is there something I can do for you, Mr. Wallace?"

"Yes." He heard the tremor in his voice and took his own deep breath. "I'd like to bring my father home."

"You want to end his hospice care?"

"No. I mean, don't they come to the home? I guess I don't really know how any of this works."

"Yes, they certainly can. I'd have to arrange for an ambulance to transport—"

"No. I'll pick him up. I want to drive him home. Can I do that?"

"He hasn't been out of bed since he's been back, Mr. Wallace."

Xavier knew letting professionals bring him home was the right thing to do. He also knew the last time Sam had ridden in the Volvo was when his only child brought him to the place he'd begged Xavier never to bring him. Though his anger for his father had not completely resolved, his guilt over taking him to Maple Grove overpowered that resentment. If there was any vestige left of the father he remembered, he couldn't let that perceived betrayal be one of his final memories.

"Can someone help me get him in the car? Please?"

"I can't endanger my staff, Mr. Wallace."

"Okay. I understand."

"Hold on." Noises in the background went muffled. He envisioned her pulling away the phone and covering it with her hand, cursing him out. She came back. "I'll help you. Between the two of us, we should be fine."

"Oh, man. Thank you, Mrs. Thomas. Thank you so much."

She told him that she'd contact the hospice agency. She wanted to coordinate a time for Xavier to come for his father and minimize the gap of care in-between. Xavier thanked her profusely and she told him again that she was glad to help. He thanked her yet again, and she hung up before he could say it one last time.

The car engine hummed in park and the fan blew stale warm air across his face. He rolled down the window again and drummed his fingers against the outside of the door. Hope and sadness churned. Sadness for the impending loss of his father, despite feeling in the last few days that he was already gone. Hope in bringing him home. Hope that things might feel as they once did, even for only a moment.

They'd sit on the couch (such as it was) and share one more meal on the tray tables in front of the television, an old fight DVD playing while they ate. If he couldn't get out of bed, he'd bring the television to Sam, put it on top of the dresser, and watch with him until he fell asleep. Either way, they'd both be where they'd been when things were right with their worlds, and that would be okay. Even if that story wasn't entirely true. Even if it was only for a little while.

Guilt strummed again though, for his mother and what she'd endured. But he reminded himself of her words and her strength. If she could forgive, then he could, too. He didn't owe it to his father. He owed it to her.

His phone buzzed again.

The fuck you at X?

> Heading back to the house
>
> That better mean the gym
>
> It doesn't

Xavier immediately regretted that response, surprised at how quickly it came, but the text had been sent. A speech bubble from Shot appeared then disappeared almost as quickly and his regret compounded. Xavier waited for a response, but nothing surfaced. He drove out of the lot and toward his father's house. He had to make it a home again.

XAVIER TOOK ONE OF THE undamaged throw pillows and put it down before he sat in the gap Loki had created. He rested his head on the edge of the sofa and counted the drop ceiling tiles. An ache settled into his neck, followed by a throb in both knees. He'd spent hours on all fours while he scrubbed the tub, stooped over as he scoured the toilet bowl and cleaned the sinks. Floors swept, bed made, he rested. That he was so fatigued and achy from such menial tasks would have surprised him had he not been as dehydrated as he was. Tomorrow, after he got his father settled, he would go to the gym and sweat off as much as he could before returning home to Sam. Then he'd drive to Jersey, to the resort hotel, where he'd get a good night's sleep before the weigh-ins the following afternoon. A thought sat him up. His neck cracked.

What if he doesn't die before then?

Yeah, what are you going to do about that?

He sat forward and massaged one shoulder. The possibility hadn't occurred to him when he'd asked to bring Sam home. How had he not thought of this? He'd been so caught up in the emotion of the reunion with his mother that he'd romanticized logic out of the equation of his father dying at home. Could Xavier even leave the house? How many hours would the hospice team be there? Would Sam die alone no matter what? Mrs. Thomas said he was on the decline. That he hadn't been out of bed since he'd returned. It sounded as if it was only a matter of time.

It has to be.

That's some cold-blooded shit right there.

He hadn't known *when* the tinnitus had returned, only that it had, in both ears now, and growing ever louder. Then someone knocked on the front door.

Though the glasswork obscured his face, Xavier knew Shot's silhouette. He cursed under his breath and opened the door. They stood on either side of the doorway in a pre-fight faceoff.

"What, you not going to invite me in? I ain't no vampire."

"Come on, then."

Shot crossed to the middle of the living room and gave it the once over.

"The fuck happened to your couch? Looks like a dog got at it." He put his hands out as though something unseen had frightened him. "Wait, where's that dog at?"

"Not here."

Shot's shoulders relaxed. "Where, out back or something?"

"Nope."

"Oh. *Oh.*"

"Yeah."

"Want to talk about it?"

"Nope."

"All right, cool."

"What are you doing here?"

"What I'm doing here is you got a fight in a few days and you ain't been to the gym all day. You're not answering my texts, or you being a bitch when you do, *and* you sending my calls to voicemail. That's some cold shit, by the way. At least let it ring through and pretend you ain't heard it."

"Pops is coming home tomorrow. On hospice. That means—"

"Nigga, I know what it means."

"I guess—I don't know, I felt like I should get the place clean, you know? And look, I'm sorry about not answering the call and disrespecting on the texts, but I saw Mom today, too."

"Auntie Ev? Where?"

Xavier motioned to the undamaged cushion on the couch. Shot sat while Xavier explained the last few hours to him. When he was done, Shot leaned back.

"That's a lot, cuz."

"Don't I know it."

"You all right?"

Xavier opened his mouth to ask Shot what he cared, other than to make sure his mind was right for the fight, but stopped. He read Shot's body language like an opponent—leaned forward, elbows rested on his knees, hands gripped opposite arms like they held space for an embrace—one meant for Xavier.

All that told Xavier that Shot did care about him, as clearly as if he'd come right out and said it. Though that voice shouted in his ears not to trust him, not to give him an inch, not to be manipulated, Xavier was comforted by Shot's question. As infuriated as he'd been with both Shot and himself for their current situation, he wanted badly for them to have the relationship that existed before the complications and accusations. Before the mistrust and the words that left bone-deep bruises. Too much had gone wrong in too short a time, and the familiarity of that love and concern from his cousin was a balm he was all too willing to apply.

"If I'm being one hundred, man? I don't know if I'm all right. Everything I think I know seems to change hourly, and I think that would probably be normal even if all of this jumbled mess in here wasn't messing with me in the first place." He pointed to his head with his index finger and made circles in the air. "It's like, whenever I'm away from Mom, Dad—hell, even you—it makes it easier to be pissed off. I can wallow in it. Like the opposite of absence and the heart growing fonder and all that. But the minute I saw Mom—man, the minute she opened her arms to me like nothing had ever changed, I couldn't hold on to that anger even a second. Even as happy as I am about seeing her right now, there's a part of me that's asking if this is just another mood swing. If this is just my fucked-up brain telling me what to think now, and that tomorrow, I'll be pissed off all over again. I don't trust it even now."

"Don't trust what?"

"Everything. Everyone. Myself. How I feel. What I think."

"You don't trust *me*?"

"Come on, man. That's not what I'm saying. Are you even listening to me?"

"I guess that's my answer."

"Shot."

Shot stood. There was no confrontation in his countenance, his shoulders relaxed, hands in his pockets. Xavier had seen this posture from opponents in the cage. Resigned. Broken. Without intention, he'd landed the blow that took the fight out of Shot, the one that made him quit. He walked over to Xavier and put his hand on his shoulder.

"It's all right, cuz. I get it."

"You're taking this the wrong way. I'm not explaining it right."

"Nothing to explain, my man. I feel you. I do."

Xavier's phone buzzed and shimmied across the top of the entertainment center. He saw it was the nursing home.

"I have to take this. Don't leave."

Shot jutted out his chin.

Mrs. Thomas gave Xavier the details for hospice as he rushed to the kitchen and opened the junk drawer. He pulled out scrap paper and scrawled down the time he needed to meet her at the facility. He thanked her, hung up, and returned to Shot in the living room. "Sorry about that."

"All good. You got shit to handle. You not going to put all that in your little reminders thing on your phone?"

"In a minute. About what I said."

"You said what you said. I ain't mad at you. Just do me a favor. Tomorrow, when they're setting up your pops in here, and next week when you having brunch and mimosas or whatever with Auntie, and you and me are whatever we're going to be when this is all done, remember who was always who they said they were with you. Who ain't never been any-body but who they told you they was, for better or for worse. Maybe there's some shit you can't trust, maybe I ain't always done right, but you could always trust me to be me. You could always trust that." He looked around the living room. "Good luck with your pops tomorrow. When you're done, get to the gym. We got to make that weight and you still looking soft."

"I don't know how quickly they'll get him set up, so—"

"See you tomorrow." He pulled the door closed behind him.

Xavier crossed the small room to sit where his cousin had and put his head in his hands. "Shit."

The quiet of the room brought the tinnitus to the fore-front, along with a renewed throb at the base of his skull. He went to the bathroom, opened the medicine cabinet, and took his pain medication, slurping water from a cupped hand to ease it down. The pain moved to his temples. Each breath shoved another knitting needle in his brain. The lights in the bathroom, the kitchen, all too bright. The burning filaments buzzed in his eardrums. He walked back to his bedroom, pulled the blinds, drew the shades, and lay in bed. He pinched the bridge of his nose and willed himself to sleep while his phone sat on the kitchen counter next to the notes he'd taken from Mrs. Thomas's call.

SLIPPIN'

Sleep brought no relief from the headache that sent him to bed. Xavier pressed the heel of his hand into the center of his forehead. The thumping stopped. Then started again. The pounding was not in his ears, but at his front door. He sat up quickly. The room turned into a Tilt-A-Whirl. The knock at the door resumed.

"Hold on!" His shout made the spinning worse. He clenched his jaw and willed the world to slow. When certain he wouldn't fall, he hustled to the front door and threw it open. A woman in blue scrubs with a bag slung over her shoulder walked back toward her car parked out front.

"Can I help you?"

She jumped at the sound and turned, her hand on her chest. "Are you Mr. Wallace?"

"Yes, ma'am."

"Oh, good, I was worried I was at the wrong house." She stepped up onto the small porch but stopped short. Xavier did not move aside to let her in.

"I'm sorry, who are you?"

She held up the ID badge that hung from a lanyard around her neck. "Donna. I'm the hospice nurse. I'm here to see your father?"

Xavier's eyes went wide. "What time is it?"

"10:45. I know I'm a little early, but I finished up with another patient near here and thought—"

"It's 10:45. In the morning?"

Donna took a step back. "A little past, yes. Is everything okay, Mr. Wallace?"

He retreated and slammed the door. No way he'd slept that long. He looked down at his clothes. Same outfit from the day before.

He fast-walked back to his bedroom when a glint of light caught his eye. Sunlight peeked through the blinds of the window over the sink and caught the face of his cell phone. Xavier walked over to see his notes from his call with Mrs. Thomas. He gripped his scalp, pulling the skin of his forehead tight. There were several missed calls from Maple Grove.

"God fucking damn it!"

The shout created pressure in his head and nausea swept through his insides. He took a deep breath, then grabbed his phone and headed for the door, just as Donna resumed knocking. He whipped it open and startled her all over again.

"Mr. Wallace, are you all right? I thought I heard a shout."

"I have to go."

He slammed the door and ran toward the back of the house. Outside and down the steps, he started the car.

Xavier turned onto the main road out of the neighborhood and looked to the rearview as he sped up the hill. Donna stood next to the open door of her car, arms in the air in disbelief. He told himself to call the agency and apologize later, then laughed at the idea that he'd remember to do so. He picked up the phone. Looking back and forth from the phone to the road, he opened his recent calls and hit send, then slammed on the brakes. The Volvo's tires squealed as the bumper stopped inches from the car in front of him. Xavier braced for impact behind him. He breathed out in relief when he saw an empty road behind him in the mirror.

"Maple Grove, how may I direct your call?"

"Mrs. Thomas, please."

"May I tell her—"

"Xavier Wallace."

The receptionist asked him to hold. He tapped his left foot against the floor and drummed his fingers against the steering wheel. The light changed and the receptionist came back on the line.

"Mr. Wallace? Mrs. Thomas has asked me to ask you if you are on your way?"

"I am. I know I'm late."

"In that case, she said she would speak to you when you arrive."

"What? Why?"

"She didn't say any more than that, Mr. Wallace."

"Then ask her!"

The line went silent. The speedometer read fifty miles per hour. Xavier passed the thirty-five sign and gently braked. "Look, I didn't mean to raise my voice. Can you please just ask her about my father?"

"I'm afraid I can't do that, Mr. Wallace. There are privacy rules that—"

"Right, great, fine. Thank you for nothing. Tell her I'll be right there." She spoke again but he ended the call and tossed the phone into the passenger seat.

She'll talk to you when you get there? What, are you in grade school now? You in trouble for being late? You got to stay after class? Who the hell does this bitch think she is?

Another emotion elbowed its way into his mind and pushed its way into his guts. In all their interactions, Mrs. Thomas had been firm, but fair. And kind in a way Xavier knew he didn't deserve. That she'd be petulant, especially now, was incongruent with all she'd shown him. Dread settled into his stomach. His chest tingled in the space above his heart. He struggled to regulate his breathing. He pressed the gas and watched the side streets, hoping he wouldn't get pulled over. He couldn't waste any more time.

Once parked, Xavier sprinted to the entrance of Maple Grove. The automatic doors slid slowly, and he turned sideways to fit through the opening. His shoulder banged off one of them and rattled it in its track. Mrs. Thomas was in the lobby with a nurse he thought he recognized. Mrs. Thomas leaned on the raised counter of the receptionist's desk. The receptionist caught sight of him and pointed him out to Mrs. Thomas. She turned to look over her shoulder, then all the way around to face Xavier. She folded her hands in front of her, the look on her face severe.

"So sorry I'm late. I don't know what happened, but I'm ready to take him home now."

"Mr. Wallace."

"He's not ready. Is he being difficult again?"

"Why don't you come with me to my office?"

Xavier laughed nervously. "Why? Is he in your office?"

"Let's just go to my office."

"No."

"Mr. Wallace, please."

"No, I'm not going into your office. I want to see my dad and I want to take him home. I left the hospice nurse waiting for me at the house."

Mrs. Thomas glanced at the nurse standing next to her. There was admonition in the look, as if the nurse had done something wrong. Xavier lost his patience with their attempts at obfuscation.

"Don't look at her. Look at me! I want to take my father home!" Mrs. Thomas flinched at his timbre. Xavier softened. "Please."

"You can't, Mr. Wallace."

"Why?"

Mrs. Thomas took a deep breath. Her face held the answer to the question that echoed in his mind.

"Can we please just go to my office?" she asked.

Her plea caught Xavier on the chin and sent him two steps back. His heels caught the carpet and he stumbled slightly. Mrs. Thomas instinctively reached out as if to catch him. He backed further away until he was close enough to one of the lobby chairs and dropped down into it. Mrs. Thomas took a seat next to him. Xavier stared at his feet. A tear fell and hit the carpet with a quiet pat before it was absorbed by the pile.

"When?"

She spoke softly. "About an hour ago." She looked up toward the nurse at the front desk and then waved to her, signaling she'd be fine. "Tanya was supposed to have called the hospice nurse to let her know. I'm sorry she came to your house."

"Did he know I was supposed to be here?"

"Mr. Wallace."

"He did. Fuck."

"Are you sure we can't go to my office?"

"Did he say anything?"

"Mr. Wallace."

"What did he say?"

She pulled at the hem of her scrubs top. "He was awake this morning. More alert than the day before. Clearer. It didn't last long, though. He asked where you were, when you were coming. Then he stopped asking. I told him I called and that I thought you'd be here any minute." She paused.

"What did he say to that?"

"Nothing at first. Just closed his eyes. I went to leave, and he said, 'It's okay.'"

"'It's okay.'"

"Maybe at the end there, he had some clarity. Maybe he remembered some of what happened. It can happen with patients sometimes. I think maybe he understood."

Xavier sat up and wiped at the bottom of his nose. "Yeah, well, nobody asked you what you think. What's that supposed to mean to me now, huh?"

Mrs. Thomas's spine stiffened. "I'm sorry. You're right. Again, that wasn't my place." Xavier chewed on his bottom lip and stared straight to the other side of the lobby. "Do you want to see him?"

Xavier stood. "No." He walked to the entrance. Mrs. Thomas called out after him. There was something about papers and powers of attorney, but her words were cut in half by the sliding doors closing behind him, drowned out by the screaming in his ears.

He headed for the parking lot. The sun seemed brighter than when he arrived. He shielded his eyes with his hand at his forehead but doing so did nothing to dam the headache filling his skull full to bursting.

In the lot sat a van with photos of dogs and cats along with a logo for an animal rescue on the side. A middle-aged blond woman with her hair pulled back in a tight ponytail coordinated volunteers who brought dogs out of the back of the van on leashes. By her side sat a blue-furred pit bull whose face had been put through its paces. Both the woman and the dog looked familiar, though Xavier didn't know why. He couldn't stop staring at either one of them. The blonde waved. The dog looked up and followed her gaze across the pavement, rose from his haunches, and whipped his tail back and forth. That she seemed to know Xavier stopped his momentum for an instant, but he kept on past them.

"Wow. Hello to you, too."

He stopped and turned. "Do I know you?"

"Is that a joke?" She narrowed her eyelids and craned her neck forward. Conscious of his swollen eyes and runny nose, he wiped at both. "Whoa, hey. Are you okay?" He looked back and forth between her and the dog. He knew he should know them and the strain to remember felt as physical as anything he'd ever done. The sky lowered until he felt it might press him through the macadam beneath his feet. Still, there was an instinct to reach out and shake the woman's hand, to squat in front of the pit and take his massive jowls in his hands and press his forehead to his. Try as he might to make them otherwise, they were strangers. The more he tried to make them known to him, the harder his head pounded, the more oppressive the sky above him until he felt crushed beneath the weight of it.

"I have to go," he said, and walked off to his car without a look back.

As HE DROVE, THE CALLS were incessant. Each time the phone buzzed, he sent Maple Grove to voicemail. The screen went dark only to light again in seconds. He'd deal with them, but not now. Not now. They called again and his thumb hovered over the green phone icon.

And what are you going to say? You going to yell at them the way your daddy did? Treat them like crap after all they done for you? For him? Man, you ain't shit. Put that phone down.

He did. After five minutes, the calls stopped. He found relief for the moment, happy to be unbothered. Then he quickly became furious at the fact that they'd given up so easily. He picked the phone up again, intending to call back and give them a piece of his mind, only to put it back in the cup holder and drive on.

He was minutes away from Manayunk when he realized

that he'd driven toward the gym. The hypnotic hum of the tires took him through the corners and curves of Lincoln Drive like a rally driver until he found himself on Main Street once again. He parked and exited the car on autopilot. He walked past the receptionist's half-hearted greeting without acknowledgment and brushed the shoulders of patrons too slow to make way as he stalked toward the locker room.

He changed into his rash guard and fight shorts. Seated on the bench he wrapped his hands, splaying his fingers as he pulled the worn cotton straps tight between the webbing, then closing them in a tight fist until the bones of his hands were densely packed together. He smacked one fist into an open hand, repeated it on the other side. He stood and walked out onto the gym floor.

Shot ran drills with Clay in the ring. Three of his protégés gathered at a corner on the floor, talking while Clay slipped and moved under Shot's focus-mitts, popping sharp counter hooks and uppercuts as he came up from beneath the strikes. One onlooker turned at the sound of Xavier's footsteps. His face swollen and distended around the jaw. Rings under his eyes, once purple, now faded to a yellowish green. At the sight of Xavier, he stood up straight. His thick shoulders tensed, pulled up near his ears. He took a step back, the calm in his voice betrayed by the rigidity of his posture. He spoke through a jaw held tight by wires.

"What up, Xavier?" Xavier didn't return Lawrence's greeting. Neither did Xavier see Lawrence's confused look as he walked past him as though he didn't know him. Xavier did not know the broken-faced man who spoke to him. Xavier had yet again been recognized by someone he did not know, but Xavier no longer cared.

Xavier walked up the steps and into the ring with Shot and

Clay. Xavier looked at Clay expectantly. Clay took his look for clowning and smiled.

"What, you can't wait your turn?"

Xavier stared Clay down, willing him to leave. Clay tried to look away, but Xavier followed.

"X," Shot said.

Xavier held the stare.

Clay stopped bouncing and held his arms out. "What?"

Shot looked back and forth between the two of them, as confused as Clay—until he wasn't.

"Go on, Clay," Shot said.

Clay looked at him, incredulous. "What do you mean, go on? We just got started."

"I said go on."

Clay looked back to Xavier, who continued his glare. Clay hissed and threw his arms up in disgust, theen stomped to the ropes and stepped through, quick-footing his way down the steps. Xavier pivoted to face Shot, who had the pads at the ready. Shot signaled to one of the boys watching and he restarted the round timer.

Three bell rings sounded, and Xavier unleashed on the pads. His long arms cut through the air. His fists struck the focus mitt's red leather circle and smacked like a baseball in a catcher's mitt. His hands came back to protect his face, the muscles in his arms coiled snakes, ready to deliver another strike. Shot threw straight lefts and rights down the middle and Xavier slipped so they only grazed his temple. The turn of his hips loaded him to deliver a chained combination. They stepped around each other and the ring in balletic movements of attack and retreat, avoid and counter.

Despite the days of dehydration and skipped meals, the acid burn in his arms and legs did not consume, but propelled. The fire did not sap his reserves but provided the combustion for an engine that drove him ever forward, each punch faster and harder than the last. The tinnitus threatened to grow louder, the pain in his heart overwhelming, so he pushed harder still, to drown the ringing with the sounds of his breathing, to hide his tears in the sweat streaming down his face.

The bell rang again, signaling the end of the round. Shot lowered his hands and turned to his corner where his water sat. Xavier pushed him from behind. The boys murmuring outside the ring fell silent. Shot turned, eyes wide. Xavier's look pleaded with his cousin. And his cousin obliged.

He stepped back into the pocket with Xavier and held the mitts at the ready. A nod and Xavier let loose ferocious combinations that sent Shot's thick arms back with each crack. He swung hard hooks at Xavier's head. Xavier wore them on his forearms before he pushed Shot backward. Shot stepped back in the pocket and swung again, this time for the body. Xavier dropped his elbows, protected his ribs, then delivered a body shot of his own. Shot winced as the strikes thundered into the thickness of his body pad. Shot brought the mitts down hard on Xavier, but his momentum would not be slowed. With each strike, the fury in Xavier's face melted into despair, as though he couldn't help but punch with all his might. The round timer sounded again, but Xavier pressed forward until Shot's back was against the corner. Xavier's hands flew from the focus mitts to the body pad until he abandoned all technique. His gloves smacked off Shot's exposed arms as he drew them in and tucked his chin. Shot whispered.

"Get it out."

Xavier groaned an agonized, guttural moan. A hook glanced off Shot's sweaty shoulder and caught him across the lip, splitting it in an instant. Shot tucked it in, brought the focus mitts closer to his face, and continued to weather the onslaught. Xavier's punches steadily lost their power as his limbs succumbed to fatigue. He threw his all into the strikes, grunting with each blow, angry with his body for betraying him in this moment when he needed it most. The punches turned into clubbing blows against Shot's shoulders and chest. His moans choked in his throat and Shot tied his arms up so he could strike no more. Xavier struggled at first to free his arms, then gave in to Shot's hold on him when he understood it for what it was. He buried his head in Shot's chest and sobbed. His legs buckled and Shot pulled him close. Shot lowered them both to the mat until they were sitting in the corner and he held his cousin's head to his chest as he cried.

DON'T SWEAT THE TECHNIQUE

The first part of their drive to Atlantic City passed in silence. Xavier had enough clothes and gear in his locker that they could leave from the gym. He asked Shot to drive. A ride alone for hours in the car his father had given him was too much to bear. Shot didn't question the request. Xavier watched the gym disappear in the rearview mirror as they turned out of the parking lot onto Main Street and made for the Atlantic City Expressway.

Xavier spent most of the drive with his head against the passenger window. He'd grown so used to the lack of air conditioning in his own car that the blasts of air from the vents of Shot's Denali were downright frigid. The sun came through the cooled glass and warmed his face. When that was no longer enough, he reached for a button on the dash and turned on his heated seat. Shot laughed and turned the air conditioning down.

"All you had to do was ask, man."

"You're driving. How am I going to complain?"

"He speaks. Thought you was going to mope the whole way up there."

"Mope? For real?"

"Come on, dude. I'm messing with you. How you doing over there?"

"I don't know."

Shot returned his eyes to the road. "Yeah, I guess that's a hard thing to know right now." Xavier didn't answer. "Look, man. I know with everything I said, it might seem like this don't matter to me, and in some ways you'd be right."

Xavier lifted his head. "Say what?"

"Slow down, before you get all heated. Let me finish. Me and your pops ain't had no love lost, we been through that. But I know how much he meant to you. I know you wanted to hate him for what he said, but I know it ain't easy for you to just shut off how you feel about him. You ain't like me, and I mean that in a good way. You my boy. If you hurting, then I'm hurting. What I'm trying to say is that I'm sorry for your loss, man. I don't know if you already knew that but I just . . . I wanted to say it. I felt like I should say it. To you."

His mother's words from his cousin's mouth. Xavier reached across the console and squeezed Shot's shoulder. "I knew it. But thank you."

"Cool. When you going to tell Auntie Ev?"

Xavier shrugged and turned back to his window. He thought he was prepared for everything that came after his father's passing, but that was because he'd imagined it happening on his terms and on his timeline. He didn't know how to tell Evelyn he'd overslept, that the sieve that was his memory caused him to leave his father to die alone when she'd asked him not to. The frustration with himself was so strong that he hadn't shared what had happened with Shot. He didn't know if Shot would judge him. He didn't know if his cousin would even care, but Xavier's own self-judgment was nearly more than he could handle, and his seams were already coming undone.

"You going to tell her. Right?"

"Can we not talk about this anymore?" The words came

out sharper than he intended and too quickly to retract. He opened his mouth to apologize but Shot cut him off.

"Okay, cool, then where's your weight at, fat ass? You looking thin, but those cheeks still too full to be on weight."

"What are you talking about?" Xavier pulled down the visor and turned his head side to side. The mirror reflected a sallow face, cheekbones prominent. As if on cue, his stomach gurgled a plea for him to fill it. The water cut had him at less than a bottle a day for fear at this stage, and at his age, his body would hold on to any water like a man rescued from the desert.

"You going to stop admiring yourself long enough to answer me?"

"Like five pounds. That is if you didn't mess with the scales at the gym to keep people coming back."

"Five is still too much."

"I'll drop two in my sleep tonight. A few more in the sauna right before weigh-ins. We'll be straight."

"We not taking chances. Not with this. We'll hit the pads one more time in the sauna suit when we get settled at the hotel."

"Man, I'm good. You're going to have me exhausted before tomorrow."

"Did you hear a request in there?"

"Yeah, all right."

Xavier returned his head to the window. Even seated in the truck, his limbs felt heavy, as if the lactic acid had already accumulated in his muscles and hardened. He was already urinating less, so there was no way to clear it from his system. He felt in his shoulder as he reached for the heated seats button that immediate burn that made him want to drop his arm for relief. His traps ached all the way up to the base of his skull, and the sensation radiated into his ears and competed with the tinnitus for space. His heart raced at the mental rehearsal of even one more session of the pads. The cab of the Denali felt small and stifling.

He opened the window a crack for air. The briny smell of the shore filtered in. He breathed deep through his nose. When his parents were still together, summertime meant trips to Point Pleasant almost every weekend. He'd race down the boardwalk the minute they parked the car, always close enough to keep them in his line of sight, though far enough away that he felt independent and brave. He always kept them close enough so he could relieve them of their single dollar bills for the games where he could win stuffed animals as tall as he was, only to end up with an armful of knock-off cartoon characters from the bottom row of prizes. A hollow victory was a victory nonetheless, particularly when he conned them both into carrying the toys when he wanted to go on the beach.

The salty sea air filled the Denali. They approached the lights of Atlantic City glowing in the oncoming dusk. Xavier didn't want the drive to end. He didn't want to check into the hotel. He didn't want to cut any more weight. He wanted to revel in that childhood recollection for as long as he could, because he knew as his short-term memory continued to abandon him, so too would the long-term. The thing that now lived in his brain would someday decide to simply wipe those recollections away. There would be no Point Pleasant. No funnel cake and pizza with cheese like magma and salty soft pretzels. No diving headfirst into waves while his parents watched, holding hands on their adjacent beach towels under a rented umbrella farther up the beach. The film reel of his lived life would unspool and collect on the floor, never to be rethreaded into the projector. He would smell the beach and it would mean nothing.

They pulled up to the front of the hotel. Shot handled the valet while Xavier unloaded their bags. A bellhop loaded them on a dolly and stood by while Shot checked them into their rooms. He gave Xavier a key, asked him if he remembered where the fitness center was, then told him to meet him there in twenty minutes. Xavier agreed.

When the elevator opened on their floor, they went their separate ways. Xavier scanned the key at the doorknob when his phone buzzed. Another call from Maple Grove, the fifth that day. He sent it to voicemail and entered his room. The king-sized bed invited him to fall backward and sleep until tomorrow. A shorter buzz vibrated.

Dont even think about sleeping

Asshole

He tossed the phone on the bed, then changed into his sauna suit, a hooded sweatshirt underneath with a T-shirt and shorts over top, then left to meet Shot downstairs. Long since used to working out in hotel gyms, he thought nothing of the other guests' stares as his vinyl suit zipped and zopped on his way to the elevator. He enjoyed their looks away. The temptation to jump his shoulders at them and snarl was almost overwhelming. He always refrained. A pleasant pre-recorded female voice in the elevator signaled their arrival at the ground floor. As the guests filed out, his brief amusement ended.

Time to go to work.

Shot waited for him at the door to the fitness center, then led him to a mirrored multipurpose room in the back of the gym. A graying white man in baggy shorts performed half-hearted abdominal crunches on a yoga mat. Hair sprouted out from underneath the shoulder straps of his ill-fitting tank top spotted through with sweat. When he saw Xavier and Shot enter, gear in tow, he quickly stood, rolled up his mat, and left the room in a near run, eyes to the floor as he exited.

Shot and Xavier watched him out, then looked at each other and laughed. Shot pulled the focus mitts from his bag and clapped them together, the sound reverberating in the room. Xavier took a deep breath and stepped into the pocket.

The first thirty seconds were sharp. Xavier's hands flew fast and free, and he allowed himself to hope in that half a minute that his fatigue was in his mind. His arms freed him of that misapprehension in the thirty seconds that followed. The gloves went from sixteen ounces to ten pounds. Blood pooled in his deltoids. Muscle fibers swelled beneath the skin, taut like plastic wrap due to the dearth of water within. He longed for stabbing pain, the type that watered the eyes yet sharpened the vision and brought everything into focus. Anything but that dull ache, that pain that spread like a migraine, nebulous with no focal point on which to apply pressure in the hopes of eliminating it. But the ache was all there was.

Shot's phone timer went off. Xavier shucked off his gloves, tossed them in a corner. He leaned against the wall before sliding down to his rear.

"That's it, Shot. I'm done."

"You hurt? You pull something?"

"Nah, man."

"Are you sweating?"

Xavier touched his hot but dry forehead. "No."

"Then get your ass up."

"Shot. I'm done. If I push it anymore, I'm not going to make the scale tomorrow. You know how they do. If I look like I can't walk on my own, or I pass out, or whatever, they'll say I can't fight. I know my body, man. I can't push it anymore."

"Unless you want your body to end up underground, you are going to stand up."

Xavier stayed seated. "The hell happened to you, man?"

"Okay, here we go."

"No, I'm serious." He walked his back up the wall until he stood once more. "I never saw anyone scare people like you did, way before they even made it to the ring. You didn't even have to talk shit. All people had to do was watch your tapes. See the trail of bodies you left on the mat. You beat them before they ever put a foot through the ropes. But now it's like these people you got in with, fixing fights and shit. It's like they pulled your teeth and—"

"And what?"

"Like they ripped out your throat. Took your bark and your bite."

"You saying I'm soft? Is that it? Because I'm trying to keep you from getting killed, I'm the punk?"

"I thought you said I had to do this to keep *us* from getting killed."

"These guys ain't stupid, X. They know if you don't work out, I'll get them someone else. They're not going to fuck with a business model that's working. You're just another Lawrence to them, dude. Except what happened to Lawrence wasn't his fault. It was yours."

For the first time in the days since he agreed to the fix, true panic gripped Xavier's heart and pushed it against the inside of his chest.

"But, Shot, you know that wasn't me, man. Not really me."

"What I know is they don't give a fuck about that, or what you're going through."

"Well, did you explain it to them?"

Shot scoffed, waved Xavier off, and turned his back to him.

"So, you just went and sold your family down the river. To save your own ass."

Shot turned. "That's what you think? Let me tell you something, cuz. If you think what it is we're doing tomorrow was the first option they had in mind for you, you best think again."

Xavier slid back down the wall again and brought his hand to his forehead.

"Yeah," Shot said. "There it is."

Xavier closed his eyes and thudded his head against the wall, sending a cascade of pain from the base of his skull to his forehead. "Shit," he whispered. Shot approached the wall. His heavy footsteps echoed. He gently kicked at Xavier's foot, and he looked up to see Shot wave him aside.

"Move, nigga." Xavier slid over and made room on the floor. Shot groaned as he slid down the wall to sit next to him. "X, you've known what I've been doing with these fights for a long time now, way before the steroids, and don't even say you didn't. Maybe you don't think you knew, but you knew. You told yourself different because we family and I appreciated you for that. You might not want to hear this, but it kind of made things easier for me to swallow."

"You're right. I don't want to hear that."

"Yeah, well. Truth is, I hated myself for a long time for getting into this side of the business, because when I was fighting, I swore to God I would never do it. I swore everything I was going to do was going to be on the level. You know this. But shit, man, when those cops took the sight out my eye? They might as well have shot me. Fact is, I wished they had killed me. When I found out I couldn't fight anymore, I didn't want to live. I think I *did* die. Know how I know? Because I don't hate myself anymore for these things I do. When you stop hating yourself for something that goes against everything you thought you stood for, you're either dead inside or you ain't the person you thought you was all along. Neither one of them is something you really want to know." They sat against the wall and stared straight ahead at the entranceway to the room. After a minute, they sighed simultaneously and Shot slapped Xavier on the top of his knee. "That's some deep shit, huh?"

"In more ways than one. How did we get here, man? This was supposed to be about fame and women and stacks of cash, retiring when we turned thirty, living off endorsements."

"It wasn't never about that for me. Don't get me wrong, it was nice, but that was almost a fringe benefit. I was doing what I loved to do. The thing I was best at. Until I wasn't. I know how I got here. Pretty sure you do, too."

Xavier turned to look at him. "You want to enlighten me?"

"Nope." Shot stood. "You right about one thing, though. No more drilling today. It's still hot as fuck outside. Keep the suit on and hit the boardwalk. Do some sprints or jog or something, get at least some sweat going. Whatever little bit you can get off. Do not drink water. Your old ass is going to hang on to every little sip you take right now."

"This ain't my first cut."

"I'll come get you in the morning."

Shot strolled out of the room. Xavier stayed on the floor. Once again, Shot's truths landed with the accuracy and power for which he'd become so infamous. They found their home in the gut with clubbing blows; their impact shivered the liver and vibrated innards until the pain spread throughout the body, devouring strength in the limbs and stealing breath until the brain said, "Go down." Already on the floor, struck by Shot's words, Xavier searched for the ability—and the desire—to get back up.

When he found them, he walked out of the fitness center and down the hall to the elevator. Once in the lobby of the hotel, he stepped out the automatic front doors. He returned

a nod from the doorman, then the valet. The air was muggy.
He took a deep inhale and again savored the saltwater smell.
Though the sun had begun its descent into dusk, it lit the
breeze on fire. If he had any fluid left to lose, it wouldn't take
much to get a sweat going. Even when he was in the wrong,
Shot was often right. Xavier hated that. He walked toward
the beach.

The boardwalk hummed. Parents laughed as their kids
cried for protection from hovering seagulls, waiting for their
chance to divebomb and snatch a bite of their towering cone
of vanilla custard. Cyclists towed tourists in rickshaws, their
handlebar bells chiming. Couples walked hand in hand.
Xavier looked back and forth, waiting for an opening to cross
the flow of traffic. He saw one and sprinted across, weaving
in and out of pedestrians, until he reached the entrance to the
beach. He knew a run there would be taxing on the legs, but
he had zero patience in the tank for a game of human Frogger
on the boardwalk.

He found a stretch of wet packed sand and trotted into a
jog. He landed with an almost flat foot, not quite on the ball,
heel always off the ground to keep from digging too deep
through the top layer. His father had taught him the technique when he'd developed shin splints in the earliest days
of his cardio training. It was the same day Xavier learned
he was a pigeon-toed runner. He thought the label an insult
until Sam explained to him some of the greatest runners of
all time had the same gait, that it seemed to somehow help
their acceleration and decreased their tendency for injury.
Xavier still felt like it was some kind of defect, yet another
strange thing about him, like having Black and white parents.
He remembered that his father had made him feel that that
was also something normal, something to be proud of. But he
didn't trust the memory. As his skin tingled with the heat that

preceded his sweating, Xavier wiped away a tear. The warm remembrance of that moment smashed up against the cold reality of what the next forty-eight hours would bring. And a storm formed.

The weight cut, the fix, and remembering all the details to make it look convincing in the middle of a fight.

His father's body, a funeral, and whether it could be afforded, and did Sam have any money left for one, and would he still sell the house now, and where would he live if he did.

His mother in his life once more, and how dare he romanticize another moment with his father. Wasn't that a betrayal to her? Was he doing it all over again when she'd opened her arms to him again without hesitation?

Thoughts and questions swirled, fronts that collided and rumbled. Each impact with the sand sent shockwaves up his limbs that terminated as pain in his temples. The muscles of his neck tightened and gripped his spine. Winded, he slowed to a stop and held himself up on his knees. With no inkling as to how far he'd run, he looked over his shoulder to see he'd cleared less than a quarter of a mile. His head throbbed and his legs ached. He conjured a thick glob of saliva and spat it defiantly into the sand.

It would have to be enough. He'd wring out what was left of himself in the sauna the next morning. Hands on his hips, he walked back to the boardwalk, head back and mouth open, filling his lungs with the ocean air. The waves crashed against the beach. A once-comforting sound now as pleasant as the static of a television without reception, the volume knob turned all the way to the right and broken off with no means of lessening the roar. And the whistle. That God-damned screaming whistle.

Back at the hotel, his headache was in full swing. Pain shot along the right side of his face and he feared another cut in his field of vision. He approached the front desk. The young woman behind the counter masked behind a tight smile her apprehension for the man in the plastic suit. She glanced behind him in the direction of the doorman, as if unsure Xavier was a hotel guest or a derelict off the street. Xavier followed her look and saw the doorman give her a thumbs up. He turned back to face her and her taut grin.

"How can I help you today, sir?"

"Aspirin. Or ibuprofen. Something. Please."

"Certainly." She disappeared behind a doorway, then emerged with a number of foil packs. She laid them on the counter. "Are you fighting at the event this weekend?" Xavier said he was. He slid the pills off the counter into his hand and turned to leave. "Oh, wait!" She went behind the door again and returned with three sweating plastic bottles of water. "Don't want to swallow those dry." She stuck out her tongue and made a face. "And here's a couple extra. You look like you could use them."

Xavier eyed the bottles. He told himself to leave them and take the aspirin with a handful of tap water, but he couldn't talk louder than the noise in his head. He collected the bottles and thanked her.

"My pleasure, sir. And good luck on Saturday!"

He waved as he walked back to the bank of elevators.

More sweat had accumulated in his suit than he'd expected, though not as much as he'd hoped. He threw the gear into a heap in the tub and pulled on his shorts and T-shirt. The bathroom lights generated a high-pitched frequency. He shut them off, then went to the bedroom curtains and drew them. Light found its way to the bottom and lent the room faint illumination. Slow to adjust to the dark, he stubbed his toe on the foot of the bed. He cursed and sat on edge of the bed and wiggled it. Not broken. What poetic justice that would have been, to have the fight ended in that way, before he ever set foot in the cage.

A soft glow lit the ceiling. Xavier swiped his hand behind him until he found his phone. There was a new voice message, added to the five others from Maple Grove. He unlocked his phone and listened, first as Mrs. Thomas made several entreaties for him to come back to the facility. There were logistics that had to be decided, papers that needed signing. The following calls marked a downturn in her mood. She informed Xavier these decisions would be made for him should he not return her calls. The final message, the one he must have missed while undressing in the bathroom, said that they'd had Sam's body removed and if his father had any internment wishes, he needed to contact her as soon as possible.

Fuck his wishes. You got your own shit. There is no "Dad" anymore. That's just a body in a bag back home. His brain jumped ship a long time ago, and now the rest is gone, too. What do you care what they do with that meat puppet?

He knew he should care. He thought he should. He thought he wanted to, but even of that he wasn't sure. The only certainty in that moment was the incessant whistle, the pressure behind his eyes, and the waves of pain. He opened all the foil packs, six ibuprofens in all, and tossed them toward the back of his throat. He swallowed hard, but they caught. Another swallow, but the coating on the pills made them stick and he fought back a gag.

He grabbed one of the water bottles from its place on his nightstand. A small sip dislodged the pills, but he didn't pull the bottle from his lips. He paused, then tilted his head back and finished the bottle in gulps. The bottle crinkled and cracked before it imploded from the vacuum of his thirst. He tossed the bottle to the floor and panted, then eyed the remaining ones on the nightstand. He already felt a little bit better. More relief awaited at only an arm's length. He just had to reach for it. When nothing else seemed louder than the noise in his mind, that relief screamed loudest.

He snatched another bottle and downed the water. The second lump of crumpled plastic had hardly hit the floor before he'd unscrewed the cap of the third, until the carcasses lay at his feet. Coolness coursed through his body as the liquid filled in the small spaces between his organs, drawn tight by dehydration and starvation. Despite the ice cold of the water, euphoric warmth spread throughout his body. His eyes rolled back under his closed lids. He dropped back to the bed and succumbed to an instantaneous slumber.

I AGAINST I

Ain't it something when everything falls into place?

Look at everything that's gone right for you now. Your pops went ahead and did you the favor of dying while you intentionally overslept. Spared you having to see him waste away, spared you the heartache of not knowing who you were, of possibly—well, let's be honest—*probably* calling you a nigger again. I know you're feeling guilty about leaving your phone on the counter on purpose, because you were too afraid to face him, so you told yourself it was my fault you forgot.

It's cool. I don't mind. That's what I'm here for. I got you, son.

We're here now, so shake it off, all this pouting and what not. Your path has been cleared. Nothing more in your way. You can start pulling the dollars you always wanted from this business. Yeah, you've got to swallow a little bit of pride to do it, but what has your pride gotten you besides having to deal with me?

Now hold on. You're not actually thinking of taking that coaching job, are you? That's *if* your mama can even line it up in the first place.

You *are*, aren't you?

Uh uh, no. No.

You mean to tell me that instead of filling your pockets

with the knots of bills Shot is tossing in your lap just to throw some fights, you want to take a job at some low-rent, two-year college while you slip into a dad-bod, sweatpants up over your gut, whistle around your neck, coaching dudes who are going to make it farther than you while you reminisce about the good old days and what could have been?

I should fuck you up for even thinking about that non-sense. Shove a knife in your eyeball straight through to your spinal cord. Not enough to kill you. Just leave you in a chair, drooling out the corner of your slack mouth, unable to remember who you are. Where the highlight of your day is when someone comes to feed you. Or when they wipe your ass. Or when they call you by your name. Or the five minutes when you might even remember what your name is.

And all that would *still* be better than your taking that sad sack job. Just hoist yourself up on a slab and roll yourself into a refrigerated cabinet, because that's the only good you'll be to yourself, you go that route.

You are a *savage*. You aren't made to be long for this world. Do you want to make your exit like some old lion in a zoo, plucked from your natural habitat to be pointed at by snot-nosed children until you eventually die from old age and a broken spirit? Or do you want to go out snarling and gnashing, taking out as many hyenas as you can?

That's where the glory is. *That's* how you were built. *That's* what you were made for. You're a man out of time, not because you don't have any time left, but because this time is not *your* time. You were born to a world that doesn't know how to let you exist in it, one that wants you de-fanged by a nine to five with shitty pay and decent benefits, all in the name of your safety, when you know good and well they want you in those safe jobs so they feel safe from you. They need you confined like they are, because your existence challenges their own.

And yes, I mean your mama when I say "they." I know you've got all the feels about this reunion, but she don't know you any better now than she did then. And yes, I also know being near her again connects you with a part of you that you felt betrayed her staying with your pops, especially knowing what you know now. It's why you laid into that boy Lawrence, and don't act like it wasn't. You always had a chip on your shoulder about that, always something to prove about your Blackness. Don't get me wrong, I was glad to be the scapegoat again, but you keep blaming me and people are going to stop believing there's a wolf in the village.

On top of all that, she still left you. Shit got hard and she bounced. What happens when things get hard again? What happens when *you're* the one in the nursing home before you're fifty because you don't remember how to tie your shoes anymore? She going to stick around then, or she going to take off? She's a sprinter. But you're so afraid of being alone that you convinced yourself that that doesn't matter anymore. Except you aren't that convinced. About the job, about the fight, or her. And you know I'm right.

Knowing I'm right might be the only thing you know for sure anymore.

ONE MORE ROAD TO CROSS

Ten pounds.

He stepped off the digital scale, watched the numbers flash until they disappeared, then stepped on again.

Ten fucking pounds.

He stepped to the toilet and threw back the lid. When the urine finally came, it was dark yellow. Almost brown.

How?

He walked out of the bathroom and paced the darkened bedroom. Hands on top of his head. The clock on the nightstand read just past 7 A.M. His head throbbed. He dared not open his curtains. He rounded the corner of the bed and something crunched underfoot. He looked down and picked up a crushed water bottle—then two more. He remembered the run. The front desk. The aspirin. He remembered one sip for the pills. And then nothing.

He did the math. He hadn't eaten, and three eighteen-ounce bottles shouldn't have added up to that. But he knew what happened. His body held onto the water and wouldn't let it go. And now his body had to listen whether it wanted to or not. Weigh-ins were eight hours away.

He'd cut ten in eight before. But that was in high school. In the days where he could eat an entire pizza before a tournament then sweat and shit it out. Those days were not these days. Every year, every fight, his body held on to the weight longer than it used to. Fought his fighting.

He picked up the hotel phone. The concierge answered before the second ring. Xavier explained that he was a fighter due to weigh in that afternoon. He needed bags of Epsom salt as quickly as they could get them to him.

Thirty minutes passed like hours. Then a knock on his door. Xavier stiffened, worried it was Shot, that he had somehow sensed that Xavier was over on his weight and had come to squeeze the liquid out of him, to punch it out of his kidneys. Xavier opened the door, grabbed the bags from the attendant, and told him to bill it to his room. He then slammed the door before the attendant could say "you're welcome."

He drew a bath. Scalding hot. Two bags of salt into the steam. Lowered in, ignored the sear against his flesh. Wait for the salt to pull the water from the skin and muscle. Spare the organs. Heart at full sprint. Running without moving. The edge of the tub too cool, he slid himself as low as his long legs would allow until his knees breached the water like two islands. When the water no longer felt hot, he stood.

Too quickly. Room spun, vision orange, fireflies in his eyes. He grabbed at the shower curtain. The plastic liner popped and pulled free from the metal rings holding it to the rod. The last few holes held. His head stopped inches from the edge of the tub. Saved his face. Saved the fight.

Equilibrium restored, he picked up the hotel key he'd set on the edge of the tub. Scraped the sweat from his skin. He dried himself from head to toe. His skin raw and tingly. He hoped the moisture in his towel was more sweat than bathwater. The scale told no such lies. Only down a pound and a quarter.

He put his forehead in his hand. Wet. The sweat continued.

A good sign, but he couldn't keep this up alone. He relented and called Shot.

Shot knocked. Xavier braced himself against the wall of the hall to the door, clad only in a towel. Shot gave him the once over.

"The fuck happened?"

Xavier licked his cracked lips.

"How much over?"

Xavier's voice rasped. "About nine."

"Nine? Nigga, you told me five yesterday. The fuck did you do?"

"I guess I had some water."

"You guess? Ain't that something. You guess." Shot paced. "Does that mean nine with them giving us the pound?"

Xavier brightened. "No."

"So, eight," Shot said. "What you standing there for? Get the suit, and bring the hoodie and sweatpants, too. We're going down to the sauna."

The thought of that wet wooden tomb set the whistle off in his ears again.

Don't even think about saying no. Get your narrow ass in that plastic suit and get to sweating. You are not going to ruin this, not if I have anything to say about it. You're done when I say you're done. I don't care how much you have to give. It's not yours to give or keep anymore.

Xavier closed the door, changed, then joined Shot in the hall. As they rode the elevator down, Xavier leaned on Shot's shoulder, but Shot shrugged him off.

"Stop that shit, man," he said, looking forward. "Someone from the commission sees that, they're going to think you cut too much to fight." Xavier straightened up. Shot looked him in the eyes. "Get it together."

The doors opened and Xavier walked beside Shot with

false bravado. A young woman walked toward them. Xavier, in a moment of clarity, recognized her as the desk attendant who gave him the water and ibuprofens. His hand shot out as she passed. He gripped her forearm, pulled her close to his face. The little skank. She knew he was a fighter. She'd said so herself. Giving him that water was thoughtless. The dumb fucking bitch. Who did she think she was? His voice pushed through his clenched jaw in a growl.

"You fucked me. You know that?"

"What? Who the fuck are you? Let me go!" She smacked him across the face, and Xavier raised his other hand. Shot grabbed it, then pried Xavier's grip from her wrist. He yanked Xavier backward.

"The hell is wrong with you, man? Ma'am, I'm sorry, are you all right?"

She rubbed at her forearm and wrist and shouted past Shot to Xavier. "I'm going to press charges, asshole!"

Xavier looked around the lobby. His rage quickly gave way to embarrassment. The commotion caught the attention of a collection of guests enjoying their morning papers and continental breakfasts. The dustup drew the doorman from his post. Xavier watched Shot go into his pocket and peel two hundreds from a roll of bills and put them in the young woman's palm. She sneered but pocketed the money.

"What's going on here?" the doorman asked. Xavier saw Shot look at the woman expectantly.

"Nothing," she said. "It's fine."

The doorman gave her a doubting look. "Perhaps you gentlemen want to get to wherever it is you're going now."

"We'll do that," Shot said. He grabbed Xavier by the arm and pulled him down the lobby toward the hall that led to the fitness center. "I don't even want to know what the fuck that was all about."

"I'm sorry."

"I swear to God, X. Stop talking."

Shot held open the sauna door. Xavier stuffed his arms in the sleeves of his hoodie. Zipped up. Pulled the strings of his hood. Drew it tight around his head and face. He sat on the bench. Felt the heat of the wood through the layers of cotton and vinyl. The thermometer read 190 degrees.

Five minutes passed. The sweat that had started upstairs wouldn't come. Then it poured from every pore. His heart pounded in his ears. Muted the tinnitus squeal. A deep breath made him gasp for another. He was drowning. The liquid air on fire. The skin on his face tightened until his lips threatened to pull away from his teeth. Fireflies returned to the corners of his vision. Shot looked through the Plexiglas window. Xavier signaled to him. Shot opened the door.

"What?"

"I can't breathe."

"Come on, then."

The cool air caressed the uncovered patch of his face. Shot led him across the gym.

"How long was I—"

"Shut up."

They stopped in front of an Airdyne bike.

"Shot, I can't."

"You won't sweat in there, you going to sweat out here. Get on."

Xavier mounted the bike. His hands hot and swollen, the handlebars like ice. The flywheel whirled. He pumped his arms back and forth. His legs spun. The fan-like front wheel generated a breeze but provided no reprieve for his blowtorched legs. The hood of his sweatshirt heavy with perspiration, he looked for a clock in the gym and found none.

It wouldn't have mattered. Shot would keep him on the bike until he dropped.

Limbs spent, he begged Shot for mercy. Granting some, Shot pointed to the tile floor. Xavier immediately went to his back. Shot left his sight, only to return with a stack of towels. He piled them on, leaving just enough room around Xavier's mouth to breathe while he cooked in his cotton igloo.

Dark.

Xavier stood naked on the scale.

When did I get off the floor? Where are my clothes?

He tried to stand up straight but couldn't. His organs shrank and pulled away from each other. Ribs touching. He looked down.

Four pounds to go.

Sauna.

Bike.

Towels.

Dark.

On the scale again.

Not in the gym.

In front of the crowd.

Am I awake? Am I dreaming?

He looked around to see Shot standing off to the side of the stage. He held Xavier's clothes and applauded, then gave Xavier a thumbs up. The crowd cheered and hollered. Xavier lowered his head and saw a hollowed tarp of taut skin where his stomach had been. He looked left and saw Shot once more. Then he saw his opponent for the first time since he'd watched all his film. Egan Finn bounced on his toes. The commissioner admonished Xavier to stay still. Then he called out a number. Xavier strained to hear over the rumble of the audience. Then the emcee shouted it out over the microphone.

"One-eighty-six, ladies and gentlemen!"

The audience exploded into applause and shouted Xavier's name. Fatigue and weakness left him then. The squeal in his ears choked out a death rattle, victim to the adrenaline bathing every nerve fiber, flooding his brain, and coating his synapses. He looked at the faces in the crowd, the flashing lights of cell phone cameras, the people pointing at him and screaming in admiration. He flexed. Every striation in his chest popped beneath the skin. He rounded his shoulders and his traps spread around his ears like a cobra's hood.

He roared. The lion bared his teeth, leapt over the retaining wall, and removed the illusion of safety from those who watched him with a mixed sense of security and superiority as he escaped his enclosure. The crowd invigorated him, returned the coil to the springs in his legs. He bounded off the scale and toward Finn, who waited for their face-off for the cameras. Xavier didn't slow as he approached, and Carson Davis put his arm out in a ceremonial gesture to keep the two from going at each other. Despite Finn waving him on, Xavier saw him take a step back.

You see that? He's scared. He's yours.

Xavier shoved Carson's hand down and pushed his forehead into Finn's, grinding it as their noses came together. Finn pushed into him but took another step back. The men in his camp rushed from behind and pulled at him.

Xavier pushed harder against Finn's forehead. "They can't save you in there, you know that, right?"

Say it. You know what it will do. Say it.

"I'm going to fuck you up real bad. Your little girl won't even recognize you when I'm done."

Eyes wild, Finn slapped his hands against Xavier's bare chest and shoved him. Xavier hardly moved. He saw that

Finn had also cut hard to make the weight and though he struck a chord with his words, there was no power in Finn's push. Xavier grinned at Finn, which only served to enrage Finn further as he struggled to free himself from his coaches. The crowd screamed at the altercation. Xavier fed off the energy. He responded with a shove of his own. Finn stumbled back into his trainers' arms. Carson, joined by security, swarmed the space between the two men. Shot's arms wrapped around Xavier and he lifted him up and away from the melee. Xavier let Shot remove him, but he never looked away from Finn. The emcee weaved his way through the fracas and put his microphone in Finn's face.

"Obviously you two had some words in the face-off. What did Wallace say to you?"

Finn pointed across the stage and screamed into the mic. "You don't talk about a man's family, dude. Especially about his kids. I'm going to smash your fucking face in tomorrow night, and you better hope the ref is strong enough to pull me off you. You're fucking dead." He smacked the microphone away and stormed off the stage, followed closely by his team and a pair of security guards. The emcee shook his head and crossed the stage to where Xavier waited, hands behind his back, amused. The crowd's favor shifted. A chorus of boos meshed with the cheers.

"Wow," the emcee shouted. "Xavier, in all the times I've called your fights, I've never seen you be anything but respectful, both at the weigh-ins and in the cage. You've been out for a year. Are we going to see something different from you tomorrow night? Is this a new Scarecrow Wallace?"

The emcee held the microphone for Xavier with expectant, electric eyes. In them Xavier saw the love for the drama, the same love he saw in the faces of the audience as they hung on his answer. Xavier winked at the emcee, then walked off the stage with Shot in tow, saying nothing. The emcee's voice echoed throughout the auditorium as Xavier took the stairs and headed backstage.

"Xavier Wallace, ladies and gentlemen! That's going to be one hell of a prelim fight, and I can't wait to see it. Next, coming to the stage . . ."

Xavier fast-walked toward the door that led to the parking lot behind the building. Shot jogged to catch him.

"X, what the fuck? Slow down, man."

Xavier heard him, though only just. The more distance he put between himself and the roar of the crowd, the louder the whistling grew. The energy he felt fill his leg muscles drained out the bottom of his feet with each step. The borders of his vision browned. That he might make it outside before losing consciousness became altogether uncertain. He picked up the pace and slammed on the metal door's release bar. The cool but humid air found no easy entrance into his lungs. He'd rushed off the stage before Shot handed him the Pedialyte. His tight muscles held his ribs in place like a collapsed umbrella, a deep breath nowhere to be found. He scanned the parking lot, saw Shot's license plate, and hurried to the passenger side of the Denali. The lights winked as Shot unlocked it. Xavier climbed up into the seat, his breathing rapid and shallow. The edges of his sight continued their close. Shot flung open the door and tossed the Pedialyte bottle into Xavier's lap.

"Chug that. Now."

The liquid sent cool tendrils up his jaw and into his temples and rested there with a dull yet welcome ache. He emptied the bottle and panted with relief.

"Now, you want to tell me what the fuck just happened back there?"

"I would love to." The borders of his vision framed nothing but Shot's angry face. "But I'm going to pass out now." And Shot disappeared in the darkness.

KICK IN THE DOOR

He stirred but did not open his eyes. His head did not throb. No whistle. The inside of his mouth no longer arid, his throat no longer swollen. He felt no pain at all, save a slight sting at the bend of his right arm. He opened his right eye and confirmed his suspicion. A needle in his vein, a bag on a pole next to the bed. Not his bed. It smelled different.

"Shot," he said, still slightly hoarse. No response. He called out louder. "Shot."

A toilet flushed and light spilled into the dark hallway, the room lit only by the flat screen on the dresser across from the bed. The weigh-ins replayed. Shot stepped out of the bathroom and came to Xavier's bedside. He examined the nearly empty fluid bag.

"God damn, man. That's the second one. I only brought three." Xavier looked up at him and Shot glared back. "Don't look at me like that. Ain't nothing in there that's not supposed to be. I would never do that without asking you. You should know that. You ain't pissing hot on my watch again."

Xavier should have trusted him. But he didn't. And he knew Shot knew it.

A knock on the door. Xavier lifted his head from the pillow. Shot peered through the peephole, then fast-walked back to the bed, whispering curses all the way. Xavier sat all the way up and braced for the vertigo.

"What is it?"

"Carson's at the door."

"So?"

"*So* I got to get this shit out your arm and put it somewhere he won't see it." He removed the needle and gave Xavier a cotton swab. "Press this on there and keep your arms crossed while you sitting there. Look natural or something."

"*Look natural?*" Xavier snatched the swab and pressed it into the bend in his arm. "God damn it, Shot. I fucking knew it. If there wasn't anything in there, then why are you freaking out?"

Another knock at the door.

"Yeah, hold up," Shot shouted. He turned back to Xavier and whispered again. "Because, bitch, IVs are illegal now because that's how people *was* sneaking steroids in. Why do you think I was doing it instead of oh, I don't know, a trained professional? Thanks for the trust, though. With your dumb ass."

Xavier's ears turned red. Shot collapsed the pole and shoved the rest of the supplies in the closet. He walked back to the door and opened it. "What up, Carson?" He stepped aside to let him pass.

"Is he in here? Where is that son of a bitch?" He rounded the corner and saw Xavier sitting on the edge of the bed, arms folded. "There he is. Holy shit. You're a fucking madman, you know that?"

Xavier looked past Carson to Shot and back again. "I am?"

"Are you kidding me? After that face-off, people are going fucking apeshit. Everybody is hyped for this fight and I do mean everybody. We don't usually get that kind of heat for the prelims. Pay-per-view buys are guaran-damn-teed to go up because of the shit you just pulled."

Xavier laughed nervously. "Huh, yeah. I bet."

"Whatever it is that got into you, man, I fucking love it. I don't know if this is Scarecrow 2.0, but you want my advice? Lean into that shit all the way. Those boos you heard up there are just as good as the cheers. Now you have people wanting to see you win *and* lose. Nothing quite like a big fanbase except a base of haters to go along with it. That means asses in seats and eyeballs on the television when you fight."

Shot spoke from behind, leaned against the hallway wall. "That mean you going to pay him for all those extra eyeballs and asses?"

"Well, look, there's no way we can attribute any numbers over the projected buys to just that little stunt. But I'll tell you this. You make the fight as exciting as that craziness you pulled on stage, light him up on the feet—hell, you knock him out? I'll make sure you get a nice chunk of change the IRS won't ever have to know about."

"Be nice to get some backend on them pay-per-view dollars," Shot said.

Carson scoffed. "Yeah, I'm sure it fucking would. Win this fight, make it exciting, and we'll see what's up for the next one."

Xavier glared past Carson at Shot but Shot gave him the high sign that now was not the time. Carson watched the unspoken volley between them, then homed in on Xavier's arm.

"What happened there?" Xavier looked down and saw the cotton puff peeking out between his fingers. He looked back at Carson, speechless. "Whatever, I don't give a shit. You just better hope you don't pop again."

"It's not a problem," Shot said.

"Good." Carson wagged his finger at Xavier, a wide grin on his face. "Fucking awesome, Scarecrow. Great fucking stuff. Get some rest. I'll see you boys tomorrow." He left the room. Shot slammed the door behind him.

"'Boys.' Every time with the 'boys.' The white guys are always 'kids,' but we're always boys. Motherfucker."

"Shot, what the hell is he talking about? What happened?"

"What do you mean?"

"I mean I literally have zero clue what he's talking about. Did I . . . what did I do?"

Shot opened his mouth to explain, then stopped when the action on the screen caught his eye. "There you go right now."

He unmuted the television. Xavier moved to the edge of the bed. He watched in horror as the events unfolded, events of which he had no recollection. The fiendish smile, the push, the colliding of foreheads like two rams jockeying for dominance.

"What did I say to him?"

"Some raw shit about his daughter. I don't even know how you knew to say something like that to him."

Xavier rested his forehead in his hand. Though the recall of the confrontation still eluded him, another memory sprouted. As he combed the internet for Finn's fight footage, he recalled an interview where he talked tearfully about his daughter and the challenges of maintaining a full-time fight career as a single father. That he used that information in such a way made him sick to his stomach. "I can't believe I did that."

"Yeah, well no one else could, either. Especially him. I actually thought that little white boy might kill you then and there."

"I would have deserved it."

"You sure about that?"

"What do you mean?"

Shot went to answer but was interrupted by another knock at the door. Xavier flinched.

"Like a SEPTA station in here." He opened the door. A woman spoke.

"You can't say hello, Shemar?"

Shot stuttered. "Hey, Auntie Ev."

Xavier craned his neck to look down the hall. "Mom?"

"May I come in?" Shot stepped to the side with a bow and a flourish. Evelyn waved him off. "Boy, please." Shot closed the door behind her. She approached the bed, arms outstretched. Xavier stood and walked into her embrace.

"What are you doing here?"

"I wanted to surprise you."

"Mission accomplished," Shot said from the hallway. "How did you even get up here?"

Evelyn maintained her hug but turned to look over her shoulder. "I know you think you all are a big deal, but you aren't *that* big a deal. I told them I was Xavier's mother and I needed to see him. Who's going to tell a little old lady no?"

Shot waved a finger at her. "Ahhh, you a hustler, too, huh? See, I come by it honestly, Auntie Ev."

Evelyn ignored him. She pulled away from Xavier and looked up at him. "I was at the weigh-in."

He sat back down on the edge of the bed. "Don't ask me what that was, because I don't know."

"I've never seen you like that."

"I know, Mom." He tapped his forehead. Touching it disgusted him, as though forced to shake hands with someone who'd betrayed him. "I told you, things aren't right up here. I just watched the replay here on the television, just now. I swear to you, I didn't even know I did that."

Evelyn sat on the corner next to Xavier. "Baby, drop out."

Shot pushed away from his lean on the wall. "Whoa, wait. What now?"

"Tell them you're sick. You injured yourself warming up. Something. You don't have to do this. I talked to the coach at the college, and he was thrilled at the idea of you coming on board. The job is yours if you want it. Stop the damage, right here and right now."

"That's not an option," Shot said.

Evelyn whipped her head around and glared at Shot. "I don't believe I was talking to you, was I, Shemar?"

Shot backed away with his hands up and snorted. "Ain't shit changed, huh, Auntie? Okay, cool. You in here now. Go ahead and ask him, then, since you don't want to hear nothing from me."

Xavier buried his face in his hands. "He's right. I can't do that."

Evelyn stood and faced Shot. "What did you do?"

"It wasn't him, Mom. This is me. This is all on me."

Evelyn maintained her mutual stare with Shot. Shot gestured to the bed. She sat next to Xavier again. Xavier looked up at her with a pained expression. Evelyn kneaded the back of his neck. He looked past Evelyn to Shot with an unspoken ask for permission to tell all.

"Go on. The fuck it matter what I got to say? Tell her."

Xavier sighed. "Mom, remember when I told you about what happened to Lawrence? Yeah, well. That wasn't the end of it."

When Xavier told her of the consequences for not throwing the fight, Evelyn silently cried. The weight of his admissions, however, did not break her posture. Despite Xavier having shared that her only child could be taken from her, she stood strong, and Xavier understood in that moment it was because she knew he needed her to. Seeing her carry the load for him, he knew had she broken down at that revelation, his own resolve would have collapsed under the strain. After all these years, after he had given up on her, he saw she was not prepared to let him bear this alone, saw she was, in fact, incapable of it.

Evelyn wiped the tears from her cheeks. A box of Kleenex appeared in her face and she and Xavier looked up to see Shot's outstretched arm, his eyes also reddened. Evelyn took a tissue and wiped her nose. Xavier breathed deep and steeled himself.

"There's something else, Mom."

She held his face in her hands. "Your father passed."

"You know?"

"Why do you think I'm here?"

"How?"

"Apparently when you first took him to stay at Maple Grove, he made an addendum to the paperwork. Listed me as a contact in case of his death. I suppose he was worried you wouldn't tell me." Xavier looked down in shame. Evelyn placed two fingers under his chin and lifted his head. "You hold your head up, son. We're past all that now. It's done."

"I'm—"

"No. What did we agree to? No more apologies."

"You're right. But, Mom, I don't know the first thing about what I'm supposed to do with him—for him—now. Funerals and all that. And the house."

Evelyn patted his knee. "I'll take care of it."

"Mom. No."

"Xavier. I'll take care of it. Let me do this for you."

He sniffed. "Thank you."

"That should free you up to do what you know you have to do."

"Mama, I know, but I can't drop—"

"Throw the fight."

"Say what?"

"Yeah, say what?" Shot echoed.

"If either of you think I'm about to lose my one and only child over this foolishness, you are sadly mistaken. Legal, moral, ethical—I really don't care. You do whatever it takes to get this done. And then it's *done*." She turned to Shot. "And I mean that, Shemar. *All* of this. It's over. The two of you are done as well." She looked back to Xavier. "You're going to take that job and you're going to get the medical attention you need."

"Mom—"

"You're going to take that job, and you're going to get the medical attention you need," she repeated. "This is not optional. You've tried taking care of yourself. Now it's my turn. Do you understand me?" The tenor of his mother's voice struck a chord that disintegrated all resistance. The grown man was still her child.

"Yes, ma'am."

"Shemar? Do you understand? After this, he is *done*." Shot looked off to the side. "Shemar." Shot pushed his tongue into his cheek, then met Evelyn's glare.

"Yes, ma'am."

"All right then." Xavier heard a note of self-reassurance in her voice, as if she said it to convince herself as much as the two of them. She stood and tossed her tissue in the wastebasket. "I imagine you two have some things to discuss. I also imagine the fewer ears the better. Deniability and all that, right, Shemar?"

"I always said you had some gangster in you, Auntie."

"I know you think that's flattering, but it's not." She stood across from Shot in the hall and took his hand in hers. Xavier watched the look of surprise on his cousin's face at the gesture. She spoke in a whisper and Xavier leaned in to hear. "See my boy through this, Shot. Please." Shot's expression was one Xavier had never seen. One that indicated he understood the gravity of her request and, what's more, accepted the responsibility. He nodded. Evelyn returned the gesture.

"And get some food in him. He looks terrible." She called back to Xavier. "I'll see you tomorrow night."

"Love you, Mom."

"Love you, too, Xavier." She placed a hand on Shot's shoulder. Shot moved as if to remove it, but instead put his hand on top of hers for a moment. Xavier watched the two of them, and while their eyes didn't meet, it was clear to Xavier that his cousin and mother *saw* each other. When he lifted his hand, hers slipped away, and she walked out of the room. Shot stared at the closed door for a few seconds, then walked over to the bed. Xavier slid down the edge to give him room and he sat. They both watched the remainder of the weigh-in repeats.

"In the replay," Xavier said. "I saw it in his face. He was scared. If this was straight up, I would win this fight."

"Yeah, I know you would."

"Yeah."

The emcee wrapped up the ceremonies and Shot stood and turned off the television. "How you feeling? Still dizzy?"

"Nah. Hungry as hell, though."

"Let's go eat, then."

"Yeah, all right." Xavier stood and followed Shot to the door.

"You know, I actually think I saw like one ab muscle in your stomach when you was up on the scale. You sure you want it to disappear again?"

"Fuck you, Shemar."

They laughed together and closed the door behind them.

ANTE UP

Xavier sat backward on a folding metal chair. His forearm rested on the back, hand outstretched, while the athletic commissioner initialed his hand wraps. He opened and closed his fingers, cotton wedged in between the webbing. His fist felt dense and compact. Shot's wrap jobs were legendary in Xavier's mind. There was security in the way he made the gauze hug the hand, pressed the bones together in a phalanx, ready to withstand the impact of whatever Xavier threw at his opponent. He'd never broken his hand with Shot's wraps, not once in all his bouts. They made his fists tightly packed plastic explosives, and he threw them with the confidence of a perceived invincibility.

Shot held open the four-ounce fingered gloves. Xavier shoved his hands in. The Velcro straps closed. Shot wrapped Xavier's wrists in the blue tape that represented his corner's color. He took his time, ensuring there were no creases, no edges that could lift and come loose during the fight. When he was done, Xavier smacked his right fist into his left palm, then right to left. He pushed the padding across his knuckles down and back. He shivered. He stood outside himself and watched as he engaged in the ritual right before his sparring session with Lawrence. His face smashed and bleeding. Unconscious and rigid on the mat. Xavier held his fist in his hand.

"You all right?" Shot asked.

Xavier blinked to rid himself of the vision. "Yeah, I'm fine."

"Where'd you just go?"

"Nowhere good."

Shot scooted his chair closer to Xavier. "Look at me, X." Xavier acquiesced. Shot looked around the room to see who of the other fighters and trainers sharing the staging area might be listening, then brought his chair even closer. He leaned in and spoke softly in Xavier's ear. "You have got to get your mind right, and right now. You feel me? What you have to do is more important than any game plan we've ever come up with for any other fool you've been in that cage with. I'm not trying to scare you right now. These are facts. You stay clear for two and some odd rounds and you done. You out from under this and you move on with your life." Shot pulled away. "You remember the signals?"

"Yes."

"Okay, good." He looked around the room again. "You ain't got to say them now. Stand up and shadowbox. Get your arms used to that little bit of weight at the end of them again. We're not going to warm up too hard. Just enough to get some sweat going."

Xavier pulled up the hood of his sweatshirt, stood, and moved to a corner of the room where a body-length mirror hung on the painted cinderblock wall. He threw half-speed punches and alternating knees at his reflection's head and body. He saw Lawrence in his mind again and stopped.

"What's up?" Shot asked.

"Nothing. Let's pummel instead."

Shot shrugged and met his cousin in a half embrace, one arm over, one arm under. With a tap on the shoulder, they began swimming their arms up, over, and through, looking for the double underhooks bear hug. They pushed and pulled, attempting to off-balance each other and gain control. There was a playfulness Xavier had forgotten, and what started as a warmup became a game between adolescent cousins jockeying for dominance and bragging rights. Sweat pooled on the top of Xavier's head underneath his hood. It spilled down behind his ears and the bridge of his nose where it hung at the tip. Neither man gave up position and they separated.

"You still can't get me," Shot said.

"You the one breathing hard, not me."

"Whatever. Keep moving. Won't be long now."

On cue, the crowd's muffled roar reached the locker room. The collected fighters and trainers looked up at the television mounted high in a corner of the room. A preliminary fight ended. Two men stood in the center of the cage. The referee held their wrists as they awaited the decision.

"Wallace," a voice shouted behind them. Xavier and Shot turned to see the fighter wrangler's head poked through the door. "You're up." Xavier and Shot followed him out into the hallway.

Another roar from the crowd. The decision had been announced. Xavier pulled his hood's drawstrings tight. In previous fights, the hood around his head took him to an imagined room, a place where he didn't suffer nausea, where anxiety dared not tread, where fear and the concept of losing were notions spoken in tongues he didn't understand. But he couldn't reach the room. The door stood closed, locked from the inside. Each time he attempted a turn of the knob, an alarm sounded, the steam whistle screaming. He pounded on the door, only to be pulled back by the gravity that formed the pit in his stomach, the electric shock of angst that traveled up and down his axons. He bounced up and down and shook his arms, as if to set loose the feelings through the ends of his fingers.

The losing fighter from the bout before came down the long hall in the opposite direction. He held a blood-stained towel over his nose and just beneath his eyes, one of which had a cavernous gash above it. The lids of the other eye had swollen shut, distended and purple from the collecting blood. The towel wasn't there to staunch his bleeding nose, however. He sobbed into the stained terrycloth. One cornerman kneaded his shoulders and spoke reassurances that echoed off the floors and walls as he kept in step behind him. Two others flanked him and attempted to keep him shielded from the view of others, to let him have a private moment in this most public hall, until he could grieve alone.

It was a sight Xavier had seen many times before. It was a thing he had experienced himself more times than he'd cared to count. The grief wasn't simply about the loss. If the fight wasn't exciting enough, if it didn't end with a knockout or a submission, then there was no bonus. None of his sponsors were approved by the promotion. After payment to trainers and taxes, undercard fighters took home far less than a livable wage. That alone was enough to make anyone emotional after losing in front of thousands of people, and Xavier had no other mouths to feed. As the fighter approached him, Xavier extended his fist. The fighter saw it and stepped around one of his entourage to move closer to Xavier. He touched his fist to Xavier's without breaking stride and they exchanged an understanding nod.

Then Xavier's music hit. DMX's "What's My Name." The chunky piano chords reverberated throughout the arena before the song was consumed by cheers and boos.

"Let's go, baby!" the wrangler shouted. "It's showtime!"

Shot clapped his hand on Xavier's shoulder. A cameraman in front of him turned on his light. Make the walk. One last time.

Xavier shadowboxed. The music did not hold its usual sway over him. It did not move him. Instead, he reviewed the plan in his head.

Weather the initial storm. Then light him up for two rounds, but not too much. Move the odds higher in your favor over two rounds. Do not give the ref an opportunity to stop the fight. Back off when he's in trouble but be slick about it. Read him. Look for him to set his feet for the big punch in the third. Give him the opening.

Walk away free.

The hallway ended. Xavier stepped under the archway that opened into the arena. Security walked alongside them, pushing away hands extended for high fives. Xavier scanned the crowd in wonder, amazed by the number of fans in attendance for a preliminary fight, surprised even more by the number of boos. Word of his taunt to Finn spread and Xavier sat firmly in the role of heel. Steroid cheat. Insulted a man's family. Involved his child. Some cheers filtered through the noise, but it was clear he was no fan favorite.

So stop trying to be one.

Xavier lifted two middle fingers as he proceeded down the aisle to the staging area just outside the cage. The jeers filled the arena, to such a pitch that Xavier imagined the dust in the girders shaking loose. He smiled. The image of his grin on the large screen above the cage incensed the crowd further. He smiled wider. He wasn't supposed to be enjoying this— but he was.

He reached the staging circle. Kicked off his slides. Unzipped his hoodie. Shot helped him get the sleeve over his gloves then pulled him in close. Over the steady din of the crowd, he shouted in Xavier's ear.

"I can do all things through him who gives me strength."

Xavier stopped bouncing. He was a boy again, in the

backseat of his parents' car as they returned from church. "Amazing Grace." The verse his father quoted to him before he stepped into the ring, onto the wrestling mat, the one he could not recall until just now. And despite all that had passed, Xavier missed his father.

Stunned at the memory's abrupt return and the sentiments that accompanied it, Xavier backed away. Shot's face revealed he knew the words would mean something to Xavier and why. Xavier blinked back tears. Shot handed him his mouthpiece. Xavier took it, then slapped hands with Shot and pulled him in for one more hug. Xavier released but Shot held on for a second more. Xavier's arms hung in the air, and he thought to engage again in the embrace but Shot pushed away from him. Xavier watched his cousin sniff once before he grabbed Xavier by the shoulder and turned him to face his cut man. He stood in front of Xavier and rubbed Vaseline into his forehead, eyebrows, nose, and cheeks until it covered his face in a sheen. Xavier regretted letting go of his cousin first, but as with so many things, the moment had passed. When the cut man finished, he stepped aside and let the referee perform his final check. No body grease, trimmed fingernails, groin cup. The ref pointed at his own mouth and Xavier flashed his mouthpiece. Satisfied, the ref signaled for Xavier to ascend the metal steps and enter the cage.

Xavier paused at the open cage door, then took a knee, though not in prayer. Six inches in front of him waited the end of his career. He never imagined it wouldn't be on his own terms, and certainly not like this, but the time for imagination had ended. No room remained in his crowded thoughts for dreams of a way out of his situation. After days of waiting filled with dread, that which he had wrought, whether intentionally or no, lay before him. He stood and entered the cage.

Taunts and cheers rose again as he circled around the

perimeter of the cage, once, twice, stopping with a ritual third. He faced Shot, who took his spot on the dais outside the cage. Xavier's music ended and the lights lowered. He hung his long arms from the top of the cage and stretched his shoulders. An Irish punk rock song came on full blast as the lights came up. Xavier glanced at the monitor above the cage to see Finn enter the arena in a near sprint. He turned back to a laughing Shot. He yelled above the din.

"I think that dude really wants to punch you in the face."

"I think you might be right."

Xavier laughed. Though a part of him still reveled in the novelty of the heel role, guilt panged for what he'd said to Finn. He'd never made fights personal, especially *that* personal. Finn was his opponent, but he hadn't deserved that. Little did Finn know Xavier would make it right as long as he could keep the instructions straight.

Xavier turned and waited for Finn to take the cage. The announcer ran down their stats, Finn paced back and forth on his side of the cage, mean-mugging Xavier, never breaking eye contact. Xavier stood motionless and rehearsed the plan.

The ref took the center. Pointed to each man to ensure their readiness.

And the fight was on.

Finn rushed to the middle, but he didn't stop there. Twenty-four hours, food, and rehydration had not stemmed the rage Xavier had stoked. Finn came forward and swung wildly. Xavier covered up and caught the blows on his forearms. He backpedaled until he felt the fence press quilt patterns into his flesh. Finn stood at distance and wailed away. One punch clipped Xavier on the ear, and he unleashed a short counter hook. It caught Finn flush on his raised chin. His knees buckled.

Xavier saw it. He grabbed Finn, pulled him into a Greco

Roman clinch and spun him against the cage, in Xavier's corner. He looked over Finn's shoulder down at Shot. They exchanged fearful looks that said the same thing.

He's got no chin. Jesus Christ, how do I drag this out if he's got no chin?

Shot called out instructions.

"Body shots in tight, X. Knee the thigh. Foot stomps."

Yes right good smart.

Xavier pressed his weight into Finn who jawed at him, oblivious to the fact that he'd almost ended up on his back counting the lights.

"Let go of me," he said. "Stop tying up like a pussy."

Knock his ass out then, he wants to talk shit.

Shut. Up.

Xavier ignored Finn as they jockeyed for head position. The shorter man, Finn drove the top of his head up under Xavier's as he ground his chin down into Finn's crown. Xavier threw shoulder shots and open-handed slaps to his ears until the ref separated them for inaction. They reset in the center of the cage.

Finn rushed forward again, chin up, pumping piston-straight rights and lefts, driving them back into the same tie-up on the opposite side of the cage.

Good. Do the work for me. Run that clock down.

Xavier spun Finn against the cage again and they resumed the grind. Finn was heavily muscled, and Xavier felt his breathing change under his weight hanging off him. When the ref forced them to reset again, Finn took a deep breath.

Not so soon. Where is your gas tank?

No bum's rush this time. Xavier bounced and looked to counter, but Finn threw out half-hearted jabs, and Xavier sensed an impending takedown attempt. Xavier stung him with jabs and kept Finn at his considerable arm's length. The connections got good to Xavier. He snapped them out faster, harder. A line of blood left Finn's nostril.

Move your Goddamned head, kid. I can't carry you this long.

Xavier threw a switch kick to the inside of Finn's leg. Finn attempted a catch, but Xavier's retraction was quick and clean. Frustrated, Finn threw a big overhand right that Xavier stepped away from. Finn followed the missed punch with a shot for the takedown. And Xavier instinctively threw a counter knee.

No.

Hell yes.

The strike lifted Finn's chin and sent him sprawling on his back. The crowd thundered. Xavier's stomach turned to icy slush. It melted when he saw Finn still conscious, though clearly dazed. Xavier stayed on his feet, in front of Finn's open guard. Finn's legs flailed until he regained enough composure to throw up kicks at Xavier's face and straight kicks to his shins. Xavier threw hard low kicks at the outside of Finn's thighs and grabbed his ankles, giving the appearance he'd attempt a guard pass. But it was all a stall. The referee watched Xavier to see if he'd engage further but Xavier ignored his unspoken question and kicked away at Finn's legs. Finally, the ref told Xavier to step back, and Finn stood.

For the remainder of the round, Xavier leapt around Finn and kept him on the outside with jabs and stinging leg kicks. The audience grew restless, and the boo birds sang their dissatisfied song. The air horn signaled a merciful end to the round. Xavier blew out in relief and realized that despite the exertion, he'd been holding his breath. The cage door opened and Shot came in with the cut man. Xavier saw Shot shove his cell phone in his pocket. Part of the plan was to check the odds after the first round. Shot set the stool down.

"Well?"

Shot iced Xavier's shoulders and spoke calmly into his ear.

"You won that round, but it was close."

The odds didn't improve.

"You're going to have to do more."

They moved closer.

"Another round like that and we could be leaving it to the judges."

Be more convincing. Put on a show. Bust him up if you have to.

"Take some chances but be smart."

Don't knock him out. No doctor stoppage.

"You feel me?" Xavier nodded. "Good. Deep breath." He poured water in Xavier's mouth and replaced his mouthpiece. "Show me something these next five minutes." He winked at him. "Have a little fun." The ref yelled for the seconds to leave the cage.

Xavier stood, ready for the last round he'd ever enjoy.

He met Finn in the center and resumed his stinging jabs. Finn had new life in him, and he moved his head more quickly off the center line. Xavier missed with a straight right. Finn caught him with a glancing counter hook to the body before coming back up top to the head. Xavier blocked the blow, but the impact sent him back a step and triggered his tinnitus. Despite the ringing, he smiled.

Okay. Now we got a fight.

They danced. Kicks exchanged to thighs, missed spinning techniques drew oohs and ahhs from the crowd. The back and forth reopened the small cut created by his father's crucifix. He wiped at the spot, and the sight of blood, though not unfamiliar, provided oxygen to the ember that had been glowing since the day his father swung his pendant at him.

Nah, you bitch. You don't get to have that.

Finn threw another leg kick and Xavier caught it and took him down. Finn grabbed around Xavier's neck to hold him in his guard. He released his clinch and grabbed at Xavier's wrist for a submission attempt, but Xavier regained his posture.

Fuck you.

Xavier brought an elbow crashing down into Finn's face. Finn cried out. Xavier looked at the red mark his forearm left on the pale skin of Finn's forehead, just above the bridge of his nose. Then he watched in horror as blood streamed from it.

The sight threw a water bucket on Xavier's stoked anger. He succumbed to Finn's defensive flailing and allowed him to break his posture. He pressed his head against Finn's chest. His hold on Xavier felt weak, but Xavier stayed there and threw half-hearted short shots to the body, avoiding his head. Then he heard the sound he dreaded the moment his elbow connected with Finn's face. The referee yelled.

"Stop! I need the doctor!"

Finn opened his legs and Xavier stood up out of his guard. He followed the referee's direction to go to a neutral corner. The ref walked Finn to the cage door and the doctor examined the cut. If he deemed the cut a danger to his vision, if Finn said he couldn't see, the fight was over. Xavier shot a nervous glance to his cousin on the opposite side of the cage, as he paced the small stretch of cage to which he'd been confined. He looked up at the clock. Just under a minute to go in the round.

Come on, come on. You're fine. You can see. Please say you can see.

The ref leaned in to hear the doctor's words. The doctor looked back to Finn.

Finn gave two thumbs up.

The arena exploded in cheers.

Xavier clenched his jaw to keep from adding a cheer of his own.

The physician left the cage and the ref positioned them back on the ground, then shouted "go." Xavier allowed Finn to pull him down against his chest again, slick with sweat and blood. Xavier stayed there and threw more do-nothing body shots. The wooden clappers cracked the ten second warning. The blare of the air horn that followed was more welcome than any noise Xavier had ever heard. He stood and jogged back to his corner. He glanced back and saw Finn slow to rise. Seeing Xavier watching him, Finn lifted his shoulders, bounded up and down, and stared. Xavier turned back toward his corner and smiled.

Atta boy.

Back on his stool. Shot in his ear.

"Almost had him."

What the fuck was that? You almost won.

"But you definitely up on the scorecards."

Odds shifted heavily in your favor.

"Do you see the opening when he throws the right hand?"

Is he telegraphing the big punch?

"Yeah, I see it."

"Good. Then this is our round. Finish him off."

Take the punch and go down.

Xavier took a final swig of water. The buzzer went off, signaling Shot's time to exit.

"It's almost over, X. Bring it home."

Unless you fuck it up. But then it's over either way, ain't it?

Shot replaced Xavier's mouthpiece and left the cage. Xavier stood and looked across the cage at Finn. His corner had stemmed the flow from the cut and wiped away the mask of blood from his face. Finn, hands up, chin down, glared at Xavier from underneath his brow. Xavier raised his hand, a request for a glove touch for the final round. Finn shook it off. The snub showed on the screen above the cage and sent the crowd into a fervor. The ref clapped his hands and pointed to the center of the cage, the signal for them to fight their final round.

Finn ran. Xavier walked.

They met in the middle and engaged in an immediate fire-fight that sent the audience to their feet. Xavier bobbed and weaved. Finn's blows hit his gloves first, then grazed his ear, his forehead, anywhere but his chin.

Not until I want you to. You don't get to have the when.

Xavier scored a front kick flush to Finn's solar plexus that drove him back a step. Then Xavier slapped him. A hard, open handed smack that reverberated louder than any punch he'd landed in the prior rounds. Finn registered a brief moment of shock, then reset his stance. Xavier waited for him to step back in range, then slapped him again. The force opened the cut on Finn's forehead.

"You going to let me slap you like that in front of all these people?" Xavier shuffled his feet. "Watch out, I'ma do it again." He watched Finn's eyes and when he saw them dart down, he whipped out another hard slap. "Oh, I did it again!"

"Keep it quiet," the ref said.

Xavier assented, his mission accomplished. Finn radiated fury and disgust, his blue eyes highlighted by the crimson flowing from the cut between them. Xavier stepped in range. The crowd booed. Finn's shoulders tensed and he ground his feet into the mat. He tapped his gloves together, a tell Xavier scouted in his fight films, a telegraph he'd watched Finn deliver throughout the first ten minutes of their bout. At the sight of the gesture, Xavier dropped his lead hand. Finn uncorked the overhand right and it smashed into Xavier's jaw.

Dark.

Light.

People screaming.

Someone punched him in the face.

Dark.

Light.

Another punch. A hand on his throat.

Grab the wrist. Throw up the legs. Trap his arm. Squeeze your knees. Arch your hips.

Feel the elbow joint pop.

Hear the bone crack.

Hear the scream.

Feel the tap.

Someone yelled.

"Stop."

"It's over."

"Let it go."

Strong black latex gloved hands pulled Xavier's legs off Finn's head and shoulders. Pried Xavier's grip from his wrists. Xavier stood and watched his anonymous attacker fall backward onto the mat where he writhed in pain and gripped his elbow.

Onto the mat. In a cage. I'm in the cage. It was the referee screaming for me stop.

I won.

Xavier fell to his knees and looked at his open hands. The crowd reached a deafening volume. Finn's cornermen and the ringside physician attended to him. The doctor attempted a manipulation of his arm and Finn yelped. Strong hands gripped Xavier's shoulders.

"Get up, man," Shot said. Xavier continued to kneel. Shot shoved his hands under Xavier's arms and lifted him to his feet. The cut man stood in front of him and pressed a cotton swab into the cut next to his eye.

"Shot."

"Not now."

The cameraman approached them but Shot led Xavier to the cage entrance. At the door, they ran into the emcee from the weigh-ins.

"What, no interview? Come on, you have to let me talk to him."

"Jaw's broke from that punch," Shot said. "Got to get him to the hospital."

"Oh, shit. Yeah, get him out of here!"

The emcee stepped out of Shot's path, but behind him, at the base of the metal steps, stood Carson in a sharp dark suit and no tie. He held his hand out for a shake. Xavier stood paralyzed. Carson looked back and forth between Xavier and Shot until Shot took his hand.

"Boys, that was fucking incredible. What a fucking fight. Listen to this crowd. A little ring rust in there, you could have finished him earlier, but otherwise you looked fantastic. How do you feel?"

He felt nothing. Not his hands in his gloves nor the metal steps beneath his feet. He moved out of the cage behind Shot as though programmed. He hardly heard Carson's question nor the shouts of the audience. Only the steam whistle, which screamed unabated.

"Jaw's broke," Shot said with greater impatience. "Got to get him checked out."

"Yeah, yeah, go ahead," he said, and stepped aside. "You better heal up quick, son. We're going to want to fill your dance card real soon."

Shot pushed Xavier in front of him and waved an acknowledgment to Carson. Xavier walked down the cattle chute back toward the locker rooms. He searched the audience for Evelyn. He slowed his pace but Shot's hand on his back urged him forward. Finn fans lobbed curses and threats as he passed through while fans of his own reached into the aisle and touched his head, his shoulders, and extended their hands for high fives. They reached the archway.

"Shot," he said again.

"I said not now. In the locker room."

Xavier's mouth went dry, his tongue pasty. They reached the locker room. A fighter and his cornermen exited just as Shot opened the door. They congratulated them on the way out and left the room empty. Xavier couldn't decide if he was relieved or terrified. Shot locked the door behind him and any modicum of relief disappeared when the deadbolt clicked home.

"Sit down."

Xavier did so.

"Did you do it on purpose?"

"Does it matter?"

"The fuck did you just say?"

"Will you believe what I tell you?"

"Did you fucking do it on purpose?"

Xavier's tears fell freely. "No, Shot. I didn't. I woke up and he was on me, and I reacted. I didn't know who he was. I didn't know where I was." He looked past Shot to a blank space on the wall, forcing himself to remember. Nothing came. "Shot, I can't even tell you what happened before that."

Shot stood in front of him. He laced his fingers on top of his head and took a deep breath. Then he screamed. Xavier flinched. Shot kicked a folding chair. It collapsed on itself and clattered against the floor.

"Shot, I'm so sorry. I would never put you in this situation." Shot barked a disgusted laugh. He paced the room with his hands on his hips. "How much did they . . . how much was on the line? Maybe we can . . . Dad's house. I can give them the money when we sell it. Will that take care of it? It's gotta help, right? They can put me on a payment plan or something, right? These guys are businessmen."

Shot stopped in front of him. "No. No, they're not."

"Oh," was all Xavier could manage. The tinnitus rang as loud as the crowd and made him lightheaded. "So—this is it?"

"God damn it, Xavier. Fuck!"

"Yeah. Right. Okay. This is it."

Shot crouched down and picked up Xavier's sweatshirt off the floor. He tossed it in Xavier's face.

"Come on."

Xavier clutched the sweatshirt to his chest. "Where are we going?"

"Nigga, I said come on. Pull your hood up. Keep your head down. People need to think you hurt."

Xavier fed his arms into the sleeves as he followed Shot to the door. Shot unlocked it and walked down the hall toward the back of the arena. Xavier pulled the hood strings tight, his hands in his front pockets. The pair fielded congratulations from production crew members as they passed. Shot thanked them. Xavier kept his head lowered. The walk down the hall felt as endless as the stream of questions about what had happened—and what was about to happen—that pushed their way through the concussion cobwebs. Xavier resisted a dry heave.

"Shot, I think I'm gonna be sick."

"No time. Get your shit together."

Xavier breathed in through his nose and out through his mouth. He saw the door and desperately wanted to reach the exit, to breathe fresh air, but the fear filling his chest left little room for anything else. Shot pushed open the back door. The light breeze had died. The humid ocean air sat stagnant. Shot weaved through the parked cars. Xavier stayed in step. He peered over the roofs of cars, turned to look behind them, to

see what, he didn't know, but his guard was up. They came up
on the rear bumper of Shot's Denali. Shot clicked the remote
and the rear door slowly opened. Then he grabbed a duffel
from the back and unzipped it.

"What's that?"

Shot pulled out a .45.

Xavier's guts knotted. The steam whistle screamed. He
vomited. The sick splashed on his toes. He wiped his mouth
with his sleeve, then put a hand up and clutched his stomach.
He stepped back. "Shot, please, man. You don't have to do
this. Jesus Christ, man, we're family."

"Xavier, shut up." Shot held the .45 out to the side. "Gun."
He set it down on the bed of the Denali, then reached back in
the duffel and withdrew a cell phone. "Burner." He set it next
to the gun. Once more into the bag. He came out with several
taped stacks of fifties and hundreds. "Cash."

Xavier shook his head. "What? I don't understand."

Shot replaced the contents of the bag, zipped it up, and
pushed the bag into Xavier's chest. "Where's your phone?"

Xavier stuttered. "I think I left it in your console."

Shot opened the driver's side door and leaned in. He came
back with Xavier's cell in hand. He dropped it in front of him
and stomped it with the heel of his boot.

"Shot, what the fuck?"

Shot stomped again. And again. The already cracked
screen splintered. Plastic and metal squeaked and ground
under his heel. Shot's stomps continued. He gritted his teeth
as his heel thudded over and over until pieces of the phone
turned to powder, until he smashed nothing but asphalt
under his foot, until his breath came out short and ragged.
When he looked up, Xavier saw tears. He'd never seen his
cousin cry. Xavier had never been more frightened. Shot
pointed at the burner.

"You don't use that phone to call me. Or Auntie Ev. Or anyone else you know."

Xavier looked down at the bag, "I don't know anybody else."

Shot held out the keys to the Denali. "Drive to the bus station."

"Shot, I think I'm concussed."

"Leave the keys in there."

"Shemar!"

"Buy a ticket with cash and get far away. Don't go somewhere you've been before. Don't open no bank accounts. Cut up your credit cards. That money will last you a while. If you need a job, get something under the table. No records."

Xavier squeezed his head. "This is a joke, right? My brain finally gave up? I'm—we're in the hospital right now and this all just in my head. This isn't real life. It can't be."

Shot wiped his nose. "You got to go. Now."

"Mom."

"She'll be all right. She's tough."

"Yeah. She is."

"She was right, too. She said after this we'd be done."

Xavier stepped to his cousin for one last hug, to give Shot the one he thought he wanted before he entered the cage, the one Xavier himself had wanted. But Shot put his hand out with the keys once more and pointed to the open driver's side door.

"Go on."

Xavier took the keys. He climbed in the Denali and started the engine. His vision vibrated. The truck cab swirled and shifted. He shook it off and put the truck in reverse. He looked at the rear camera. Shot was already gone.

Xavier backed out of the space and onto the main drag before he realized he didn't know where the bus station was and pulled over. He typed it into the Denali's GPS. As it calculated the route, he reached into the bag, retrieved the burner, and powered it on. He found the notes application and typed furiously. When he was done, he took a screenshot, saved the image as the home screen for the phone, then tossed it back in the bag. His destination set, he pulled back onto the road and drove for the bus station.

EVERYDAY STRUGGLE

Xavier leaned against the wall and stared out at the sea of faces seated throughout the restaurant. A voice called out to his right.

"Jake. Jake. *Jake!*" A pale pair of fingers snapped in his face. He blinked and turned.

Xavier stared at the man to whom the fingers belonged. His name tag read "Vick." "Earth to Jake. What's your deal, man?"

"Don't put your hand in my face when you want to get my attention. That's my deal."

"Then try answering me when I call you." Vick peered at him. "Are you high?"

Xavier snorted. "No, I am not high."

"Well, whatever, yo. My ten top just got up and they left that table a fucking mess. I swear, we should have a cutoff for how many kids are allowed at a table. Fucking Cheerios everywhere. I don't think they even ate any of them. Anyways, help a brother out, huh?"

"Yeah, sure. *Brother.*" Xavier slung his white towel over his shoulder and grabbed his empty bus pan.

"Oh, and hey, I'm pretty sure I heard the mom say one of her little shits puked on the floor in the bathroom. So, if you can check that out when you're done."

"Yep."

"You da man, Jake." Vick put his hand out. Xavier let it hang there and walked away. Vick had a habit of attempting some complicated choreography every time he shook hands with Xavier and code switched whenever he spoke to him. Always his "brother," always "da man." He reminded Xavier of someone, but he could never quite place who. When he thought hard, when he seemed close to recalling, a disproportionate rage swelled, and he envisoned visiting violence on Vick. When he saw images of Vick, bloody and battered, his face became unfamiliar, but his visage was accompanied by a familiar unease and he gave up trying to remember.

He was obligated to tolerate Vick's soft shoe. Vick's father owned the tiny North Dakota diner and agreed to pay Xavier under the table. He also owned the twin across the street and let Xavier pay month-to-month. Vick's cultural appropriation was the price of anonymity.

Xavier reached the catastrophe that Vick's customers had left behind and groaned. He pulled out his phone to check the time. The screen lit up and he read once more the list he'd created the better part of a year ago and looked over his shoulders.

No calls.

No bank accounts.

No credit cards.

You're Jake.

The screen went dark. He didn't recognize his reflection in the screen. Though he'd maintained his subterfuge in his new town, there'd been some early near misses. Before he'd grown his beard and hair out, a random local asked him if anyone had ever told him how much he looked like Xavier Wallace. He'd laughed it off, told them, "Yes, all the time." Mercifully, the lie had been enough to satisfy their curiosity. He had wondered if they heard his heart pound.

He still struggled with the alias. He and Shot had loved *Training Day*. Shot did a mean Denzel and used to holler "Jake!" at Xavier when he was too hard on himself in training, when Xavier had gotten mad at him for no reason, or when he knew his cousin just needed a laugh. He missed Shot's laugh. Once he swore Shot was there. He watched the back of his head as he sat, facing away from him in a booth. Xavier whispered his name, and the wraith turned. Shot looked back at him, a bullet hole in the middle of his forehead, the whites of his eyes red with blood, and said, "What up, Jake?" The vision had been so real, Xavier dropped his bus pan, shattering the plates within.

The dinner rush had come and gone. Xavier cleaned the table. The fights started at seven. The sooner he got to the venue, the sooner he could weigh in and have something to eat. The smoker fights held there required a same day weigh-in, though they never really enforced anything if a fighter was off. They simply left it up to the other fighter if they wanted to keep the fight. They weighed in on a cheap old bathroom scale with a dial and needle before they stepped off to be examined by whichever paramedic got the call to play ringside physician that night.

Xavier always made weight. It was the principle of the thing. He was reliable, and the promoter kept giving him fights. Tonight, he would compete for a title. Xavier didn't care one bit about a belt. Fighting was the only time he didn't hear the steam whistle. The only time the headaches moved to the background. So, he fought as often as he could. However, the more he fought, the worse he got, which made him take more fights just for some kind of relief, no matter how temporary. At least that's what he told himself.

The table cleared, Xavier took the bus pan back to the kitchen, loaded the dishes into a rack, and sent it through the machine. He rinsed out his tub, set with a stack of others, and pulled his apron off over his head. He waved to the line cooks who wished him luck on his way back out of the kitchen. As he reached the front door to the diner, someone tapped his shoulder.

"My guy," Vick said. "The bathroom? The puke?"

"Shit."

"Dog, between you forgetting your shifts and not hearing me call your name? I'm starting to think you got that CTE or whatever."

Xavier glared. Vick's father had been more understanding about his forgetfulness than he would have ever expected— until he saw a black and white photo in a glass case behind the register. Vick's father, in the ring, arms raised in victory. In front of the photo, curled up on itself, rested a Golden Gloves pendant.

"What? I'm just playing—I mean, I'm just kidding. You know. Just messing. Around. My bad. Sorry."

He turned away from Vick and disappeared inside the bathroom.

THE FIGHT WAS HARD. TOO hard. His opponent was a step up in competition. Younger than Xavier by fifteen years, he saw in him the potential to be a middleweight contender, undoubtedly on his way to *The Show*. He had fast feet, faster hands, and those hands landed like mortar fire. They found their way through Xavier's defenses. If Xavier covered his temples, he adjusted with uppercuts. Protected his chin, he got slammed in the temple. When he got tired of Xavier tying him up, he fell back on his wrestling and slammed Xavier to the mat with vicious double leg takedowns. For everything Xavier threw at him, the kid had an answer.

But Xavier would not go away. He bit down on his mouthpiece and took whatever the kid had. Xavier knew he wouldn't walk away with the belt, but he was going to make the judges tell him so. As they waited for the decision, the tinnitus sparked so loudly it produced pain. He stuck his finger in his ear, convinced he'd draw it back bloody, that his eardrum had finally split open. The ringing had never come on this quickly after a fight. When they announced his opponent as the winner and raised his hand, Xavier lost vision in half his right eye.

He changed and boarded the bus for the ride back home. His vision had not returned. His hands trembled and he could not make them stop. He massaged his sore knuckles. The sack of fluid under his eye pulsed in rhythm with the hematoma forming in his thigh from the heavy kicks he'd absorbed. The scream continued unchecked.

The bus pulled up to his stop. He grabbed his gear, along with the "go bag" Shot had given him, and got off. Far from the threats back home, paranoia still reigned. The bag went with him everywhere. He stepped gingerly off the bus and limped the block back to the twin home.

The house had a shared front porch, separated by wooden bannister. Xavier's neighbor Teddy was an EMT who worked odd hours. Late nights when Xavier couldn't sleep, he'd find Teddy on his side of the porch with a cigar and a beer in a rocking chair. Xavier didn't talk much when he joined him outside, and Teddy obliged him with quietude. They often sat in silence. He'd listen to the gentle creak of the wooden planks while Teddy rocked. Some nights Xavier fell asleep right there on the porch.

Teddy gave Xavier the usual nod as he saw him approach and winced when he saw Xavier's face. Xavier forced a weak smile. Teddy raised his beer can as an offering. Xavier waved it off. Teddy nodded again and Xavier unlocked his door.

The wooden screen door slapped shut behind Xavier and he cringed. The normally benign noise was piercing. The moon shone in through his window. He left the light off, threw his bag on the sofa, and dropped down onto the stiff cushions. He pressed the heels of his hands into his forehead, hoping the pressure would relieve the pain, but the bruises there kept him from pushing too hard. He closed his eyes and rested his head on the back of the couch. The tinnitus alternated roars and squeals. He ground his teeth fit to crack them. His still trembling hand touched the go-bag. He felt the stock of the .45 through the fabric.

"You sure about that?"

Xavier lifted his head at the sound. He opened his eyes and his vision blurred. An easy chair sat in a darkened corner of the small living room where the moonlight didn't reach. Someone sat in it.

"Shot?"

Silence. Xavier leaned forward. "Shot?" Still nothing. Xavier swallowed hard. "I know you're not there." He ground his finger into his temple until the tip bent back. "I know you're in here."

"You sure about that?"

"Yeah. Yeah, I'm sure. You told me not to, but I checked the internet at the library here. Just the once. Saw you died. Killed yourself. The article said CTE. 'Damage from years of boxing.'"

"Do you believe it?"

Xavier's sobbed. "No. I knew your head wasn't like mine. I knew it was them. Because of me. Because you let me go."

"But I'm here."

"I wish you were. I miss you. I miss Dad. I miss Mom. I wish

I'd never gone to see her. I can't remember the things I need to remember, and I can't forget what I want to forget. I wish I could forget her. I wish I could forget you. But here you are."

"Why am I here?"

Xavier let loose a whispered wail. "I don't know."

"Yes, you do."

"I can't. I'm scared." The tinnitus screamed.

"If you wait, you won't be able to hear me."

Xavier looked to the ceiling. "Help me."

"I can't."

"But I can."

A knock sounded and Xavier jumped. He wiped the tears from his cheeks and sat up. Before he could speak, Teddy cracked the door and stuck his head in.

"I don't mean to intrude, but, uh . . . well, I thought I heard crying. You okay?"

"I'm fine, Teddy. All good."

"I can . . . is there someone I can call?"

Xavier thought about the reminders on his phone. "No."

Teddy flipped on the lights. Xavier looked across the room to the empty easy chair. He looked down to his left. Next to his leg, hidden from Teddy's view, was the .45. Out of the bag and in his hand. Teddy surveyed Xavier's face and Xavier saw his concern.

You're tired.

"I'm tired, Teddy."

It's time to rest.

"I just need to rest."

"Okay," Teddy said. He turned to leave.

It's almost over. Bring it home.

Xavier's tears streamed again.

"Hey, Teddy." Teddy stopped. "Can you turn that light off for me?"

Teddy looked around the room. "Sure." Teddy flicked off the switch and closed the door behind him.

"Thank you."

Xavier placed the .45 in his mouth. The barrel was cold. The pop was loud. And the screaming stopped.

ACKNOWLEDGMENTS

To readers, booksellers, and reviewers everywhere: without you, I don't get to do this thing I love. Thank you for the time and effort you put in boosting and supporting, as well as providing feedback on my work. All of it makes me want to work harder at my craft and I'm grateful for you all.

To my agent and friend, David Hale Smith (aka DHS): thank you for your tireless work, editorial input, and advocacy on my behalf. You always make me feel like I'm your only client. Of course, the incredible Naomi Eisenbeiss might have a *little* something to do with that.

To my editor, Juliet Grames—there is no other way to say it: working with you has made me a far better writer. I'm truly fortunate to have worked with you. Thank you for everything.

To Bronwen Hruska and the stellar Soho Press team: thank you for taking a chance on me and this novel. Publishing with you has been nothing short of a dream accomplishment.

To Harriet Wade, Poppy Luckett, and everyone at Pushkin Press—it was a privilege to work with you all again and I hope to do so many times over in the future. My mornings were always brighter when I saw an email from you in my inbox.

I was fortunate to have several beta readers and I am eternally grateful for their input. Special thanks go to Ted

Flanagan and Brannan Sirratt. Your willingness to seemingly drop everything to read my latest installments as this book took shape continues to fill me with immense gratitude. Your honest and direct opinions were critical, and you both helped me to write the book I wanted to read.

To the healthcare providers, particularly to the Black and Brown brothers and sisters: on a daily basis, you put your physical health, mental well-being, and—more often than not—your dignity on the line in caring for the most vulnerable. I love and appreciate you for all you do.

Thank you to the amateur, student, and professional athletes who put it all on the line for our entertainment; special thanks to those who use their platform to speak out against inequity and injustice.

There are many others to whom I owe much. In fact, I'm fortunate enough to have so many that it would be impossible for me to list them all here without the inevitable glaring oversight. Know that if you've been a part of my journey, whether in writing, on the mats, or in friendship, I am eternally thankful for your presence in my life.

Finally, to my beloved, JJ, Miles, and my Peanut, Michelle— I love you three beyond measure. With you beside me there's nothing out of reach. Thank you for loving me the way you do.

ALSO BY
JOHN VERCHER

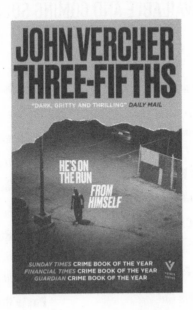

"Searing . . . mesmerising" *SUNDAY TIMES*

"Incredibly suspenseful" *ATTICA LOCKE*

"Lucid and harrowing" *OBSERVER*

Pittsburgh, 1995. Twenty-two-year-old Bobby Saraceno is a biracial black man, passing for white. Bobby has hidden his identity from everyone, even his best friend and fellow comic-book geek, Aaron, who has just returned from prison a newly radicalized white supremacist.

During the night of their reunion, Bobby witnesses Aaron mercilessly assault a young black man with a brick. In the wake of this horrifying act of violence, Bobby must conceal his unwitting involvement in the crime from the police, while battling his own personal demons. This is a harrowing story about racism and brutality that is more urgent now than ever.

AVAILABLE AND COMING SOON
FROM PUSHKIN VERTIGO

Jonathan Ames

You Were Never Really Here
A Man Named Doll
The Wheel of Doll

Sarah Blau

The Others

Zijin Chen

Bad Kids

Maxine Mei-Fung Chung

The Eighth Girl

Amy Suiter Clarke

Girl, 11

Candas Jane Dorsey

The Adventures of Isabel

Joey Hartstone

The Local

Elizabeth Little

Pretty as a Picture

Jack Lutz

London in Black

Steven Maxwell

All Was Lost

Louise Mey

The Second Woman

Joyce Carol Oates (ed.)

Cutting Edge

John Kåre Raake

The Ice

RV Raman

A Will to Kill
Grave Intentions

Paula Rodríguez

Urgent Matters

Tiffany Tsao

The Majesties

John Vercher

Three-Fifths
After the Lights Go Out

Emma Viskic

Resurrection Bay
And Fire Came Down
Darkness for Light
Those Who Perish

Yulia Yakovleva

Punishment of a Hunter